AS LONG AS YOU LOATHE ME

Also by Swati Hegde

For Adults

Match Me If You Can

Can't Help Faking in Love

AS LONG AS YOU LOATHE ME

SWATI HEGDE

Delacorte
Romance

Delacorte Romance
An imprint of Random House Children's Books
A division of Penguin Random House LLC
1745 Broadway, New York, NY 10019
penguinrandomhouse.com
getunderlined.com

Editor: Alison Romig
Cover Designer: Trisha Previte
Interior Designer: Michelle Canoni
Production Editor: Colleen Fellingham
Managing Editor: Tamar Schwartz
Production Managers: Natalia Dextre and Shameiza Ally

Library of Congress Cataloging-in-Publication Data is available upon request.
ISBN 979-8-217-02816-0 (trade pbk.) — ISBN 979-8-217-02817-7 (ebook)

The text of this book is set in 11.25-point Fairfield LT Std.

Manufactured in the United States of America
1st Printing

The authorized representative in the EU for product safety and compliance is Penguin Random House Ireland, Morrison Chambers, 32 Nassau Street, Dublin D02 YH68, Ireland, https://eu-contact.penguin.ie.

Random House Children's Books supports the First Amendment and celebrates the right to read.

For Anahita,
who loved these messy queer girls before anyone else did

CHAPTER ONE

"You Belong With Me (Taylor's Version)"
by Taylor Swift

Meera

You know that moment in every love story when the protagonist realizes they're *this* close to losing the love of their life, so they have to do something really drastic to get their happily-ever-after before it's too late?

As I sit beside Sushant on the school bus, listening to him go on and on and *on* about looking up date-night restaurants in New York for him and his girlfriend, I realize one thing: This is that gotta-win-my-love-back moment for me.

Except, well, Sushant was never really mine. He's always been Lucy's. Goddamn Lucy.

"And, yeah, you have to book a table, like, four months in advance, but they apparently have the best steaks in the—" Sushant pauses when he notices my quirked eyebrow. "What?" He shows me the restaurant. "Look, it's so close to this romance-only bookstore. I could take Lucy there before dinner."

"Why are you planning this already?" I ask. "You don't even know for sure if you're both going to college in New York."

Sushant frowns. "Of course we are. I'll get that scholarship any day now, and Lucy's got the perfect application for NYU." He brightens. "So, what do you think? Should I add a reminder on my phone to make a reservation for our first night there?"

I shake my head indignantly as I look over the restaurant menu, wishing I could shake some sense into him instead. "Two hundred dollars . . . for a steak? What, is it gold-plated or made of diamonds?"

He blinks in confusion. "Meera, I've always wanted to take Lucy to a fancy restaurant, and it sucks that we don't have one here in town. Maybe in New York I can give her the kind of romance she deserves."

"Yeah," I snap, "and I'm sure the gigantic New York rats and the muggers on the streets won't bother you at all on your romantic date nights."

Sushant bites his lip, clearly at a loss for words. The bus lurches to a stop to pick up another student, and I take the opportunity to collect my thoughts before speaking. "Let me get this straight: You're giving up your scholarship to Berkeley to move three thousand miles away from home to the most expensive city in America . . . because you want to buy your girlfriend overpriced steaks? Do you hear yourself right now, Sushant?"

He frowns at me. "I do, and it sounds like the perfect future to me. A future with Lucy."

Scoffing, I lean back in my seat and turn my gaze to the window. "Cool." I can feel his questioning eyes on me, but I plug my earphones in and blast my favorite Spotify mix—EDM songs, of course—loud enough to drown out the thumping of my heart.

He's moving. In a few short months, I'm going to lose the only boy I've ever loved to the only girl I've ever hated. Just my lousy luck.

I know what my father would say. Appa's voice rings in my ears, calm and spiritual as ever: "Hate is a strong word, putta. Hate carries negative energy. Your higher self knows love is the only real force and hate is simply a manifestation of your own insecurities."

But what does he know about heartbreak? Appa and Dad were high school sweethearts, each other's first love, and they've never had to fight anyone or anything in their quest for happily-ever-after—except perhaps Appa's traditional South Indian parents. But even *they* warmed up to the idea of having a son-in-law instead of a daughter-in-law shortly after I was born through artificial insemination and surrogacy.

As for me? I'm fighting persistently frizzy hair, a depressingly low peg on the high school social hierarchy, and, worst of all, the most beautiful, smart, perfect girl there ever was: Lucy Hughson.

The bus finally pulls into the high school parking lot, and Sushant turns to me, smiling. "See you after football practice? Gianni's Pizza? I need help studying for the French midterm."

"I have plans already," I lie stiffly, slinging my backpack over my shoulders and following him down the steps of the bus. He's now whistling to the tune of some random song. It never ceases to surprise me how quickly this boy lets conflict slide. If I were in his place, I'd be paranoid wondering if my since-fetuses neighbor was mad at me.

But Sushant? He doesn't care. He has other things to worry about, after all. Like his girlfriend, whose Honda has just pulled into its designated parking spot under three shady trees. Nobody else parks there. It's an unspoken rule that the best parking spot on campus is reserved for our darling head cheerleader.

Sushant squeezes my shoulder before heading over to Lucy. She gets out of her car and gives him a hug and a kiss that lingers. I avert my gaze, teeth gritted, and tighten my grip on the straps of my backpack. I have to do something to stop Sushant from making the biggest mistake of his life—giving up everything for a girl who could never deserve him.

"You're joking, right?" My more socially acceptable friends (and by that I mean "just as unpopular as me") stare at me, wide-eyed, when we congregate at our adjoining lockers and I fill them in on my vague plan to break up the It Couple.

"I'm not joking," I say, shrugging. "I can't let the love of my life slip through my fingers."

Ron blows a strand of his shaggy, straight brown hair out of his eyes and leans against his locker. His pale, freckled nose has a smudge of white sunscreen on it. He speaks before I can point it out. "We're seventeen, Meera. We have a long way to go before we meet the loves of our lives."

"You know who she's going to bring up," Valeria mumbles

under her breath. She's snacking on a Snickers bar from the candy collection stashed in her locker, one toned arm resting on her hip.

I raise a finger to shush them. "Need I mention my parents? They locked eyes across a crowded, noisy classroom on the first day of senior year over twenty years ago and knew they were meant to be."

Valeria shoots Ron an I-told-you-so look, then sighs. "We've discussed this. Sushant doesn't know you are meant to be. Hence, your parents' example doesn't apply."

"I thought you'd accepted your fate as his neighbor and nothing more," Ron says, chuckling. "What changed?"

He's right. Since we became friends a little over a year ago, they've heard me rant about Lucy and Sushant's relationship over and over, but apart from one (failed) attempt to get Sushant to notice me romantically, I've been all talk, no action.

I blow out a breath. "The entire bus ride, he wouldn't shut up about how excited he is for their perfect future in New York, and yet I vividly recall him telling me three years ago that he never wants to leave the West Coast. She's clearly brainwashing him."

"That was three years ago," Ron points out. "He might have changed his mind."

"Because she forced him to change it." The first bell rings, and I lead us down the hallway. "Maybe Sushant doesn't know it yet, but she's not the one for—"

My words are cut short when Lucy walks past us with her

new best friend, Natalie—my replacement. Oh yeah, did I forget to mention that? Lucy and I were once inseparable, until she unceremoniously friend-dumped me.

Lucy's head is held high, and a designer purse hangs from one wrist. She's too cool for backpacks. Her red hair is beachy-wavy today, and she shows off four-inch heels and a short skirt that fits her like a dream.

And here I'm wearing an oversized black T-shirt, faded blue jeans, and five-year-old sneakers whose soles are glued on.

Right before the queen bee turns the corner, she looks over her shoulder. Our eyes meet, and I narrow my gaze. Her green eyes flicker with a difficult emotion I can't quite place, and then she's out of sight. The sound of her heels echoes long after she's gone.

"Sushant belongs with me," I say, glaring at the space Lucy just deserted and ignoring the little annoyed murmurs my friends let out. "And I'm going to prove it to him."

Lucy

I can feel Meera Rao-George's gaze—or should I say "glare"?—on me as Natalie and I walk down the hall. It's hard to shake off the guilt I feel for what I did. Not just the guilt of ending our six-year friendship with no warning, but also the guilt of becoming this popular version of myself that I always knew she would despise.

I know, because I despise it too. Before I joined the cheer squad, I was just another invisible face in the high school crowd, but I had one perfect person with whom I could let my walls down and be my anxious, introverted, happy self without judgment.

Until my feelings became . . . complicated, and I had to shut her—and the world—out for my own good by changing everything about myself. Being popular comes with invitations to parties and access to booze, but it also brings with it the chronic fear of never being able to show people who you really are and wondering if that's for the best . . .

"So, do you know when you'll hear back from NYU?" Natalie asks, nudging my foot with hers once we're sitting at our usual desks in class. "Although part of me wishes you hadn't applied to a college so far away."

I cock my head at my friend. "New York is where my dream job is. You know that."

She tugs on a coil of her curly black hair. "I know, and you're gonna publish the best books someday. It's just . . . I don't know what I'll do without you."

My throat catches as I shrug nonchalantly. "Who knows? Without me around, you might rule Madre Maria."

Natalie has a dreamy, reverent look on her face when she says, "Nobody can replace you, Lucy."

Natalie's going to community college here. It's crazy how

many people from high school plan on never leaving this small town, where everybody knows everybody's business and no one can keep a secret for longer than a week.

But I've kept my secret for *years.* Meera's glare flashes before my eyes, and I push the image away. I did the right thing cutting her out of my life. Maybe it hurt her, but I had no choice. I couldn't risk anyone finding out.

There are only four people in Madre Maria who are queer *and* out, and my mom hates them all. Two of them are Meera's dads, and the other two are seniors who are just as eager as me, no doubt, to leave this place behind as soon as they graduate. The people of Madre Maria aren't openly bigoted or anything—not even my mom, whose discomfort around people of color or queer people is hard to sense unless you know her like I do. It's just . . . people talk, and being queer is unfortunately fodder for "hot gossip." And I'd rather they gossip about my taste in designer clothing and my very cute, very serious relationship with my boyfriend, instead of the fact that I might be—

"Anyway," Natalie says, bringing me back to the present moment, "I hope things work out for you. You deserve the kind of life you want."

I smile. "Yeah. A new life with Sushant in New York is exactly what I want."

Natalie doesn't know my secret. She thinks I want to get out of here because New York is where the publishing industry is. Which, in my defense, is sort of true. But I also need to leave Madre Maria and be far away from Meera for the sake of my sanity.

As much as I love my mother and appreciate how hard she works to provide for us as a single parent, being the daughter of a divorced Christian life coach for Jesus-loving moms—yes, that is a thing, apparently—is not fun. At all. I'm not religious anymore, but I tolerate going to church every Sunday because that's the only real face time I get with my mom. Once she was done mourning the most serious relationship she'd ever had, she made use of her psychology degree and became a fiercely passionate life coach. Although she tries her best to maintain a work-life balance, her calendar is booked out and busy with client calls every day of the week. It's funny: Mom got custody of me after the divorce, but my dad is the one who has more time on his hands to talk to me. Not that I bother picking up his calls. If he wanted to be a part of my life, he should have just . . . stayed. Nine-year-old me will never forgive him.

During lunch, Sushant shows me a list he's made of the best restaurants in New York, from a French restaurant next to a bookstore to a gourmet Korean barbecue place with dishes I've only ever read about on food blogs. My heart skips a beat at how much this boy loves me, at all the things he does for me unprompted and how eager he is to begin our next chapter in New York. Sometimes I'm so overcome with affection and love for him that I forget I only started dating him to keep my secret. My initial plan was to end things after a few weeks, once Meera stopped talking to me for good. But then things changed, and somehow, Sushant became the boy I wanted to spend all my days with. Now he is undoubtedly my favorite person in the world, and I know I'm his.

"So?" Sushant's eyes flicker with excitement as he watches me flip through the photos. "Where should we do our first NYC date night?"

I set the phone aside, graze the side of his stubbly dark jaw with my fingers, and peck him on the lips. "I love you for making these plans already, but we both need to get into college there first."

He takes my hand in his and kisses my fingers. "We will. You're a shoo-in with your grades and essay, and as for me"—he shrugs—"Coach is talking to a bunch of scouts from New York, and he's really optimistic."

"He is?"

"Yeah. I mean, if Berkeley wanted me, other schools will too. Hopefully Syracuse."

"That's still four hours away from New York City," I say, my shoulders sinking.

"Hey." He smiles at me. "I'll make the drive every weekend to meet you at your dorm. We'll figure this out."

"Thank you." I squeeze his hand as a warm feeling swells in my chest: love, an emotion I never thought I'd feel again. This love is calmer, softer, sweeter than the passion for Meera that once drove me crazy. My breath hitches at the thought of my ex–best friend. Tears prick my eyes, and I blink them away and take a bite of my salad, hoping a change of topic is in order. Thankfully, one of the other guys on the football team brings up the game next week, and the conversation shifts.

Later, like almost every day after school, Sushant heads off to football practice after kissing me once on the nose, twice on the cheeks, and thrice on the lips: our own little tradition. Natalie gushes about how cute we are, and then she and I head to Café Kismat for our caffeine fix. I used to go to Meera's parents' café so often when we were besties, and I've kept the habit going despite our friendship breakup. Nobody else in town makes iced coffee like Mr. George, while Mr. Rao's tarot readings are always spot-on. Besides, Meera knows when I drop by, and she avoids the after-school shift like her life depends on it.

Most casual dining places in town are either macrobiotic, vegan, paleo, or somehow all three. Café Kismat, thankfully, is none of those. The problem is, the café has probably never seen a busy day because of Madre Maria's obsession with extreme fad diets that you'd wish would go out of style. I mean, Natalie's cat is vegan, for God's sake. I once tried explaining to Mrs. Copps that it's important for Buttons to have meat, since he is, you know, a *cat*, but she only laughed it off and promised me she knows what's best for her fur baby.

I pull up in front of Café Kismat in my Honda, park on the street, and then lead the way inside. The refreshing aroma of coffee beans and something floral and spicy coupled with the cool blast of air-conditioning are heaven to my senses.

The café is dimly lit by only twinkling yellow fairy lights and a few low-hanging orange bulbs. Incense sticks burn beside the counter, and an aromatherapy diffuser emitting rosy fumes changes colors from blue to green and back again near the toilets. The music is the same as always: instrumental versions of Bollywood songs. I recall that the song currently playing is from Meera's favorite Shah Rukh Khan movie about reincarnated lovers. That was the first Bollywood movie we ever watched together, soon after my dad moved out, on one of our countless sleepovers over the years. She'd told me that same night that Sushant reminded her of SRK with his dimples and messy hair, which was why she'd crushed on him so hard.

I wonder if she still likes Sushant.

My stomach twists in that familiar knot spurred by guilt, anxiety, and shame. *Don't go there. You did what you had to do to push her away, and it led to you falling in love with the boy you're going to end up with. It's okay.* I exhale softly through my teeth and sidle up to the counter with a forced smile, hoping my anxiety lets go of me for once. "Hi, Mr. George. How are you today?"

Mr. George pushes his thick rectangular glasses up his pointy nose and grins down at us. "I'm lovely, sweetheart. The usual, I'm guessing?"

I nod, and Natalie clears her throat. "Please make sure mine's—"

"Almond milk, no sugar. I remember." Mr. George's eyes are bright as he scribbles our orders onto two cups and passes them to the lone barista on duty. "Why don't you kids take a seat?"

Natalie and I claim our favorite table in the center of the café, where you get the best view of not just the floor-to-ceiling glass windows but also the little TV behind the counter, where a rerun of a cricket match is always playing. When Sushant and I first started dating, I knew nothing about cricket, but his whole family is obsessed with it, so I've started paying attention to the sport.

The barista calls out our names a few minutes later. I bring our drinks over: a large iced ginger turmeric chai latte for me and a medium iced coffee with almond milk for her. I wish Natalie didn't feel the need to stick to this difficult vegan/no-processed-sugar diet when away from her mother's prying eyes. But as we both know, nothing ever stays hidden in Madre Maria.

We sip our coffees while Natalie scrolls TikTok and I read a book from my vast collection of Jane Austen retellings—our usual routine once we get to the café.

As I turn over to the next page of the romance novel, I spot Mr. Rao at his little spiritual abode in the corner where he sometimes holds mindfulness classes or reads tarot for customers. He notices us and waves us over. There's nobody else in the café besides us—seriously, how do they make profits or break even?—so we get up from our seats, leaving our stuff on the table, and walk over to the tarot corner, to Mr. Rao.

"When was the last time I drew cards for you both?" he demands as he expertly shuffles a deck of pink tarot cards.

"Last week?" I guess.

Mr. Rao chuckles, his mustache twitching. "A reading is well overdue, in that case." He has at least twenty different tarot decks in his collection, and the one he's using for today's reading is pale pink with gold edges. This entire corner of the café is lined with huge chunks of raw crystals on display, including amethyst, rose quartz, citrine, and a few others that are pretty but I can't name. Natalie and I carefully sidestep the crystals and sit cross-legged in front of Mr. Rao.

"So, Natalie," he says, sorting the cards in his hands as the orange light from the bulb above our heads shines onto his bald spot, "what's on your mind today?"

Natalie sneaks a look at me and then tugs on her lower lip. "I want to know what life is going to look like for me after graduation. When Lucy's gone."

I press my hand into hers and let out a sad smile. We grew close shortly after I realized it would be impossible to hide my secret if I stayed best friends with Meera. Natalie had always been chatty with me since middle school, when we bonded over our love for floral-print clothing, so I decided to befriend her during camp the summer before my big fight with Meera. Natalie, who was already popular, got me onto the cheerleading team and made me who I am today. I'll forever be grateful for her.

Mr. Rao shuffles the deck one last time and lets a card fall out onto the blue velvet–carpeted floor. He turns it over and grins. "The Star!" The card pictures a woman clad in pink clothing raising her arms to the sky with a giant gold star peeking out from behind her.

Natalie claps her hands. "That sounds like a good card, right?"

"One of the most favorable cards in the deck, I'd say."

Mr. Rao closes his eyes briefly, then says, "I feel like you're really afraid of what the future holds for you."

She bows her head and runs her finger along the floral pattern on the carpet. "I am. Like, I don't have any dreams, you know? I don't have a real passion. I don't know where I'm meant to go, unlike Lucy."

"No matter what you believe about yourself, putta," Mr. Rao says, using that South Indian nickname he loves to use for kids and teens, "this card is telling me the Universe has your back. Inspiration is coming in divine time. You'll know what you're meant for when you're ready, and then you'll be unstoppable."

Natalie squeals loudly and dances around in place. "That's exactly what I wanted to hear! Thank you, Mr. Rao!"

With a grin, he turns to me. "And you, Lucy? What question do you want answered?"

I ponder his question for a moment. I already know where I'm going and who I want to go there with. But what happens before that? Graduation is still months away. "What's in store for me during the rest of senior year?" I ask finally.

Mr. Rao shuffles the deck vigorously, mumbling under his breath, "What have you got for Lucy, cards? What is coming up for Lucy this school year?"

A card flies out of the deck and into my lap. I turn it over and gasp.

The Tower.

Natalie and I exchange glances. Even with our little knowledge of tarot, we both know the Tower is not the happiest card. I mean, one look at it tells you it's scary: a large tower being struck by lightning with fire blazing out from the windows.

"Ah." Mr. Rao's eyes glint. "This year is going to be liberating, putta."

I scan his face to see if he's joking. "I thought the Tower is about things going to ruin. Things ending. Going from hero to zero."

"Indeed." His eyes glaze over, a ghost of a smile on his face. "But you must remember: A phoenix can only rise from the ashes, renewed and reborn, after first burning to nothing. A year from today, you're going to be grateful for this card and everything it holds for you."

I gulp, taking the card, which feels surprisingly heavy in my hand. The golden edges catch the light and shimmer. Mr. Rao has never been wrong, not with a single reading, in the six years since the café opened.

This time, I hope he's only half right. I want to be liberated. From Meera, from this town, from this false persona I've adopted. But I do not want to burn to the ground and then rise up. I want to soar without having to fall first.

And if there's anything the past year has taught me, it's that I am luckier than most. Good things just happen to me. I get everything I want without having to work too hard for it—the grades, the accolades, the boyfriend.

One tarot reading cannot change that. I won't let it.

CHAPTER TWO

"I Miss You"

by Clean Bandit feat. Julia Michaels

Meera

Valeria and Ron are not impressed when they walk upstairs to my room and see the words *THE PLAN: DATE SUSHANT & DESTROY LUCY* written on the whiteboard hanging on my wall. In the background, music—the one thing I can't live without—plays from my speakers.

"You're kidding, right?" Valeria groans. She bites off a chunk of roasted peanut chikki—my go-to Indian sweet treat to make whenever I'm stressed—and chews furiously. Her metabolism is sky-high and her blood sugar too low, so she needs to snack every hour to avoid getting cranky and woozy. Over the past year of our friendship, I've learned to always keep food within reach of her. I love to bake and cook, and although Appa and Dad won't let me experiment with the café menu just yet, Valeria loves taste-testing my recipes.

I stand in front of the whiteboard and lift my arms in a ta-da sort of motion. "It's time to turn the social hierarchy upside down. It's time for the nerd to get the jock."

Ron plops himself down on my bed and studies me with a funny look. "But your grades aren't good enough for you to be a nerd. If anyone qualifies for that label, it's Lucy, with her straight A's and her—" He shuts up when I narrow my eyes at him. "Sorry."

"As I was saying . . ." I gesture for Valeria to join Ron. "I can't sit around and let Sushant move to New York and lose all my chances with him. The Date Sushant and Destroy Lucy Plan begins now."

"'Destroy' is a terrible, hateful word." Valeria scrunches up her nose from where she sits on the bed. "Maybe 'dethrone' would be kinder?"

"Who are you, my father?" Regardless, I erase the word *DESTROY* and replace it with *DETHRONE*. Then I set aside my red marker, pull the cap off my favorite blue marker, and draw three stick figures under the heading on the whiteboard. "Now, there are three people involved in the Plan: me, Sushant, and Lucy." I pause to regard the sketch. Damn it, Lucy is the best-looking one, even as a stick figure. Deciding to let it slide, I press on, using arrows to emphasize my point. "We have to find a way to (a) elevate my social standing, (b) bring me and Sushant closer together, and (c) make Lucy undesirable to Sushant."

I pause to see if my friends have anything to add. They're staring blankly at the multiple arrows on the whiteboard, so I continue. "Let's start with Lucy. How do you bring down the queen bee? You cut off her resources—"

Ron looks at me sheepishly and raises his hand. "Uh, may I interject?"

"Sure."

"Why does this feel like a rehash of *Mean Girls*?"

Valeria bursts out laughing and winds an arm around his shoulder. "Oh my God, it totally does!"

I study my unevenly painted turquoise nails, embarrassed. I did an at-home manicure last week using a YouTube tutorial for reference. It did *not* turn out well. When we were best friends, Lucy always did my nails. "I might have watched a few scenes of *Mean Girls* on the bus ride home for . . . inspiration."

My friends dissolve into a fresh bout of laughter, and I put my hands on my hips and clear my throat so they'll look back at me. "You know, Lindsay Lohan's friends in the movie were a lot more supportive than you two."

I'm only half serious. Ron and Valeria have been my lifelines since my fight with Lucy. We'd always had adjacent lockers, so I used to pass by them every morning before class, but it wasn't until two weeks into junior year that we actually spoke to each other. I'd noticed Lucy and Sushant pressed up against his locker at the other end of the hallway, and I'd slammed my own locker shut, my fists balling as my teeth gritted.

Ron jumped. "Geez, calm down," he said, clutching a hand to his heart while Valeria nearly dropped her books.

"I can't calm down," I snapped, turning to them, "because my best friend is making out with the boy I love who has no idea I love him, and now he's dating her, and, oh, did I mention that the best friend in question no longer wants to talk to me or tell me why our friendship is over, and I don't know what I did to deserve *any* of this?"

They exchanged wide-eyed glances while I breathed in and out, trying to slow my racing heart. *Great going, Meera,* I thought. *They probably think you've lost your mind.*

Valeria shut her locker softly and placed a hand on my shoulder. "That sounds rough. You're Meera, right?"

I nodded slowly, blinking back tears. "And you're Valeria and Ron? We had English together last year."

"That's right." She sighed. "Do you . . . want to talk about it?"

"Maybe. I don't know." I lowered my gaze to the floor as a tear fell down my cheek. Ugh. Crying was the worst.

Ron shrugged. "If you want someone to talk to, the guidance counselor's office is in the next building—" He yelped when Valeria elbowed him.

"Don't you start." She rolled her eyes at him and said to me, "Why don't you join us for lunch today?"

I bit my lip, my eyes going back and forth between them. "Thanks, but I don't want to be the third wheel."

"We're not together," she said as Ron laughed next to her, "and besides, I could use some girl talk for a change."

I wiped my cheek as the bell rang, a soft, warm feeling in my belly after far too long. "All right. I'll see you both at lunch."

Now, back in my room, I wait for my friends to stop laughing at my Plan. Finally, they straighten up, and Valeria finishes her last mouthful of chikki. "Okay, sorry. We're listening. You have to cut off Lucy's—"

Appa's voice interrupts us as my door creaks open. He must have just come home from the café; he smells like incense. "Cut off Lucy's what, now?"

I nearly drop the marker in my haste to kick my father out of my room. "Appa, you're supposed to knock!"

"The door was ajar!" He steps back, hands raised, then twirls his mustache with amusement as his eyes fall on the whiteboard. *Shit.* "If you like this boy," he says slowly, "just tell him."

"He's madly in love with Lucy!" I exclaim, pushing Appa away from my bedroom. "It's not that simple."

Appa opens his mouth to speak, but I swing the door shut in his face and bolt it for good measure. Then I spin around. "Well, then. Where were we?"

"Look, I don't think your *Mean Girls*–esque plan is going to work in this situation," Valeria says, one hand on her head. "You need to get in with the popular crowd before you even have a shot at 'dethroning' Lucy." She makes air quotes around the word "dethrone." "Besides, Sushant's not a shallow guy who only cares about reputation. He'd date you as long as he were single and had feelings for you."

I pull my desk chair over to the center of the room and sit down, nodding. "You have a point. How do we make Sushant have feelings for me, then?"

Ron rubs his chin with his thin fingers, pensive. "We already tried the makeover route. Didn't work."

In March, when Sushant eagerly told me it was his six-month-iversary with Lucy, I asked Valeria's sister—who runs Madre Maria's best salon—to give me a makeover from head to toe, hoping the clichéd teen romance trope would work in my favor. I ended up with dark brown layered hair and blond highlights, my glasses swapped for contact lenses, and an intensive wardrobe change that included switching my comfortable and casual all-black attire for spaghetti-strap tops, bright colors, and heels. *Kill me now.*

The result? Sushant gave me a confused look the next time he saw me on the bus and said, "Why do you look so . . . weird?"

I remember tossing my freshly styled hair back and saying, with as much faux confidence as I could, "I'm simply leveling up my appearance. Don't I look hot?"

He chuckled before brushing my hair out of my face, sending tingles down to my very cramped toes in those heels. "You look good as you are. It's pretty obvious you're uncomfortable in that getup. Aren't you?"

Once we reached the school building, I wiped off the makeup, grabbed my handy spare sneakers from my locker, and decided that if he thought I looked good as I was, it wouldn't be long until he'd fall for me too. He just had to realize it.

. . . Nearly ten months later, the boy still hasn't come to that conclusion.

"Maybe you could assist the cheerleading team, or join one of the other clubs the popular kids are in." Valeria chews on her lower lip. "Then you'd be able to have lunch with Lucy and Sushant."

I fold my arms over my chest and scoff. "Forget a cartwheel. I can't even do the tree pose from yoga without falling flat on my face. We"—I think for a moment—"have to break them up so I can slide into the empty space in Sushant's heart—"

Ron's phone buzzes, and he stands up. "My little brother needs help with his math homework. I'm out." He gives me a hug, then nudges Valeria. "Want me to drop you off at home?" Ron's the only one of us who has a car, a hand-me-down from his older brother, who's a sophomore in college.

Valeria gives me an apologetic look and stands up too. "I'd like a ride, yeah." She wraps her arms around me and whispers, "We'll figure it out, okay?"

I press my face into the crook of her shoulder. "Thank you." I don't quite believe her, but sometimes you have to keep going even when you have zero faith. This is one of those times.

Lucy

Mom's voice echoes off the walls when I unlock the front door and walk into the living room. Although she does her Zoom calls from her home office, which is at the far end of the first floor, you can't miss her loud, exaggerated, chipper life coach voice no matter which corner of the house you're in.

"Oh my goodness, Karen, this is a completely safe space," she's saying to one of her clients as I walk into the kitchen to pop a frozen pizza into the oven. "You don't have to censor yourself in front of me . . . or anyone, for that matter."

I want to smack my head against the refrigerator door. Obviously, Mom never discusses her life coaching clients' problems with me—confidentiality and all that—but I can guess that poor Karen is crying crocodile tears because her kid got told off in class for being homophobic or something.

Mom's clients aren't ever from here. She makes it a point to work with Christian clients "around the world," as long as that excludes Madre Maria. But from the little sneak peeks I've gotten of her clients based on their social media testimonials, I know they're all middle-aged straight white women who love Jesus, dote on their kids, and resent their ex-husbands. Just like my mother.

I'm biting into the second-to-last slice of pizza when Mom finally exits her office, stretching her arms. She's got a bright pink blazer on, very Reese Witherspoon in *Legally Blonde*, and she brightens when she sees me—and the pizza.

"You'd better be saving that slice for me," she declares, grabbing herself the final slice along with some utensils. "I had three back-to-back calls today, and that meant no time for lunch. Helping other women is more important than food, you know?"

"You can't help them if you're low on energy, though," I say, pouting. "Take care of yourself like you take care of them."

"I'll try, sweetheart." Mom beams at me, then cuts a small piece of pizza with her fork and knife and daintily takes a bite. "How was your day?" she asks as I put my plate in the sink and run some water over it.

If she were open to the vastly different experiences of people from other cultures and faiths, I'd tell her about Mr. Rao's tarot reading and how afraid I am of my Tower moment happening. Instead, all I say as I walk back to the kitchen island is "School was fine. I went to Café Kismat with Natalie for iced coffee after and read a book."

Mom tuts. "That café is so . . . eccentric. I don't see why you like going there, honey. There are other places that serve coffee in town."

Eccentric. A faux-polite way to say "people of color." I study the edge of my nail. "They have the best coffee, Mom. That's all." *And it's my only link to my ex–best friend.* But I don't dare say that part out loud.

"You know"—she sets her empty plate aside and puts her hands on her hips—"I was so happy when you and that Meera girl stopped being friends. I don't like her family or that café one bit."

"Mm-hmm," I say as my stomach drops. I take her plate and put it in the sink too. I grip the edges of the sink with my fingers, forcing my nervous system to calm down. *Inhale . . . exhale. Inhale . . . exhale. Inhale—*

"Anyway, your father called again today," Mom says dispassionately. She picks some lint off her blazer and sighs. "I wonder if his new boo knows how often he calls me."

My teeth clench. He called me last week too, but I let it go to voicemail and deleted the message without listening to it. I have no interest in talking to him or the woman he chose over us. I haven't met her, nor do I ever want to. "Did you pick up?" I ask.

She huffs. "Yeah. Apparently, your grandfather passed away and left your father a good chunk of money. It came as a surprise to him too."

My grandparents and Dad had a falling-out shortly after he graduated high school. Dad didn't want to talk about it, and we never visited them, although they live in California too. Still, my heart pangs in my chest. I never got to meet Grandpa, and now I never will.

I swallow, then ask, "Are we going to the funeral?"

"No, he didn't invite us." Mom rolls her eyes. "I suppose he just called to rub it in our faces that he's rich now."

I tighten my hold on the sink. It's not that we're poor or anything. Mom's business is thriving, what with the long hours she puts in, and the alimony checks help, but our designer clothes are all secondhand, and we've had to put off much-needed home renovations for a couple years now.

Good for Dad, though. He'll probably be able to give his future kids not just his time and attention but also an Ivy League education. Lucky them. Before he blindsided us, he was an incredible father, and I was the biggest daddy's girl. He surprised me with a new toy with each paycheck, took me to Disneyland every other month, and bought me cotton candy to cheer me up after an attendant said I wasn't tall enough for the "big-kid rides." He'd read bedtime stories to me, stroking my hair as I fell asleep. He was the one who got me into the reading habit I'll never let go of.

I guess that was all just an act.

"Well, honey, I'll get back to work." Mom gives me a kiss on the cheek before heading to her office for her next coaching call, and I unclench my hands and go upstairs.

My room is small but cozy, with plenty of natural light and breeze. I draw the curtains open and let cool air drift into the room from my window. I don't hang photos or nail paintings anywhere, unlike Natalie, whose room is filled with posters of her favorite artists—Megan Thee Stallion, Beyoncé, Tyla. My floral pink wallpaper decks up my bedroom well enough. What does overwhelm my room is my white wooden bookcase crammed with literature of all kinds. From classic works and romance novels to young adult and sci-fi, I've got quite the collection. The one thing most of them have in common, though, is that they're either written by Jane Austen or are inspired by her works.

Sushant can never understand how I read so much. Sometimes I manage to finish a hundred books a year while he's read maybe four books in his whole life. He especially can't figure out how I juggle it alongside cheerleading and school and, well, our relationship.

But until I can leave Madre Maria, books *are* my escape.

I fall onto my bed, snuggling into the white comforter, and take three more long, deep breaths until my heart stops racing. Then I grab my laptop. Like every day recently after coming home, I check the status of my application to NYU.

Nothing yet.

I bite my lip. I've applied to one other college here in California, UCLA, only because Mom said I needed to have "safety schools" and because she hates the idea of me leaving the state. If I don't get into the English lit program at NYU, I'll move to the city with Sushant anyway. Take a gap year, wait tables at coffee shops, babysit for young parents, pay my bills somehow—and then reapply the following year.

I'd do anything to get out of here and to New York. Nowhere else. It has to be New York or no dice. Someday I'm going to be a big-shot editor at a publishing house. And, sure, I've done enough research to know there's not much money in it, but there's heart and hope and passion. My biggest dream is seeing my name in the acknowledgments section of a wonderful book, acquired by me, written by an author I absolutely adore. And New York can bring me closer to that dream than any other place can.

My phone buzzes with a text from Sushant. Check your email babe! 😘

He's sent me the list of restaurants he was showing me at lunch. I text back a heart. I love that he's as thrilled about New York as I am, but, gosh, it's next to impossible for two college kids with no family money to go to any of these places. I don't even know if Mom has enough in savings to help pay for my college tuition and housing.

As for Sushant, his folks run a chain of small electronics stores in and around California, initially started by his late grandfather. They're doing well for themselves, and they've promised Sushant they'll support him through college. He once told me Indian parents don't like the idea of their kids being independent and "leaving the nest" at eighteen.

But there's a huge difference between paying for his room and board and paying for a New York City lifestyle, and I don't want to put them through that. Sushant and I are starting a new life together. We love each other enough to find a way to fund it.

Love, unfortunately, doesn't pay the bills.

Sighing, I open a fresh tab on Chrome and search for Madre Maria job listings.

CHAPTER THREE

"Look What You Made Me Do"

by Taylor Swift

Meera

I'm expecting Appa to bring up the Plan he spotted on my whiteboard sooner or later, given his nosiness. What I don't expect is for him to ask me about it at the breakfast table the next morning with Dad right there.

"So, putta, do you want to tell your old men about this plan you've devised?"

I narrow my eyes at his betrayal and focus on feeding masala dosa to our Boston terrier, Raj, who we adopted four years ago. He laps up the food before scurrying over to his water bowl.

Dad is quiet but staring at me, waiting, which makes it clear they've already discussed this behind closed doors and have jointly decided to confront me about it. "Well?" He quirks a brow beneath his glasses.

Sighing, I relent. "I'm just trying to have a proper high school experience. This is my last chance to make some real memories."

Dad studies me for a moment, then pops a piece of spicy yellow potato wrapped in the crispy dosa into his mouth. Over the twenty-plus years my parents have been together, Dad's spice tolerance has vastly improved, which is great because I love cooking spicy dishes. "And plotting to take someone down is the way to do that?" he says quietly once he swallows.

When I don't respond, they exchange helpless glances. "Look, putta." Appa scratches the side of his receding hairline. "I understand you're upset that the boy you like doesn't feel the same way about you, but breaking two people up is not the right thing to—"

"She knows I love him, Appa." I slam my fist on the table, ignoring the pain that shoots up my arm. "She was my best friend. Sushant was all I talked about for, what, three years? And then she goes to camp the summer before junior year, barely texts me, and the next thing I know, she's dating him, and we're not even friends anymore. She's a bitch, but nobody's willing to do anything about it but me."

Dad coughs, his eyes steely. "Language."

Appa puts a hand on Dad's wrist to pacify him, then turns to me. "If Sushant is meant for you, nothing can keep you apart. The Universe—"

I interject before he can get started with that useless speech about divine timing again. "I can't sit around and wait for the Universe any longer." I take my spoon out from my bowl of sambar and tap it on the plate to emphasize my point. "Sometimes you have to make. Stuff. Happen."

My parents look at each other, presumably having one of

their usual telepathic conversations: eyebrow movements, twitching lips, and short exhales. Then, finally, Dad nods. "You're almost an adult. You get to make your own choices."

"But don't lose yourself in trying to win your love," Appa finishes. "Then you'll be left with nothing, and even your Angels won't be able to help you."

I stand, wipe my mouth with the back of my palm, and sling my backpack over one shoulder. "I already have nothing," I declare furiously, "which means there's nothing to lose."

Dad audibly sighs as I leave my plate on the dining table and storm outside to catch my bus. Sushant is already waiting by the sidewalk for the bus and me, bouncing back and forth on his toes.

"Morning," he says cheerfully, showcasing those deep-set dimples I'd love to stick my pinky finger into. "Breakfast?"

"Masala dosa, sambar, coconut chutney," I list, going along with our daily pre–bus ride tradition. "You?"

"Aloo parathas with homemade butter and mango pickle, plus a tall glass of lassi." He licks his full lips—my stomach flutters at the sight—and rubs his muscled abdomen. "Dadima went all out today."

Sushant's parents are usually busy with their electronics store and taking care of his seven-year-old brother, Dheeraj, so his grandmother is the one who takes over kitchen duty. I love her food—no Punjabi restaurant can match her authentic home-cooked meals—but unfortunately, I barely ever get invited to Sushant's because Dadima doesn't like my family. It might have to do with the fact that she's seventy years old, narrow-minded, and silently judges my parents' totally queer marriage. And she probably doesn't want to encourage a friendship or a potential relationship between Sushant and me.

The bus arrives, and we take our usual seats in the middle. Sushant gets out his French notes and starts going through them since midterms are coming up, so I put my Spotify mix on shuffle and stare out the window at the passing houses and people watering their plants or mowing their lawns.

We drive past Lucy's house. The light-blue-and-gray paint is in desperate need of a fresh coat, and the grass on her front lawn is slightly overgrown. Her mother, who goes by her family name, Ms. Miller, must be swamped with her coaching clients. Lucy's car isn't in the garage, which means she's on her way to school too.

I grind my teeth and think about Appa's words, which are the opposite of wise: "Don't lose yourself in trying to win your love." Ha! I'm a nobody. I have nothing at stake here, so I have to try. I look up at the sky through the window, bright blue and not a cloud in sight, and say a silent prayer to my Angels, who I have a love-hate relationship with: *If you're done drinking your mai tais and chilling in heaven, I'd appreciate a little help here—maybe some sort of divine intervention. Give me a sign that you have my back. Please, you lazy fucks.*

Then I bite my lip. *Sorry for calling you lazy. Thanks in advance for your help!* I turn back to the front of my seat and smile at Sushant, still busy with his notes. Something tells me the Universe is on my side. I just need to keep my eyes peeled for the signs.

Lucy

Today has already been insufferable, and it's barely eight in the morning. I tap my heel against the marble-tiled floor of the waiting room outside the vice principal's office, trying to yawn discreetly.

I was up late last night, working on the routine for today's cheerleading practice, studying for midterms, and going through the two job listings in town that seem like a good fit for me. And now, after a meager four hours of sleep, I'm supposed to show some new kid around for the entire day.

Vice Principal Montgomery didn't tell me much about him, except that he's an exchange student from Paris and it's his first time in America. I have no idea what he looks like or whether he speaks any English. All I know is this: He clearly doesn't care about my schedule, since he's ten minutes late.

I'm about to give up and head to class when the door opens and Meera walks in. Her worn-out sneakers screech to a halt as she spots me, her gaze hardening. Behind her is an athletic boy who I'm guessing is the exchange student. He's around medium height, with dark brown skin and curly black hair styled with gel. He's wearing a mandarin-collared shirt and well-fitting jeans, and, damn, it's true what they say about the French being attractive as hell. This boy is beautiful. "So, this is the vice principal's office?" he asks Meera, who's still looking at me.

I force myself to stifle another yawn and walk over to them. I nod politely at Meera, who only folds her arms and stares me down, and then I turn to the exchange student. "Julien, right?" I attempt to say his name the way our French teacher would: *Zhoo-lien*. Hopefully I didn't butcher the pronunciation too much.

"Yes," he says, his eyes lighting up as he leans forward and kisses me on each cheek. I jerk back a moment too late and grin embarrassedly, my face coloring. His cologne smells divine.

Julien mumbles out an apology. "Sorry, it's a force of habit," he says in a French accent. "You must be Lucy."

"So, you're the one showing him around, then?" Meera's got one eyebrow quirked, a soft smile playing on her lips. "For the entire day?"

I nod again, and she beams at me, which is jarring because she hasn't done that since before the first day of junior year, when I told her, in front of the whole school, that I'd outgrown our friendship. My insides churn at the memory, my throat catching as I recall the way tears streamed down her face. And Meera *never* cries. I shove my anxiety down.

"You're in good hands, Julien," she says, the grin now spreading fully across her face. "I'll leave you both to it."

She turns around and walks out, closing the door softly behind her.

Julien heads to the administrative assistant's desk to get his class schedule while I rack my brain, wondering why Meera's being nice. I'm still staring at the door when Julien taps me on the shoulder. I jump. "Shall we?" he asks.

"Sure." I bite the inside of my cheek, dazed, and lead the way to English class.

As we walk, Julien hands me his schedule and chatters on about this town and how welcoming our people are, the bright, sunshiny warm weather, the places he wants to see, the American family he's staying with—God, the guy just won't shut up.

I mumble out "hmm"s and "uh-huh"s as I look at his class schedule. They've put him in almost all the same classes as me, which means I'm going to have to be his "friend" for a lot longer than just today.

Great.

Natalie sits upright at her desk when she sees us walk into class. No, it's not just her, because the noise of twenty restless teenagers dies down at the sight of Julien Perrin. Heads turn. Whispers echo. Someone even wolf-whistles.

"Who's this?" Natalie asks, eyeing Julien curiously.

Julien starts to move toward her, presumably to greet her in the French way, then bites his lip and simply holds out his hand. *Hmm. Character growth.* "Julien Perrin, from Paris."

"This is my best friend, Natalie," I say, because she looks too transfixed by his accent to speak or return his handshake.

"Enchanté." Julien smiles, and I swear to God, his teeth sparkle like diamonds.

I settle into my seat and take out my books while Natalie

asks him about Paris and if it really is like how it's depicted on that superpopular Netflix show.

"That show is bullshit." Julien's all riled up now, his forehead wrinkled and his eyes narrowed. "You should never trust foreign cities shown from the American gaze."

"Absolutely. You're so right," Natalie mumbles. She plays with a lock of her hair. "Do you have a girlfriend back home?"

Well, that escalated quickly. I try not to snort with laughter. Julien tells Natalie about his recent breakup with his girlfriend—I catch her holding back a smile—and proceeds to chat her ear off throughout class, something she doesn't seem to mind in the slightest. The English teacher has to shush him twice.

If only Natalie and I had more classes together. But, no, I have to bear the brunt of Julien Perrin's loquacious ass for two more hours, until we can break for lunch and he'll get to bother someone else in the cafeteria.

Until then, God help me.

CHAPTER FOUR

"you were good to me"
by Jeremy Zucker and Chelsea Cutler

Meera

I all but pounce on my friends when they get to our usual lunch table in the corner of the cafeteria. "You will not believe this!" I exclaim, and Valeria almost drops her tray in surprise. "There's a hot new French exchange student in town!"

They both sit down across from me. Ron takes a bite of his sandwich and frowns. "Wait, so you're over Sushant?"

"I don't blame her," Valeria says, setting her head on her hands and sighing dramatically. "The new guy is so gorgeous. He even has a sexy name. Julien Perrin."

"No, the Plan is still on," I say hastily, brushing my hair from my eyes and grinning at them. "But guess who's in charge of showing Madre Maria's newest hottie around?"

Their eyebrows scrunch up for a moment before it dawns on both of them. "Lucy," they say in hushed voices.

"Yep."

"Oh yeah, I saw him sitting beside her during Algebra. He

wouldn't stop talking to her." Valeria has a dreamy look in her eyes as she fans herself. "That French accent, my God."

After I sip some of my chocolate milk, I lean forward on the table and lower my voice, but the excitement in my tone remains. "You both know what this means for the Plan, right?"

"What?"

"I can use Julien to break them up!"

Ron's mouth drops open, revealing chewed-up bits of meat and lettuce. I avert my gaze to Valeria, whose eyes are wide with disbelief. "Shit," she whispers. "Meera, that's . . . that's diabolical."

I toss my hair back over one shoulder proudly. "I know, right?"

"I didn't mean that as a compliment," she continues, shaking her head. Mayo and marinara sauce are oozing out of one side of her sandwich and dripping onto her fingers, but she doesn't notice. "There's got to be a better way to do this than bringing an innocent stranger into the Plan and potentially setting him up for heartbreak."

"Like what?" I groan and plant my face on the table. "I thought about it all night and came up with nothing."

Ron rolls his eyes, but Valeria snaps her fingers. "I got it. My sister told me Lucy applied for the receptionist position at the salon. She's looking for a job."

"So . . . ?"

"So"—she grins—"you can offer her one at Café Kismat. Keep your friends close and enemies closer, right?"

"She must have applied to a lot of places." Ron shakes his head. "And if there's one thing we know, it's that Lucy *always* gets what she wants."

"I'll tell Rosa not to hire her." Valeria thinks for a moment. "And as for the rest, we'll figure it out as we go along."

"Thanks," I say, clasping her palm with mine and squeezing. "But I'm still going to figure out if I can use Julien to break them up."

"I can't . . . I can't even." Ron shakes his head and busies himself with his phone. He looks pissed. I mean, I get it. This isn't a pretty plan, or even a nice one. But playing nice hasn't gotten me anywhere so far—and after the way Lucy hurt me, she deserves nothing short of the heartbreak she put *me* through.

Being a Mean Girl might not be the worst thing if it means I can get even. Right?

My friends discuss a new sci-fi show they're obsessed with while I try to see what's going on at the It Crowd table. Lucy's sitting next to Sushant, of course, but on her other side is Julien. He's talking to the table at large, and people are listening with rapt attention. Sushant leans back in his seat and laughs loudly at something Julien says. But Lucy is focused on her meal, and even from a distance, I can see a tic in her jaw. *Oh no.* I know that look.

Lucy, popular as she may now be, has always been an introverted woman of few words. When we were friends, she was chatty around me, in the comfort of my home or the café, eagerly telling me the plot of whatever book she was reading or her in-depth analysis of the latest Taylor Swift album. I don't care much for books or pop music, but seeing her in her natural element and knowing our friendship was what put her at ease . . . It made me long to hear every word that came out of her mouth.

I bite the inside of my cheek, shaking off the nostalgia and the ache in my stomach. *This isn't the time for that, Meera.* I'm sure she's just as talkative with darling Natalie now, since they're best friends or whatever, but new people are an acquired taste for her. Julien has probably gotten on her nerves already. His looks won't be enough to drive a wedge between her and Sushant.

So, until she warms up to Julien, I'll have to find another way to put the Plan into motion. And maybe Valeria's idea can work.

The problem is, Café Kismat doesn't have an opening for a job. Given how Appa and Dad refuse to talk to me about our finances and never let me near the accounting books on my shifts, it's pretty clear the café's not doing well. We don't have the budget to hire anyone new. Right now, there's only one employee apart from the three of us: Danny, the barista who handles the afternoon-and-evening shift. He works two other jobs so he can make enough to pay for college next year. There's no way my conscience would let me sabotage his future just for the sake of the Plan.

Which means I have to convince my parents to create a new job opening at Café Kismat. One that is the perfect fit for Lucy *and* brings in more profits for the café.

Lucy

I'm exhausted by the time cheerleading practice is over and I take a quick shower. The lack of sleep last night (and the headache I got listening to Monsieur Won't-Shut-Up all day) doesn't help my anxiety over my first job interview.

Once I'm parked outside the library, I look at myself in the rearview mirror. The concealer is doing a half-decent job of hiding my dark circles, and the subtle eyeliner helps. I definitely look the part of a library assistant with my red hair up in a tight bun and my white button-down shirt tucked into one of Mom's old pencil skirts.

I clear my throat and smile at my reflection. "You've got this," I whisper. "Mrs. Fields loves you. You know those bookshelves better than anyone else in town. You're a shoo-in."

With trembling hands, I close the car door behind me and walk into the library, taking deep breaths to quell the churning in my belly. My brain is in overdrive with anxiety, thinking about all the ways I could fuck this up. What if I puke on myself midway through the interview? Mom would kill me if I ruined these shoes. What if Mrs. Fields expects me to work shifts right after school? I'd have to choose between this and cheerleading. What if that damned tarot card reading comes true and all my dreams of going to New York are shattered?

"Lucy, what a pleasure seeing you here!" Mrs. Fields is kind as ever. She pushes her glasses up her nose and studies me. "You look so pretty. What's the occasion?"

My forehead wrinkles. "I'm here about the library assistant position? The application said I could come in for an interview around this time."

"Oh! One minute, dear." She presses a button on the telephone that sits on the desk.

A buzz sounds, then a woman's clipped voice. A voice I unfortunately recognize. "Yes?"

"Sharon, are you still taking interviews for the assistant position? Lucy's here."

"Uh . . ." There's a pause, and I hear the rustling of papers through the intercom before Sharon replies. "I was about to take a break, but, yeah, sure. Send her in."

Mrs. Fields claps her hands and smiles at me. "Best of luck. It's the office that's down the hall, to the left."

I already know this, but I thank her anyway and head past the bookshelves to Sharon's office. My throat feels tight; my mouth is dry. I lick my lips and swallow.

Sharon is the head librarian here, and I wasn't expecting her to interview applicants. I figured she'd be busy with administrative work. She doesn't particularly love me. One time, she saw me eagerly checking out a romance novel with a shirtless guy on the cover and said, tsk-tsking, "Are people still reading that trash?"

I'd forced myself to smile and replied, "Uh, I guess," and

she shook her head and walked away in a huff. She's one of those literary MFA grads who turn their noses up at anything commercial or, God forbid, entertaining.

The interview starts out well enough. Sharon asks me a few things about myself, my hobbies, and whether I know my way around management software tools and databases.

"I'm a quick learner," I say. I keep my hands clenched in my lap, my right thumb tapping along the knuckles of my other hand to keep me grounded. "And considering I want to work in publishing someday, this would be such a great opportunity for me."

Instantly I feel like I've said the wrong thing. Sharon's features twist into a smug "gotcha!" kind of expression. "Publishing, huh?" She leans forward and appraises me. "What kind of books would you acquire? The kind you read? Bodice rippers?"

"I—" I swallow, my mouth dry as I think hard. I know I can turn this around by giving her the answer she wants to hear: hard-hitting, intellectual nonfiction; character-driven literary fiction; and stories that inspire change and revolution. But I can't bring myself to lie.

"Sharon, I know you're not the biggest fan of commercial fiction," I say, trying to choose my words carefully, "but books that spark joy and love are just as important as books that start conversations. In fact, I don't think the two are mutually exclusive. A book can be entertaining and also thought-provoking."

She doesn't agree; I know that for a fact. But to her credit, she nods and smiles politely. "That's an interesting perspective. Lucy, what's the last five-star book you read?"

Simple question. I devoured a book in one sitting just two nights ago. I open my mouth to answer, but suddenly my mind is blank. What are words? What book did I read? Who wrote it?

"I—I—" My grip on my left hand tightens.

She waits patiently, one eyebrow quirked.

I gulp, then get the words out. "*Prada, Purrs, and Prejudice.* It's a contemporary take on Jane Austen's book." After a moment, I add, "Sorry, I'm a bit nervous."

Sharon definitely knows this book. It's a young adult romance with an illustrated pair of heels and a cat on the cover that I borrowed from this library. And judging by the little sneer on her face, she isn't impressed. "Lucy, thank you for applying," she says, giving my résumé one final look before setting it aside. "We'll let you know in a few days."

That's obviously code for "you didn't get the job." I smile at her and slowly stand up. "I'm grateful for the opportunity." I pause, wondering if she wants to shake hands, but she doesn't even get up. *Ouch.*

I leave the room, closing the door behind me. Mrs. Fields looks up as I walk past her desk, but I don't stop to engage in chitchat. I get into my car, lay my head on the steering wheel, and exhale through my teeth. I'm definitely not getting that job. Which means I have to ace the other job opening: the receptionist position at the Cut & Color Salon.

But when I get home and call them to ask when I can come in for an interview, the lady on the phone—who I presume is Rosa, the salon owner—asks for my name, then hesitates and says I wouldn't be a good fit.

"Wait, how do you know that?" My voice shakes. "You haven't interviewed me yet."

"Uh, you're in high school, right?" She sighs. "We need someone full-time."

"But the job listing on the website stated it's a part-time position on the weekends—"

"We didn't update the listing. I'm sorry, Lucy."

Before I can try to convince her to hear me out, she hangs up the phone. I yell curses into my pillow so Mom, who's on another coaching call in her office, won't overhear the barrage of deeply non-Christian swear words coming out of my mouth.

I pull the comforter up to my chin and close my eyes, letting a few tears wet the pillow under my head. There's bound to be another job opening in Madre Maria sooner or later. I could ask around at school or find a remote job I could do from my desk.

My phone buzzes. I wipe my eyes and check it.

Sushant:

Dinner at my place tonight? Maa and Papa miss you . . . and so do I 😘

I smile and text back, Yes please. I miss you too

Sushant:

I love you 😍

I pause. Although we've been together for so long, saying those words back to him often makes my stomach lurch because I know that our relationship started with a lie. But there's nothing more real to me now than the tender feelings in my heart for him, and I deserve to love and be loved by this perfect person. So, smiling, I text back, I love you too 🥰

CHAPTER FIVE

"The Way I Loved You (Taylor's Version)"

by Taylor Swift

Lucy

"Have some more, Lucy. You look so thin," Sushant's grandmother insists. She puts another tandoori chicken leg on my plate and adds a big dollop of mint chutney beside it for good measure.

I smile at Dadima and murmur a polite thank-you. Dinner at Sushant's place means I have to mentally prep myself to survive a never-ending meal. From fresh, fluffy rotis and lamb curry to lentils and a whole cooked tandoori chicken, the dinner table is jam-packed with Punjabi food. There's barely enough room on the table for the six glasses of Thums Up (India's favorite fizzy cola, I've been told), one for each of us.

"So, Lucy, how's school going?" Mrs. Khera asks fondly as she dips a piece of chicken in mint sauce.

I swallow a particularly juicy morsel of meat and nod. "It's going well, Mrs. Khera."

"I've told you before, call me Ritu Aunty." She makes a

tutting noise. "We don't do those formal salutations under this roof."

"Sorry, Ritu Aunty." I smile weakly.

"This supercool French exchange student showed up to school today," Sushant says. His plate is already empty, save for the meat bones—so naturally Dadima leans over and tosses him another piece of tandoori chicken. He dives right into his third helping of dinner and adds, his mouth semi-full, "His name's Julien, and he's hilarious. Isn't he, Lucy?"

"Uh-huh," I say, suppressing the urge to roll my eyes. There's still a dull ache in my head. I have to somehow get out of being Julien's tour guide. Maybe I can sic Natalie on him. Or Sushant, since he loves Julien's sense of humor so much.

"Oh, the French are really rude. And Paris is so dangerous!" Mr. Khera lowers his voice as though the neighbors will overhear. "I remember when your mother and I went to Paris for our honeymoon and we almost got mugged."

He goes off about the honeymoon mugging incident, a story I've heard at least five times before, and as the whole table laughs and interjects in Punjabi every now and then, I simply nod and smile.

Sushant's little brother, Dheeraj, catches my eye from across the table and shrugs apologetically. He gets how overwhelming these loud family dinners can be. The seven-year-old kid and I are the only introverts at this table.

Sushant was a nervous wreck the night I first met the Kheras, over a year ago. He'd never dated seriously before, much less introduced a white girl as his girlfriend to his parents. But his family warmed up to me even before dinner was on the table.

I don't have to wonder why. Meera told me, back when we were friends, that traditional desi families often like their sons to date quiet, polite girls who don't talk back to their elders.

"That's why Sushant's folks never invite me over although we're neighbors," she'd said that night as the credits rolled on yet another one of her favorite Shah Rukh Khan movies, this one following the arranged-marriage-to-lovers trope. "I'm too much for them."

Even then, in the dim room lit up only by the glow of the TV, I wanted to close the distance between us. I wanted to cup her cheek with my hand and tell her, *You're not too much; you're perfect, and screw anyone who thinks differently.*

But all I said was "Is that why you won't tell him you like him?"

"Come on." She snorted and tossed the last kernels of her homemade caramel popcorn into her mouth before settling into the soft fabric of the couch. "He's way out of my league. Have you looked at him? Have you looked at *me*?"

"I have," I said, taking her in. Her dark brown skin, her wavy black hair tied in a loose braid, and the sharp jut of her collarbone. *She's so beautiful.* When would she see herself the way I did?

Meera sighed loudly and turned toward me, so I averted my gaze to the empty bowl of popcorn and stood. "Let's clean this up and go upstairs."

She was asleep within seconds of her head hitting the pillow. I stayed up for a whole hour, though, tossing and turning beside her, wondering when and how I had developed feelings for my best friend.

A girl who was in love with the boy next door—not me.

"Lucy?" Dadima's voice jars me back to now. She's standing beside me, one hand on my chair. "Are you finished with dinner?"

I look down at my half-full plate. Sushant told me his parents hate wasting food, that it's bad manners to leave the table with food still on your plate. But my stomach is squirming and sweat pools at the base of my neck, so I nod. "Yes, I'm done."

Dadima pinches my cheek and shakes her head sadly. "You need to fatten up, my girl. Come home for aloo parathas sometime."

"I will." I rise, throw the rest of my food in the trash, then put my plate in the sink. I offer to help with the dishes, but Mrs. Khera drives me out of the kitchen, thanking me but also reminding me I'm a guest in their home.

"Ready to get going?" Sushant asks as he puts on his shoes at the door. One of his hands is on his belly, somehow still flat and chiseled despite the filling meal.

"Yeah." I say goodbye to the Kheras—lots of hugs and kisses ensue—and then I'm in Mr. Khera's car, staring out the window as Sushant drives me home. He turns on the radio to an electronic dance song by Gryffin. Gryffin was Meera's favorite artist back when we were best friends. A few years ago, she'd wanted to go to LA to attend one of his DJ concerts, but her parents had said no. She'd cried on my shoulder for a whole hour.

I wonder if she still uses that coconut shampoo.

The car brakes to a halt, and I put a hand to my heart and gasp in fright. "Sorry," I mumble when I realize we've reached my driveway. "I was lost in thought."

"About what?" Sushant unbuckles his seat belt, leaning forward. He moves some hair away from my face and studies me glumly. "You've been distracted tonight."

"I'm anxious about New York." I nibble on a fingernail before remembering my expensive manicure. "And the tarot reading."

"Come on, babe." He throws his head back and laughs. I told him about the Tower card reading over lunch, and he said I was overreacting. Sushant doesn't believe in tarot, or spirituality, or any of the things Café Kismat represents. He doesn't even like *coffee.*

"I know you think tarot is nonsense," I say, threading one hand into his curly hair, "but Mr. Rao's never been wrong before. He predicted I'd win homecoming queen, remember?"

"Anyone could have predicted that." Sushant scoffs. "You're the best-looking girl in school." But his eyes soften, and he kisses me, his warm hand cradling my neck, and we only break apart a minute later to catch our breaths. Kissing Sushant always soothes my anxiety, and tonight is no different.

He kisses me goodbye in his standard fashion—nose, cheeks, lips—and doesn't pull out of the driveway until I close the front door behind me.

Mom's talking loudly in her office again. From the gap between her door and the wall, I see her recording something for her social media audience. I go upstairs without disturbing her, choosing instead to text her, *good night, I'm home!* I change into my favorite silk pajamas and scroll through Instagram while lying in bed.

Sushant posted a selfie with the football team, his goofy, dimpled smile out in full glory. I like the photo, marveling internally at how handsome my boyfriend is, and move on. Natalie's cat, Buttons, is playing with an empty paper bag on her Stories. I react with a heart-eye emoji. Some authors I follow did a live stream together, so I make a mental note to watch it when I have more time.

Before I exit the app, I check Meera's profile. I'm careful not to click on her Stories ring or like any of her posts. I don't want her knowing I sometimes still look her up online.

The most recent photo on her feed is from a few days ago, featuring three cups of coffee—one Americano, one latte with whipped cream, and one large iced ginger turmeric chai latte. Her friends Ron and Valeria are tagged, as well as Café Kismat's IG page.

Has Mr. George told Meera I still always order my favorite beverage, the one she introduced me to? Does she know that we have the same drink order even now? Sighing, I turn off the lights in my bedroom and put on a Spotify playlist I created last year—it's titled "MRG" and has all the Gryffin songs Meera used to play on loop—and then I curl into a fetal position as a tear falls down my cheek.

It's been well over a year. She has new friends now, friends who would never break her heart to hide their secrets like I did. She's happy. She probably doesn't miss me.

I should stop missing her too.

Meera

Weekends are when the café is comparatively busier, so I'm on duty at the counter alongside the barista and Dad. Appa is sitting in his little tarot corner, doing a reading for two customers. Instrumental music plays from the speakers: the theme song from one of my favorite Bollywood movies, in which a former convict stops at nothing to hunt down the cops who killed the love of his life. The smell of the incense Appa burned earlier this morning is slowly dying out.

I'm putting a few drops of lavender and peppermint essential oils into the diffuser by the toilets when the door opens and two people walk in. I nearly fumble with the dropper in my hand at the sound of Lucy's soft, girlish voice. "And guess what? They didn't think I could prioritize washing dishes over my manicure, so they didn't even interview me. Jerks!"

My ears prick up. So she *is* still looking for a job. Valeria's sister turned her down and hired someone else, but I don't know if Lucy has any other leads. I crouch down beside the wall, hoping I can eavesdrop for a bit before they notice me.

"You could just ask your mom to help you pay for New York." Natalie puts her purse down on their usual table and crosses her legs. "Didn't she make six figures from her business last year?"

"She had to pay most of it to her virtual assistant and social media manager, and then there's her accountant," Lucy explains with an exaggerated sigh. "Apparently, a coaching business can't be run by one person alone."

"What about asking your dad?" Natalie suggests. "He's been calling you so often . . ."

Lucy laughs sarcastically. "Mom thinks he's only calling to ease his guilt, not to actually make an effort with me. She's probably right. I mean, he didn't even *try* to get joint custody."

I cough silently, trying not to inhale the fumes of the diffuser blowing right into my face. Last night, after scribbling on the whiteboard and erasing bullshit ideas over and over, I managed to find an activity that could bring in profits, one that only Lucy could do well enough—and to top it all off, it's something she'd love.

Except I haven't discussed this with Dad or Appa yet. I'm not sure if I should create a presentation on Canva to convince them or if a simple sit-down conversation could do the trick. Regardless, I have to think and act fast. Lucy's clearly desperate for a job.

"Meera!" Dad calls out from behind the counter. The coffee machine whirrs and splutters. "What are you still doing there? We have customers!"

"Sorry, Dad." I walk over to the counter, cringing, and take my spot at the empty cash register. Danny must be in the kitchen, doing the dishes. "Won't happen again."

Dad studies me, perplexed. He must have been expecting a retort, but I need to be on my best behavior. I smile brightly at him and turn to Natalie, who's waiting patiently. "Hi, Natalie," I say. "The usual? Iced coffee, almond milk, no sugar?"

She nods, but her eyes are on the chocolate chip cookies on display. "Get me a cookie too."

"Those have sugar," I remind her, frowning. "And dairy. And eggs."

Natalie shoots Lucy a furtive look and lowers her voice. "It's not for me. Lucy's having a bad day."

"What happened?" I feign curiosity as I ring up her order.

"She's looking for a part-time job someplace in town, but there are no openings. If only y'all were hiring." Natalie shrugs. "She'd love to work here."

At that, Dad looks up, adjusting his glasses and peering at her. "We'll let you know if we ever need more hands on deck."

Natalie smiles back at Dad. "Thanks, Mr. George. Oh," she addresses me, "did you include Lucy's drink?"

"Uh, no." I shake my head, trying to recollect her order. All I can remember is what we both used to drink when we were friends: iced ginger turmeric chai lattes. Since I avoid Lucy whenever she's here, I haven't acquainted myself with her new fancy order.

Natalie scrunches up her nose as she thinks. "It's an iced ginger something chai latte? She's been drinking it for years. I figured you'd know."

My jaw nearly drops as my stomach does a weird flip. She still drinks those? If our friendship was something she could "outgrow" so easily, why wasn't the drink that I introduced her to?

"Meera"—Dad prods my shoulder—"bill the order."

The cash register beeps as I print the receipt and hand it over to Natalie. She stands between the counter and their table, where Lucy is busy reading a book. I can't make out the title or the cover, but she's got the faintest of smiles as she turns the page. Her shiny red hair hangs in waves around her face, and as she pushes a strand back and looks up, she catches me staring at her.

I'm embarrassed, but I choose to sheepishly grin and wave. "Hey," I call out.

Lucy turns to look behind her at the glass wall, perplexed. Our usual routine is ignoring each other when we cross paths, but if the Plan is to work, I need to change that.

"Are you talking to me?" she says, raising a perfectly shaped brow.

"Am I not allowed to?" The retort slips from my mouth before I can think twice.

She shrugs and returns to her book. Natalie's still waiting to pick up their order, but when she gets a phone call, she excuses herself and heads outside. As soon as the door closes behind her, I spin around and mumble in Dad's ear, "Please don't be mad at me for this, but I'm going to offer Lucy a job."

"What?" he says. "Why would you do that?" His voice is low and quiet, but the creases on his forehead deepen. Dad's been in the food-and-beverage industry for decades, so his hands don't shake as he pours coffee into the cups. I could probably announce I'm pregnant with Shawn Mendes's child and he still wouldn't mess up the orders.

I glance behind me. Lucy is still occupied with her book, Natalie's outside, and the rest of the customers are either sitting on the other side of the café or getting a tarot reading from Appa.

"Meera." Dad sets the iced coffee cups on the counter and folds his arms, glaring at me. "What's going on in that head of yours?"

I'm about to admit it's for the Plan, but that's a recipe for disaster. I don't want a rehash of Appa's speech over breakfast the other day. Nope. I need to make something up. "You and Appa were right about my Plan," I whisper. "It's a horrible idea. I don't want to graduate without making things right with Lucy, and she clearly needs a job. Can we please help her?"

He opens his mouth, closes it, and lowers his gaze to his Crocs. "That's very sweet of you, but we don't have the budget for another barista."

"It's not a barista job. I promise this will only bring us more money. I promise," I repeat when he still looks dubious. "Just give it a few weeks. And you can cut her pay from my allowance if you want to."

He takes off his glasses and cleans them with the side of his shirt, thinking. His eyes go back and forth, and he casts a glance at Appa, who's laughing as he shuffles cards in the corner. Finally, Dad nods. "Okay, go ahead. But you're going to have to explain this to your Appa on your own."

I squeal as softly as I can and serve the drinks and cookie to Lucy's table, since she's busy reading. Natalie walks in and takes a sip of her iced coffee. "Ah, coffee," she says, licking her lips. "The elixir of life."

"Thanks, Meera," Lucy says without raising her gaze from the book.

I need to find a reason to start a conversation with her. Something that'll make her reply to me. So I say, "I didn't realize you still drank chai lattes."

She lets out a soft exhale and nods, closing her book. "Yeah." She sips her drink from the straw and shrugs. "It's a good drink. Mr. George makes them well."

"You will not believe who I was just on the phone with," Natalie says, completely ignoring me and tugging on Lucy's arm. "Julien! He wants to hang out!"

"Really?" Lucy gives me a pointed look. Clearly, this is a private conversation.

Sighing, I step back, tray tucked under my arm. I should give them their space. Maybe I can find a better time to offer her the job. School on Monday, or the next time she's here for a drink.

But why wait? I've got Dad's permission. I have to do this before she ends up taking another job. And I have to get straight to the point. So I clear my throat until they both look at me, and then I say, "Lucy, do you want to work for Café Kismat?"

CHAPTER SIX

"After You"

by Gryffin and Jason Ross feat. Calle Lehmann

Lucy

I'm eagerly listening to Natalie talk about the annoying French boy she's crushing on when Meera speaks and my brain shuts down.

Natalie pauses midsentence, probably just as shocked as I am. She knows about my history with Meera, how empty this café always is. She knows it makes zero sense for Meera to offer me—*me!*—a job at her parents' café. They don't need another barista. Hell, they probably can't afford another barista.

My mouth is still agape. I can't seem to close my jaw. I set my iced latte aside and wipe a shaky hand on the fabric of my short denim skirt. "Are you offering me a job, Meera?"

"Yeah." Meera smiles. "Dad and Appa came up with a new business model, and I thought you'd be the perfect person to help us with it."

I look from Natalie to Mr. George, who's listening in, and then back to Meera, blinking slowly. "I . . . I don't know. Um, what—what business model?"

"It's a book club." Meera hesitates, then grabs a chair and sits down beside me. "You'd pick something for people to read every month with a proper book club discussion at the end, and we'd try to invite the author to chime in, maybe over Zoom or in person—"

I'm still processing the fact that she's talking to me. Her words are making sense, but they're going way over my head. "A book club?" I repeat.

Meera nods, but Natalie interjects, "Wait, so how much would you pay her?"

"Does"—she looks back at Mr. George, who's got one eye on us as he cleans the coffee machine—"twenty dollars an hour work?"

My eyes widen. That's about the same pay as the library job, and this one actually sounds fun. I love the idea of spearheading a book club. Madre Maria has a ton of book lovers, but there's no real community aspect to it.

And this book club job would involve a lot less time being around Meera compared to if I were a barista. There doesn't seem to be a catch here, and my mind is yelling that this sounds too good to be true. But if I have to choose between "too good to be true" and "no way to make any money for New York," I'll go with the former. So I say—

"Yes." I clutch the romance novel I was reading to my chest and nod at Meera. "I'll take the job."

Meera screams in delight and holds her hand out for me to shake. I ignore it. Being friendly with her will get me nowhere. She doesn't seem to mind, though. She claps her hands eagerly, then stands. "We'll send you all the details by tomorrow. I'm so excited!"

"I can see that," I mumble.

A few customers walk out through the door after having their tarot cards read, and Mr. Rao pauses in front of our table. He's frowning. "What's going on?"

Meera cringes. "Appa, can I talk to you and Dad for a bit? In the kitchen?"

Mr. Rao and Mr. George exchange glances, then nod as one unit. The three of them go inside while Danny, the barista, returns to the counter.

Once they're inside, Natalie squeezes my arm. Her brown eyes are lit up with excitement. "I can't believe Meera would do that for you."

"What do you mean?" I ask her, blinking.

She smiles. "When I was at the counter, I told them you were looking for a job. Mr. George said he'd let you know if they had an opening. And then, two minutes later, Meera offers you a job based on a new business model? They obviously made that job up on the spot to help you out."

I raise my eyebrow. She's right. That doesn't make sense.

"I know things haven't been great between you and Meera." She links her fingers with mine and squeezes. "And I know you don't want to talk about why your friendship ended. But"—she sighs—"she clearly still cares for you."

My head throbs with all this confusing new information. Why would Meera do this for me? She hates me. And after how I stole her crush and ended our friendship, why shouldn't she hate me? I open my novel again to the bookmarked page and shrug, trying to look nonchalant. "Well, that's nice of Meera, but it doesn't change how things ended." I straighten and shoot Natalie a wink. "She'll never replace you."

"Of course not." She clears her throat. "Now, back to Julien—can you believe he wants to get vegan Froyo with *me*?"

Meera

Appa stands tall, tugging on his graying mustache, his frown growing deeper and deeper as Dad fills him in on what just happened with Lucy. Dad turns to me every few seconds, hoping I'll chime in, but I avert my gaze and stare down at my sneakers until Appa's rarely used stern tone fills the small kitchen.

"So we've just hired Lucy for a job we don't need with money we don't have?"

Dad gives my shoulder a rather hard squeeze. "Care to speak up and fill in the gaping holes in this new business plan of yours, Meera?"

"Sure, Dad." I fold my arms and quirk a brow at them. The past few minutes have solidified the belief that this plan will help not just me but Café Kismat too. "The only other book club in town is at the library. It's quiet, it's uneventful, it's boring. A book club for teens—hosted by Madre Maria's head cheerleader, of all people—would bring in students from every clique."

Appa and Dad exchange a brief look. Then Appa shakes his head. "I don't know anything about books, authors, or book clubs. Neither does your dad. Nor do you. This is only going to make us—"

"But Lucy does," I insist. "Give her two book club discussions. This is my way of helping her *and* bringing more customers to our café."

"You're being irrational," Appa says thickly. "You haven't seen our accounts. We don't have the money to experiment like this—"

"Maybe we don't have the money to experiment because we *never* experiment," I shoot back, my voice rising. "Apart from your tarot readings, which you've been doing since we opened shop, have we ever done anything different from other cafés in town? Changed the menu, even?"

"Meera," Dad whispers, his eyes on the door leading back to the café, "lower your voice."

I let out a whoosh of breath and say, my words softer, "You don't trust me or my recipes? That's fine. But I know this book club is a genius idea."

"We're open to your recipes; it's just not the right time—"

"Two months," I say. "That's all I'm asking for."

Appa rubs along his bald spot, his shoulders sinking. "All right. Two months."

"Thank you." I head back out, fastening my Café Kismat apron tighter along my waist, and as I wait by the counter for new customers, my gaze falls on Lucy holding—but not reading—her book. Her unmoving eyes are glued on a spot a few inches above the book's spine, and she's not even paying attention to Natalie talking loudly about how cute she finds Julien.

Oh, damn it. I grit my teeth. Julien can't be dating Natalie. He needs to be the wedge that drives Sushant and Lucy apart, not the person warming the fourth seat on their double date. I'll have to figure something out. God, why can't getting revenge just be easy?

As if she senses me looking, Lucy glances up at me. "Hey, Meera?" she calls out. "Can you come here for a moment?"

"Sure," I squeak. I walk over to her table and hesitate before taking a seat. "Did you have any questions about the new job?"

"Why me?" She bites her pink lower lip. "Why not someone from the literary club or the school yearbook?"

I swallow, and her eyes zoom in on the movement. Squaring my shoulders, I fumble for words. "Well, I know you've always wanted to work with books, and I don't have any other friends who are readers, so—"

Her eyebrows shoot up. "So we're friends now?"

Natalie sucks in a breath, looking between me and her.

I've honestly outgrown our friendship. The words Lucy once said that stabbed me in the back resurface to the front of my mind. If I want this Plan to work, I have to be nonchalant. Thankfully, Dad comes to my rescue, calling for me when a customer enters the café.

"No, I guess we're not friends," I finally say to Lucy, standing. "I'll email you with more information soon. Welcome to the Café Kismat family."

While I ring up the customer's order, Lucy returns to staring blankly at her book. I busy myself with grinding beans, the whirring of my thoughts louder than the coffee machine. There's so much riding on this Plan now: not just my future with Sushant, but also the success of the café that has been my family's second home for years.

Universe, you better not fuck this up for me.

CHAPTER SEVEN

"she's all i wanna be"
by Tate McRae

Meera

I sit cross-legged on the carpet in front of the couch, making adjustments to a flyer I created on Canva for the book club while my favorite Bollywood movie from the late 2000s plays on the TV. Seriously, Shah Rukh Khan is a gift to humanity.

My phone buzzes, and I pick it up to see a message from Lucy. I'd asked her earlier if I could use one of her photographs for the flyer.

Now I stare at her reply, my jaw slack. It's a picture of her at Café Kismat, and it's exactly what I need to make the flyer pop. In it, her head is bent low, tendrils of her wavy red hair framing her face as she reads a popular romance novel with an illustrated cover. She looks beautiful, like she does every day of her life. My face flames, a prickly sensation gnawing at my stomach. Jealousy? After all, she's a perfect, ethereal being, and I'm a mediocre human—

"How are the flyers going?" Ron asks from the couch, prodding my shoulder with his large—and clearly unwashed—foot.

I swat his leg away and turn to reprimand him. "Don't touch me with your smelly feet!"

He scoffs, although he's smiling. "You're the one imposing this no-shoes-indoors rule on everyone who walks in."

"Because wearing shoes inside the house is disgusting," I snap. It's one thing Appa has ingrained in me since I was a mere toddler. "Do you know how gross the outdoors can be?"

Beside him, Valeria says, deadpan, "Meera, it's a known fact white people don't wash their legs in the shower. I bet Ron's bare feet are worse than the outdoors."

"Wait, what?" Ron jerks his feet up off the floor and inspects them. "You don't have to wash your feet separately in the shower. The soap lather runs down your legs and does the cleaning on its own. Right?" He looks to us expectantly.

My jaw has fallen open while Valeria just looks defeated, like she can't believe we're friends with someone who doesn't know the basics of personal hygiene.

"Whatever. We need more snacks." Ron shoots off the couch and heads to the kitchen.

I rub the side of my shoulder, deciding to focus on my work. I upload Lucy's picture onto Canva and paste it into the center of the flyer, and, damn, it makes the entire page come to life. Her fiery red hair, the pink and blue of the book cover, and the faint but luminescent orange lighting in the backdrop—nobody with eyes could look away from this flyer.

"Great job," Valeria says, bending ahead toward where I sit on the floor, her eyes on the laptop. "And I'm not just talking about your graphic design skills. I still can't believe you roped Lucy into this. I thought she hated you."

I shoot my friend a proud look. "Clearly, I can be quite convincing."

"Or Lucy was just that desperate for a job." Valeria laughs and then sits back, focusing on the movie. I've seen *Om Shanti Om* at least a hundred times before. Right now, we're in the midst of an especially fun song-and-dance sequence in the almost-three-hour-long cinematic masterpiece. Shah Rukh Khan is shirtless in this one. What a sight to behold.

Ron comes back with a platter of cheese and fruit. He sits down, pops a square piece of watermelon into his mouth, and moans very unsexily. "How does your family always have the best fruit?"

The flyer is ready to be printed. I set my laptop aside and look at the platter he's balancing on his lap. Hands on my hips, I say, "I bought all that cheese to try out some recipes for the café."

Valeria grins. "So you finally convinced your parents to let you change the menu?"

I lick my dry lips. "They'll only give in if the book club goes well."

"It will," Ron says as he nibbles on a small block of Emmental cheese. "And obviously, I'm happy to volunteer as a taster for the new menu."

"Now your foot isn't the only thing that smells in here." Valeria shifts from the middle to the other end of the couch, but not before taking a piece of apple from the platter with a smile. We both know Ron got the platter to satiate her constant hunger cravings.

The smell of cheese doesn't bother me, so I sit between them and draft a text to Lucy, attaching the flyer as a PDF file. Does this look ok? Thanks for all your help, by the way 🙂

Then I shake my head. *Baby steps with the pretend niceness, Meera,* I remind myself. There's no need to make her suspicious. And I'm not supposed to be asking for her approval. I'm the employer here—or, rather, Dad and Appa are, but I'm representing them, so I can't be talking like that.

Meera:

Here's what it'll look like. Thanks for all your help!

The song ends, and Valeria boos when SRK appears onscreen again but wearing a shirt this time. "Can we replay the song?" she asks, swiping a blueberry from the platter.

Before she can reach for the remote, Ron grabs it from the coffee table and sets it next to his knee. "This actor's, like, sixty years old. Show some respect for the elderly, Val."

"He was only fortysomething when they filmed it," I say, jumping to her defense.

"And we weren't even born yet." He finishes the last of the cheese and gives the platter, still half full of blueberries and pears, to an eager Valeria. "Have you both thought about who you'll go to senior prom with?"

I bite the side of my cheek to keep from smiling too wide. "If all goes as planned? I'll go with Sushant."

"I'll probably just go with you," Valeria says to Ron with a heavy sigh. "High school boys are so immature, and you're the only one I can tolerate for longer than ten minutes."

Maybe she doesn't spot the upward tilt of Ron's lips as he shakes his head and returns to watching the movie, but I do.

Ron and Valeria have been best friends since middle school. I didn't know them except on a first-name basis at the time, and I've often wondered if one of them sees the other as more than a friend, especially with their never-ending banter and teasing over the past year of our close friendship. And neither of them has dated seriously, choosing instead to spend all their time with each other—or me.

I think now I finally have my answer. For Ron's sake, I hope Val feels the same way.

Lucy

As I sway slowly on the large wooden swing in our backyard, soaking in the sunset that turns the sky pink and orange, I look at the flyer Meera texted me on my phone. The picture of me, taken by Natalie last year, fits perfectly with the color scheme and overall vibe of the ad. Meera's done a great job from what I can tell, given my zero design experience, but it's finally sinking in that this is real. I have a job now. And it involves working with the one person I've been running away from since junior year.

"Hey." Sushant joins me on the swing, which creaks under the weight of his all-muscle body. He catches a glimpse of my phone and does a double take. "*This* is the job offer you wanted to tell me about?"

"Yep." I start to bite the side of my blue-painted nail, then pull my finger away. "It's not ideal, but it'll do."

Sushant takes the phone from me and zooms in to read the text on the flyer. "Not ideal? Are you kidding? You love books, you love Café Kismat, and you love—"

"I don't love Meera," I say quickly, before he can finish speaking. Saying those two words together—"love" and "Meera"—in the same sentence makes a shiver run down my spine. It's terrifying to even think that I once believed those words to be true. *Not anymore,* I tell myself. The only person who gets my love now is Sushant. Rightfully so.

"I was going to say, you love leading people. Like with the cheer squad." He strokes the side of my cheek with his long fingers, a lazy smile on his lips. "And you'd be so good at this. Besides, whatever fight you and Meera had was a long time ago. Maybe now you two can make amends and become friends again."

"Maybe," I lie. It's easier than explaining it to him. I can never admit the truth to him. If I do, he'll hate me, and I wouldn't blame him for it. Shifting my gaze to the slowly dipping orange sun on the horizon, I add, "You and Meera still take the bus together, right?"

Sushant nods. "Yeah, why?"

The words fall out before I can stop them. "Does she ever talk about me?"

"Uh." Sushant laughs weakly, rubbing his hands along his jeans. "Sometimes, when I bring you up in conversation. But otherwise, not really."

I hold my head up high, although my stomach deflates. "Good. That's what I was hoping for."

The backyard door slides open, revealing Mom in her faded pink flowery apron that only ever sees the light of day when Sushant comes over. "Dinner's ready," she announces, and wipes a bead of sweat from her forehead. It's a hot day, and our AC needs fixing. "Hurry up before the food gets cold."

"We'll be right there, Alice," Sushant replies, grinning at her.

She beams and heads back into the house. Mom loves my boyfriend. The first time I brought him home to her, she was suspicious—Sushant's not white, after all, nor is he Christian, and after the way Dad walked out on us, Mom's not particularly fond of most men. She hasn't gone on a single date since the divorce. Her one true love is life coaching.

But Sushant did all the right things and charmed her within minutes, despite her hesitations: He raved about her somewhat-above-average cooking, which is why she now only ever makes dinners for him; he complimented her for being a self-made woman helping her clients be their happiest selves; and, most importantly, he nodded and made all the right sounds of reassurance and empathy when Mom ranted about Dad trying to interfere in our lives while still dating "that home-wrecker."

By the end of the night, Sushant earned the right to call my mother Alice, and he hasn't called her Ms. Miller since. I still wonder if he's uncomfortable around her—she's not exactly subtle when it comes to her more backward views. But then again, Sushant is too kindhearted to notice anybody's flaws.

Midway through dinner, as our plates of meat loaf and roasted potatoes start to empty, Sushant nudges my shoulder and says, "Did you tell Alice about your new job?"

I shoot him a warning look, but it's too late. Mom looks up from her glass of red wine and asks, "You got a job, Lucy? I didn't know you were looking for one."

"For about a week now," Sushant tells her excitedly as he finishes the last bite of his potatoes. "It's the perfect job for her."

Mom leans forward in her seat, seemingly eager. "Oh, Lucy, your first job! Where are you working?"

I gulp down some root beer to stall for time, then grip the side of the chair with my fingers to stay calm and composed. The cool wood and the leathery cushion, warm under my weight, ground me. "It's at Café Kismat. I'm in charge of their new book club."

My mother looks from me to Sushant, who still has the

biggest grin on his face. Slowly, her lips press into a wide but fake smile, clearly only for his benefit, and she sets her wineglass down. "You definitely would be great at that," she agrees. Then she exhales and reaches for our empty plates. "You kids done?"

"Thanks, Alice." Sushant isn't fazed—he doesn't know my mother like I do, after all. Mom obviously doesn't approve of my working at a café run by two gay men, one of whom is Indian and spiritual, but she can't say that in front of Sushant. She can't say that, period. I'll probably be subjected to snarky, passive-aggressive retorts during church on Sunday morning instead of hearing her actual opinion on the subject.

Mom retires to her office to prep for her "busy and money-making week ahead"—her words, not mine—and Sushant kisses me goodbye on the front porch in his usual fashion. Before I turn to head inside, he tugs me back into his arms. He locks his lips with mine once more, one of his hands cupping the back of my neck and the other sliding under my top, his hand warm and big, over the cup of my lacy bra. I pull away seconds later, toying with the collar of his shirt, not meeting his eyes. "It's late," I breathe.

"It's late," Sushant agrees. His voice is heavy with lust. "I just wish we could have some . . . alone time."

"Soon," I promise him, pecking him on the cheek and going back inside. I lean against the closed door and wipe my clammy hands on my skirt, breathing in and out, deep and slow, for three counts.

Sushant and I haven't . . . gone very far. Natalie doesn't

get why I want to wait—she thinks it's a rite of passage that you must cross before college and wishes she had someone to love like I do—but the thing is, I don't know what's stopping me, either. It's not that I only like people of one gender. I like people for who they are and how they make me feel, and Sushant is the best person I know—so, yes, I *am* attracted to Sushant. I *do* have feelings for him. Maybe it's scary because I know my initial reasons for dating him weren't genuine: I was only trying to hide my secret and find a way to sever ties with the girl I loved, and what better cover than to date the popular hot guy Meera used to like? Like they say, two birds with one stone.

In my heart, though I wouldn't call our relationship passionate, I know Sushant and I are great together. We're happy; our love is constant and consistent. We aren't a roller-coaster romance with exhilarating ups and downs. We're stolen kisses on Ferris wheels, giggles and cheers while go-karting. He's my best friend and my favorite person, but . . . he will never compare to her.

The way I felt about Meera was all-consuming—borderline euphoric. Every slumber party left me restless and aching to kiss her forehead as she fell asleep, to caress her cheek when her eyes twitched from bad dreams. Every accidental brush of our fingers when we both reached for a bowl of popcorn made me wonder if she'd be just as nonchalant if I touched the nape of her neck, pressed my lips to hers. Every second of every day I spent with her held the impossible, unattainable promise of the kind of love I'd never get to share with her.

She will never be mine to keep, and I'll never be hers. It was sensible of me to end our friendship so publicly and so horribly that she would never dare let me into her life again.

I only hope this job at Café Kismat doesn't change anything. Because as long as she loathes me, I'll be safe. I can't risk losing Sushant. More than that, I can't risk losing myself in Meera. Again.

CHAPTER EIGHT

"Better Than Revenge"
by Taylor Swift

Lucy

"Hmm." Natalie peers at the flyer as we wait in line for the three buses taking the seniors to the Museum of Modern Art. "This is weird."

Meera has been handing out the book club flyers to everyone in school all morning. The QR code on the flyer links to Café Kismat's Instagram, where more details are available, including the book I chose for our first meeting two weeks from now. Obviously, it's my favorite young adult retelling of *Pride and Prejudice.* The head librarian who ghosted me after my interview might find this choice *silly*, but, hey, it's my book club, and I'll run it how I see fit.

"What's wrong?" I raise an eyebrow and try to see which part of the flyer Natalie's looking at. Is there a typo? Or some sort of problem I should have pointed out to Meera?

"This!" She points to the photo of me front and center on the flyer, a grin on her lips, which are red to match my look this morning. "I took this picture of you, and I don't get photography credit?"

I put my arm around her waist and press my cheek against hers. "You're adorable. Want me to announce to the whole school that you took this photo?" I raise my voice. "Hey, everyone—"

With a laugh and a shake of her head, Natalie asks, "Listen, do you need any help with the book club? I'm gonna be there on the day of, obviously, so if you want someone to take photos for Café Kismat's Insta—"

Meera must have overheard her, because she springs in front of us out of nowhere and says, "Natalie, that'd be great. I was going to ask Danny to handle the photos for social media when he's not busy making coffee."

"I'll bring my camera," Natalie says, smiling. Then she pats the side of Meera's arm almost . . . patronizingly? "Thank you for doing this for Lucy. She's my best friend, and I'm so grateful to you for offering this job to her even though you two aren't close anymore."

Maybe Natalie doesn't see how Meera's face crumples, for the smallest of seconds, at the phrase "she's my best friend." To her credit, Meera only nods politely and steps back to where her friends are waiting. "Cool. I'll see y'all around."

Shit. My eyes burn with tears that I refuse to let fall. Hearing someone else call me their best friend must have stung. I know, because every time I go through Meera's Instagram and see a new photo of her with Ron and Valeria, my heart breaks a little. When she indirectly called me a friend that day at the café, I had to rein in the hope fluttering in my chest. There's no room for it anymore.

Anyway. I sigh out a deep breath and choose to let it go. Natalie's looking at Café Kismat's Instagram page, probably to familiarize herself with their branding and style, so I search the line of students for Julien Perrin. He's my study partner for Art History—not to mention Calculus and Chemistry—so I have to write a report with him once we're done with the school trip. It's a pity he's not my partner for French; there's so much I could have learned from him. If only he'd talk as much in French as he does in English.

I spot him walking up to Meera, perhaps asking if she's seen me. She nudges her head in my direction, then gives me a little wave and a wide grin, even though we literally spoke a minute ago. Confused, I wave back.

"Hello, Lucy, Natalie." Julien makes a show of sticking his palm out to Natalie, then laughs when she eagerly returns the handshake. "I'm learning the American way of life already, aren't I?"

I press my lips together. "Yeah, if this were a job interview, maybe."

Natalie throws her arms around Julien and hugs him tight until he puts a tentative hand on the small of her back. Pulling away, she beams. "That's how we do it in Madre Maria." It's not, but I bet she'd use any excuse to touch him. Honestly, I don't blame her.

Julien smiles approvingly. "You smell lovely, Natalie. Like spring is coming."

I make a snort-like noise that comes from the back of my throat, then put a hand over my mouth and control my giggle. They'd be so cute together. Natalie might actually be able to tolerate his speed talking.

When the bus drivers call for us, we pile into the buses. Natalie and Julien laugh and chat about Paris the whole way there, and I play Taylor Swift on my earphones, pretending it's the soundtrack to their budding romance.

About an hour later, we're walking into the art museum. The chaperones, including our Art History teacher, Mr. Lany, lead the way through the exhibitions. They talk about brushwork, color gradients, and the meaning behind each frame hanging on the walls, but my mind is on the upcoming book club discussion. Café Kismat already got two hundred likes on the announcement and sign-up post. Sharon is going to be pissed when five or six teens walk in asking if the town library has a copy of *Prada, Purrs, and Prejudice.*

I grin just thinking about it.

We pause in front of a large pink sculpture of a woman made entirely out of what looks like rose quartz crystal. It reminds me of the woman from the Star tarot card that Mr. Rao pulled for Natalie all those weeks ago. "This is beautiful," Julien breathes, and hands me his phone. "Can you take a picture of me with it?"

"Uh." I hesitate, spotting a signboard behind us. "I don't think photography is allowed in this museum."

His eyes widen. "Really? That is not the case in my favorite museum back home. America is an interesting country."

He takes his phone back and continues walking. After one last look at the rose quartz sculpture, I follow behind.

As Julien starts a conversation about the aforementioned museum in Paris and how it's his go-to first-date place, I tune him out somewhat as my eyes find Meera with her friends. They're speaking in low voices and hanging away from the rest of the students. Meera's study partner is a few paces behind them. They collectively look my way, as if they're talking about me, then avert their gazes when I raise a brow at them.

"—and my ex-boyfriend was obsessed with this one painting that never made sense to me," Julien says, and my attention springs back to him. Did he just say—

"Boyfriend?" I ask, my voice dropping automatically. If he's sharing this with me in confidence, I don't want to out him.

"Yeah, ex-boyfriend." Julien looks unfazed, speaking at a normal volume.

"But you said you broke up with a girlfriend before coming here . . ." I trail off awkwardly when he wrinkles his nose.

"Is this how all Americans perceive sexuality?" he wonders aloud, clearly disapproving. "Lucy, I am a person, and I am attracted to all kinds of people. What matters to me is what's in here"—he puts a hand over his heart—"and not anything anywhere else. And I think that's a beautiful way to love, is it not?"

"Oh," I whisper. My pulse speeds through my veins, my head spins just the slightest bit, and I can tell from Julien's widened eyes that my face has probably drained of color. What he just described, that sounds like—it sounds like *me*.

"Lucy, are you all right?" Julien asks. He puts a hand on my shoulder and looks around. "Would you like some water?"

I wave off his concerns as I regain control of my senses. "I'm fine. I just— So are you, um, bisexual? Since you like more than one gender?"

Julien stops in front of an oil painting that shows the dark silhouette of two people kissing in front of a red background that fades to white. He smiles, and it's like a mask has come off to reveal who he truly is. "I'm pansexual, Lucy."

"Pansexual," I whisper. The word feels familiar, even though I don't quite know what it means, and it wakes up some part of me that has lain dormant, unconscious, ever since I closed the door on my friendship with Meera. It tugs at my heartstrings, seeps its way into my bones, and lights me up inside exactly the way it's lighting up Julien right now.

"To me, it means I'm attracted to people for who they are on the inside, regardless of gender," Julien says, drawing himself up to his full height. "I prefer labels that empower me, and this one does exactly that."

"It does," I agree softly. "When did you—"

"Seniors, this way!" Mr. Lany yells, and the spell breaks. I clear my throat, raise my head ever so slightly, and remind myself that thinking like this is not going to help me. That's not an option. Not for me.

"Come on," I mumble to Julien from the corner of my mouth, whipping out a small notebook from my purse. "We should take some notes for the report."

Julien frowns. "All right." He pulls out his phone and opens a voice recorder app, and we spend the rest of the museum tour ignoring the giant elephant in the room.

Meera

When Ron and Valeria go ahead to catch up to Mr. Lany, I ditch my study partner—a studious guy named Henry, who'll hopefully write the report for both of us—and walk over to Sushant. He stands with a girl I don't know in front of a statue of a stork carrying a bag in its mouth. But instead of a baby, the bag holds a decaying skull.

"This is art, huh?" I say, elbowing him in the side as a greeting.

"Apparently." He smiles, those beautiful dimples peeking out, and looks around the room. "Where's your partner?"

"He's taking notes for us." I scratch the underside of my neck and turn to his study partner. "Hey, I'm Meera." She's clearly popular, given her lean legs and flowing blond hair, so of course she gives me a weird look and stalks off with her notepad and pen.

Sushant puts a hand to his firm stomach and laughs loud enough for the sound to echo in the room. When someone shushes us, he bites his lip and gestures for me to keep walking with him. "You like art?" he asks.

I shrug. "I'm not much of a visual person. Does music count as art?"

"It does. Music is definitely art." We stop in front of a vase that has a naked man popping out of its depths. Sushant looks around surreptitiously, then pokes the man's left nipple. "Boop," he says.

Now I have to keep myself from laughing. Gosh, this boy is perfect for me. I bet Lucy wouldn't have laughed at that. She could never get his jokes like I do.

"Who's your favorite musician?" I ask Sushant. One of the teachers spots us hanging back and directs us to the line of students. We reluctantly follow.

He shrugs. "I don't have one. I guess I don't listen to a lot of music. You?"

"Gryffin," I answer instantly. When Sushant's brows furrow, I add, "He's not super popular, so you probably don't know him. He's a DJ who collaborates with all these nonmainstream, thoroughly underrated artists. I've discovered a ton of singers thanks to him."

"No, I know him." Sushant grabs his notebook and pretends to write something down when Mr. Lany walks past us, although I don't bother. "Lucy has a whole playlist full of Gryffin songs on our shared Spotify."

I'm not the most emotional person on the block, but a blend of confusion and anger surges through me. Confusion, because I didn't think EDM was Lucy's thing. She always preferred Taylor Swift, whose music I don't care for. And anger, because the love of my life has a shared Spotify account with the girl I hate? Wow. She's really got her manicured nails in him, doesn't she?

Not for long.

"The playlist has a weird name too," Sushant goes on as we catch up to the front of the group of students and our partners walk closer to us. "It's called 'MSG' or something like that. I asked her what that means, but she said it's a reference to something personal. Maybe that's Gryffin's real name?"

"No, but whatever," I reply, already mentally done with this conversation. Julien and Lucy are a few feet ahead of us. They're not talking to each other, but the little psychic ability I've inherited from Appa tells me there's some sort of weird energy between them. Emotional tension? Sexual chemistry? I can't tell. "Hey." I nudge Sushant, switching to speaking in Hindi so no one can eavesdrop. "What do you think of the new kid?"

"Julien?" Sushant says his name in his usual Indian American accent instead of its correct pronunciation. He might be trilingual like me—he speaks English, Hindi, and Punjabi; I speak English, Hindi, and Kannada—but we both suck at French. Another thing we have in common. "He's a hoot," he says in Hindi, following my lead. "I love that guy."

"Lucy seems to like him too," I say, trying to gauge his reaction from the corner of my eye. "I hope you don't feel threatened. I mean, he is really hot. And nice. And funny."

Sushant's face seems expressionless at first, but I catch his jaw growing tight. He switches back to English. "He's all right, Meera, but he's not a threat. I'm all those things too."

As my study partner walks toward the exhibit in the next room and gestures for me to follow, I turn to Sushant one last time and say, "I'm glad you're so confident in your relationship. If I were you, I don't think I would be."

I don't turn back to see his reaction. I don't need to. The seeds of doubt have been sown—and with any luck, they'll sprout into jealousy soon enough. *Thank you, Angels.*

CHAPTER NINE

"A Little Bit Yours"

by JP Saxe

Lucy

"That was a fantastic service, wasn't it?" Mom says, a wide grin on her face as we step out of church together on Sunday morning.

"Mm-hmm," I say, returning her smile. "Pastor Rick got personal during his sermon today for a change. He's usually so much more reserved."

She stretches her arms and takes in the bright sunshine. "Yes, it was just what I needed to hear after the exhausting workweek I had. How about you, honey? How's school going?"

We walk ahead, falling into our usual postchurch ritual of catching up on everything from the previous week. I tell her about the changes I made to the cheerleading routine for the upcoming game and what homework assignments I'm working on. My voice quivers while I tell her about the museum trip, and my thoughts are on the conversation with Julien that felt both eye-opening and unfinished. Thankfully, Mom doesn't seem to pick up on it. "Enough about me," I say as we round the corner. "What's new with you, Miss Life Coach?"

"Well, I wrapped up my coaching with Susan after five months of working together, and I'm onboarding three new clients on Monday." Her eyes, sunken and tired as they may be from her workaholic ways, light up with a smile. "Sometimes I can't believe I get to do *this* for a living. Ten years ago, I thought my only purpose in life was being married to your father. And now . . ."

"Your clients are lucky to have you," I say, bumping my hip against hers.

She winks at me. "I know, honey."

We look across the street at the sound of barking, and Mom's shoulders stiffen. Mr. George and Mr. Rao wave at us while their dog, Raj, yips and jumps at the sight of me. When I used to hang out at Meera's place, Raj hardly ever left my side, following me everywhere with his wagging tail—even to the bathroom. Meera often joked that maybe he'd been my dog in a past life.

I haven't seen Raj in forever, and he still remembers me. God, I love that dog. "Hi, buddy!" I call out, blowing kisses at him, and he dashes forward, straining the leash Mr. George is holding in a tight grip.

Meera's dads cross over to our side of the street, wide smiles on both of their faces. I notice Mom's eyes zeroing in on their interlocked fingers, and I swallow, my throat dry. This is going to be . . . uncomfortable.

Raj bounds over to me and falls at my feet, his tongue hanging out. I reach down and rub his belly, but I'm keenly aware of the tension in the air as Mom makes small talk with Mr. Rao and Mr. George.

"Yes, everything is great," she says, her words clipped. "I hope your café is doing well."

"It is, thanks," Mr. Rao says. "We're thrilled that Lucy is our newest employee!"

At that, I straighten, my eyes lifting, and Raj whines at the sudden loss of attention.

Mom clears her throat. "Yes, she told me about the new book club. Sounds fun. Well"—she turns to me, taking my hand in hers—"if you'll excuse us, we should be heading home."

Mr. George nods and pulls on Raj's leash again. Next to him, Mr. Rao rubs his bald spot, a sad smile along his lips. "We'll see you around, Lucy. Have a great Sunday, both of you."

Mom is already tugging me away, so I give them a quick wave and resume listening, albeit half-heartedly, to my mother's upcoming plans for her career as my stomach squirms with guilt.

Meera

I swipe my hand along my forehead, catching a bead of sweat. I'm standing by the stove in our kitchen, making dosas for my friends as they "ooh" and "ahh" at the process. We were going to grab breakfast at the local diner, but there is a ton of chicken curry left over from last night, and Appa didn't want it to go to waste. Ron seemed intrigued by the concept of dosas, so Dad asked if I'd cook for us all.

"Interesting," Ron says, tearing off a piece of the first dosa from his plate. "It's like a savory Indian pancake."

"Nah, the consistency is more like a crepe," Valeria says as she watches me spread the rest of the dosa batter in concentric circles around the pan with the back of the ladle. "Hey, Meera, why haven't we ever had dosas at your place before?"

"Uh, I don't know." My hand nearly shakes as I push down on the batter. The only people I've ever made breakfast for are my parents . . . and Lucy. We'd hang out in the kitchen early in the morning after our sleepovers, talking about music and books and Bollywood. I'd show her the best way to prepare South Indian breakfast dishes—everything from dosa and idli to uthappam and pongal—and she would try her hand at it for half a minute before deciding it was best to leave it to me, the expert. Appa and Dad would join us soon after, and we'd all sit at the dining table like we were a family.

Shit. Lucy really had been my family, in so many ways. She'd been the best friend I'd always wanted, the best friend I've ever had, the one person who I thought I could count on forever. And now—

I cough and wipe my eye, pretending the tear is from the heat of the stove. "Hey, Val, can you pop the chicken curry in the microwave? It's on the middle shelf in the fridge."

She and Ron go over to the fridge while I flip the dosa over and gather my thoughts. It's been almost a year and a half since my friendship with Lucy ended, and I haven't let myself walk down memory lane in a very long time.

I just have to make sure to keep that silly, irrational, nostalgic part of me squelched down, especially with the book club coming up soon. I'll be in close proximity to Lucy over the next two months. She might fool all of Madre Maria into thinking she's the nicest girl in town, but not me. Only I know her for the backstabbing queen bee she is.

And that's how it needs to be, Meera, I remind myself over the beeping of the microwave. *No matter how much you miss the old Lucy.*

The front door opens, carrying with it the sounds of Dad's jingling keys, Raj's barks, and Appa's shout of "We're back!"

"That smells delicious," Dad says, walking into the kitchen. "Hope you kids haven't started without us."

I turn and gesture for him to grab a plate. "It was difficult, considering Ron wanted to taste-test everything, but we waited."

Ron sheepishly pulls his finger away from the chicken curry bowl. "Sorry."

Laughing, Valeria helps me set the table while my parents wash their hands. I toss a piece of chicken into Raj's food bowl and join everyone for breakfast. The curry—Appa's special recipe—tastes even better this morning with the chatter of so many people at the table. Ron can't stop reaching for more while Val tells us about her mother's chicken dish that resembles this one.

As I'm finishing my final bite of chicken and dosa, Appa says, "Putta, it's nice having your friends over for breakfast again."

Dad adds, "Speaking of which, we ran into Lucy and her mother during our walk. She's eager to start working with the book club."

My stomach coils. "I'm glad," I say, midswallow, as I exchange glances with my friends, "that she's looking forward to it."

"Of course she is." Appa stands, taking his and Dad's empty plates to the sink. "This is a lovely thing you're doing for an old friend, putta."

Ron chokes, nearly spitting out bits of chicken. Valeria hands him some water, and he apologizes, coughing and hacking. "Tiny chicken bone," he mumbles.

Dad shoots him a weird look but says nothing, only joins Appa at the sink. I sigh and turn to Ron. "You okay?" I ask.

He nods, still holding the empty glass. "Sorry. The food was delicious, though."

"Seconded," Valeria says. She puts a hand on my shoulder. "How are you feeling about the book club?"

I shoot a glance at my parents, who are laughing about something together in the distance, and lower my voice. "I'm scared no one will show up, but we've had a decent number of RSVPs on Instagram."

"We'll be there," Ron says as his phone chimes. He swipes

along the screen. "Mom needs me to do a grocery run. See you, Meera. Val, you coming?"

"Yep." She gives me a hug. Then my friends say bye to my family and head out. I go upstairs to my room just as Ron's car backs out of the driveway. I stand in front of the whiteboard, my eyes boring into the words *THE PLAN: DATE SUSHANT & DETHRONE LUCY* as my heart pounds faster and faster.

Two years ago, the only plans in my life were about movie marathons with Lucy and saving up for EDM concerts. If fifteen-year-old Meera Rao-George saw me now, she'd think I was the worst person in the world. After all, she wouldn't let anyone *think* bad thoughts about Lucy, forget *do* bad things to her, without giving them the evil eye and a heavy dose of karma.

But that Meera Rao-George is as dead as the Lucy she was best friends with.

Nodding, I uncap the black marker tacked onto the whiteboard, crack my knuckles, and get down to business.

CHAPTER TEN

"The Story Of Us (Taylor's Version)"
by Taylor Swift

Meera

In the six years since Café Kismat opened, I have never seen all our tables occupied. Dad sectioned off a space in between the tarot corner and the counter with four tables for the book club—we got twelve RSVPs—but the room is packed with at least thirty members who showed up last-minute, eager to discuss the twists and turns of *Prada, Purrs, and Prejudice* with Lucy.

And, of course, they're all sipping iced coffees. *Our* iced coffees. Natalie's here with her camera, taking photographs every few minutes, after having set up my phone in a corner to stream the discussion live on our Instagram. She's really great at it. I wonder if it's something she wants to pursue as a career or if it's just a hobby.

The door opens, and another two people walk in. Even Appa, who usually sticks to bookkeeping and tarot, has to help out at the counter today because Dad, Danny, and I cannot possibly take this many orders or make this much coffee.

It's funny so many people are actively contributing to the discussion questions, considering we only gave them two and a half weeks to read the 250-page book. I'd thought nobody would finish reading it so quickly, but clearly, I was wrong.

Lucy sits in the middle of the crowd, clad in flared pants and a yellow crop top, her legs crossed and her eyebrows furrowed. "What did everyone think of Wick and his betrayal?"

"Oh my God." Amy from the theater club rolls her eyes exaggeratedly. "I thought Wick was so cool up until I read Darcy's DM to Liz."

"And he just kept getting worse and worse," the swim team captain says, nodding in agreement. He's the sole guy here apart from Ron and Sushant, who must only be here for moral support—he doesn't even have a copy of the book with him as he sits next to Lucy with a glass of water because he hates coffee. "I was afraid for poor Lydia, backed into a corner like that. Thank God Darcy helped her with the abortion."

Lucy's eyes sparkle as she listens to everyone chime in with their thoughts. Someone who's read the original Austen novel talks about the modernization of what constitutes, in their words, social suicide, and Lucy nods, encouraging them to elaborate. She's enjoying every second of this—and I hate to admit it, but so am I, even though I've never read Jane Austen and I only flipped through this month's book.

About fifty minutes into the discussion, Lucy introduces the book for the discussion happening next month. "We're taking a much-needed diverse turn this time, and Mr. Rao will certainly enjoy this one." At that, Appa looks over at the book she's holding up. "This desi young adult romance talks about astrology and destiny in the contemporary world and shows the reader what it's like for Indian American teens to come to terms with their identity and culture."

I lock eyes with her from across the table I'm cleaning, and she adds, "Meera, I'd love to get your thoughts on this one, if you'd like to join us next time."

Luckily, I don't drop the tray of dirty dishes in my hands. For the first time since the conception of the Plan, she's being nice to me. It's jarring. I smile and nod, although having the eyes of over thirty popular teens on me makes the hair on the back of my neck stand. "Sure."

As the discussion wraps up, I take off my apron, hang it behind the counter, and walk over to Ron and Valeria's table. Just like Sushant came here for Lucy, they came to offer moral support to me. "So, this went well," I say as I plop down on the empty chair next to Valeria.

"Very well." Ron nods and claps softly. "What's the next phase of the Plan?"

I blow out a breath. Over the past two weeks, I scribbled nonstop on the whiteboard and got plenty of use out of the eraser. But I've finally settled on the four steps of the Plan, and they seem foolproof, albeit challenging. Step 1: Keep your enemies closer—book club. Step 2: Inner circle—get invited to parties. Step 3: Become Sushant's confidante. And Step 4: Break them up. I haven't yet figured out how to successfully complete each step, but playing it by ear and trusting my gut seems to be working well for me so far.

"I need to get more popular," I finally answer, jiggling my foot under the table. "And the way to do that is to get invited to parties. Somehow. Hopefully."

"Ooh, that sounds fun," Valeria gushes. "I can't wait to get superdrunk on disgusting beer after we all score invites!"

Ron smirks and punches her playfully on the shoulder. "And I can't wait to hear you rant about your first-ever hangover the next morning."

She glares at him in mock anger. "Oh, you'd better be prepared to nurse me back to health, mister. I won't be a fun patient."

I excuse myself and return to my shift while they continue obliviously flirting with each other. A few of the book club members are at the counter, ordering another round of coffees.

While Danny and Appa ring up the orders, Dad pulls me into the kitchen and hugs me. Tightly. I'm taken aback, and just as I start to return the gesture, he holds me at arm's length and peers at me from under his glasses. "Meera, your father and I were not at all sure about this idea of yours."

"Dad—"

"But we have to admit, it worked just as you'd predicted." He wipes a tear from the side of his eye. "Business has never been this good. So, thank you, kiddo. I love you."

I take his hands in mine and grin. "I love you too, Dad. Does this mean I get to make some changes to the menu?"

"Oh, why not?" Dad squeezes my fingers, chuckling. "You're going to run this place when we're old and gray anyway. Might as well get a head start, hmm?"

When I head back into the café, a huge grin on my face, my friends are preparing to leave. "Rom-com marathon tonight at my place, seven-ish?" Valeria suggests, while Ron swings his car keys around on his finger. "There's, like, a bunch of new movies on Netflix."

"Only if at least one of them is Bollywood," I say, wrapping my arms around them in a group goodbye hug.

"The marathon's gonna last a full twenty-four hours, then," Ron quips, eyebrow quirked. Valeria smacks him on the back, and laughing, they head out to his car.

I turn to get back to my shift and bump heads with Lucy. "Ow," I groan, rubbing the side of my forehead. "That hurt."

She winces. "Sorry." But she doesn't step aside to let me pass. At my frown, she laces her fingers and asks, "You still do Saturday night movie marathons, then?"

When we were friends, every Saturday night was movie marathon night. Mostly Bollywood with subtitles on for Lucy's sake, but the occasional classic teen rom-com too. I swipe a lock of hair behind my ear and duck my head, nodding. "I do. They're fun."

"Yeah, they are."

I look up, and she's staring at me, her face blank, but I notice her kneading her thumb into her knuckles, which is something she does when she's . . . nervous. Why is she nervous?

The swim team captain walks over to us, breaking our

staring contest, and puts his arm around my shoulder. "Hey, Meera."

"Uh—I—hi, Seth," I blubber. Oh my God. The hottest guy in school has got his arm around me. I can see the outline of his abs through his fitted shirt, and his muscled bicep is resting on *my* body. *Holy fuck.*

"That was a great discussion," he says, looking between me and Lucy. "I'm definitely going to borrow the desi book for the next one."

Wow, his arm is heavy. I try not to fall from the weight of it while Lucy nods politely and says, "Thank you for coming, Seth."

Finally, he steps away, hands in his pockets, and turns to me. "So, there's a party at my place tonight. Feel free to drop by."

"Like, as a guest?" My eyebrows feel like they've shot up into my hairline. "At—at your party?"

Lucy bites her lip, but a beautiful grin peeks out anyway. I side-eye her.

"Yeah, as a guest, obviously," he confirms, then heads for the door. "I gotta go. See y'all tonight!"

Oh my God. The superhot captain of the swim team wants me to come to his *party*. At his *house*. Step 2 is happening already. "Bye!" I yell after Seth in the most high-pitched, squeaky voice ever. Then I turn to Lucy and grab hold of her hands without thinking twice. "I just got invited to Seth fucking Simons's party," I whisper, bouncing on the balls of my feet. "Lucy, do you know what this means?"

Her wide eyes fall to our hands, and she jerks hers away

and wipes them on her pants. *Ouch*. "That you'll have to miss it because you have plans with your friends?"

This is when three things hit me: (1) My instinctual reaction to gush about this to Lucy is inappropriate, considering she's my sworn enemy; (2) I'm going to have to ditch Val and Ron for the first time ever; and (3) I just got invited to a fucking party at the fucking swim team captain's house. *Oh my God*.

Lucy

I lean back against the car's headrest, eyes closed, while Sushant drives me home. My skin still tingles where Meera touched me. I can't help but press my hands along my clothes, trying to get the imprint of her fingers off me. But it doesn't work, because she's imprinted in my mind too.

I clench my jaw. She still does Saturday movie nights. With her new friends. Do they love Bollywood as much as I do? Do they laugh when Meera jumps around and mimics the wacky dance moves during the song sequences? Do they stand and join in like I used to?

"Hey, mind if we take a detour?" Sushant asks, and I rouse from my thoughts. He's turning the car away from my house. His phone, open to his family's group chat, rests on his lap.

"What detour?" I rub my eyes, pretending like I've woken up from sleep, and look around. We're pulling onto the street that leads to his house.

Sushant turns to me, his dimples deepening. "My family will be out until the evening for Dheeraj's piano recital."

My heart clenches painfully. I know what he's implying. An empty house means we get all the alone time he wants. We want, I mean. I want it too. I just don't know if I want it right now.

It's terrifying to think about losing my virginity. Is it because I grew up Christian? My mother never had the Talk with me, not even when she met Sushant. Maybe she thinks taking me to church every Sunday will keep me chaste.

I know I'm not ready to have sex just yet, but it's only a matter of time . . . Sushant and I will move in together eventually when we go to New York. I do love him. So why wait?

Sushant pulls into his driveway, switches off the car engine, and turns to me. After I unbuckle my seat belt, he licks his lips and tugs me in for a kiss. I wrap my hands around his shoulders, feeling the heat between our bodies. I can't tell if the energy coursing through me is fear, excitement, nerves, or a combination of all three.

His mouth traces my jawline, my neck, my shoulder. He stops right below my collarbone. "Do you, um"—his voice is hoarse against my chest—"want to come in?"

I pull him up to face level and kiss him. "Yes," I breathe.

It's time.

Sushant unlocks his front door and calls out for his parents and Dadima. The house is silent and dark, and nobody answers. He grins and scoops me into his arms. "I love you, Lucy," he whispers against my mouth.

"I love you too." I press my lips to his neck, and he carries me to his bedroom. He kicks the door open, and we enter the room I've only been in a few times before—other rare instances when he was home alone. But my eyes linger not on his unmade bed or the freshly cleaned laundry sitting in a basket on the floor, but on his window.

The window that faces Meera's house. She's not home; her shift at Café Kismat must not have ended yet. But I can see the dark blue walls of her bedroom and the faint edge of the whiteboard that faces her bed. I spent hours in that bed, laughing with her, looking at her, pining for her.

Sushant sets me on his bed and notices my slack jaw and where I'm looking. "Sorry, I should close the blinds," he says, laughing. "Never done this before."

The room plunges into darkness as he tugs the curtains over the window. I force myself to laugh back, but my limbs are rigid, my heart pounding, as a bead of sweat drops down the back of my neck. What am I doing?

Sushant joins me on the bed, his gaze dreamlike. "So, where were we?" He pushes my hair off my right shoulder, dropping kisses on my exposed skin. It feels good—being with him always does—but a million thoughts race through my mind as his touch hardens and his kisses deepen. Am I really going to have sex with my boyfriend today? Right now?

He pulls me over him, whispering, "You're so beautiful."

My body says, *No, Lucy, you can't do this; you're not ready just yet.*

His hand snakes along my hips, hot and eager, the words "I love you" on his lips, but his warm touch still makes me shiver. My mind says, *Yes, it's logically the right time; you've been together for over a year now.*

He pulls his shirt off and tosses it to the ground. I stare into his hooded eyes, and my heart says, *He doesn't even know your relationship was once a lie. If he knew, he would leave you. As he ought to.*

Just as Sushant pops open the button to my pants, I sit up and push away from him. "No, Sushant, wait." I breathe as a wave of panic sweeps over me. "I'm sorry, but—I—I can't do this."

"Lucy." He stands, giving me some space, and just when I think I've upset him, he kneels in front of the bed, tapping the side of my cheek. "It's okay. We don't have to."

I nod, but when I look up, my foggy eyes find the window behind Sushant, and now my head is spinning and my heart is hammering and I can't breathe and—

"Hey, hey, it's okay." Sushant helps me sit on the edge of the bed and puts my head between my knees. "Relax. I'm here. It's okay."

I surface two minutes later, my breathing steady again, tears streaming down my face. "I—I should head home. Seth's party is in a couple hours, and I need to shower first."

"Okay, let me just get the car keys—"

"I can walk," I reply, and Sushant's face falls. Before he can say anything, I peck him on the lips and leave his bedroom. To his credit, he doesn't chase after me or ask if we're still going to the party together. He knows when I need space and when I don't.

As I walk past Meera's house, her dog, Raj, must sense my presence, because he yips and barks from inside, but I purposely don't look at her front door. I've hurt Sushant enough today. I don't need to hurt myself too.

CHAPTER ELEVEN

"Nostalgic"
by ARIZONA

Meera

It's embarrassing to admit, but in my seventeen years of existence, I've never been to a party like *this*. I've obviously gone to PG birthday parties where you eat cake, drink iced tea, and go home before sunset. And I've been to one other house party with alcohol, but that was way tamer and back in freshman year.

It's past nine p.m. now, and Seth's house party is a jungle of horny, drunk teenagers getting hornier and drunker with every passing minute. A couple from the theater club is going at it in one corner of the living room, while the screaming and yelling football team plays beer pong in the kitchen.

I spot Sushant cheering with the rest of the jocks as someone from the game chugs his beer. I wave eagerly, but Sushant doesn't notice me, so I drop my hand and hope nobody saw that.

Weaving through the crowd of dancing cheerleaders, I turn my head to search for Julien. The book club has been wildly successful, and I've clearly arrived at Step 2 of the Plan.

But I have a long way to go if I want to see the Plan through to the end. And the way to become Sushant's confidante is to bring jealousy and suspicion into his relationship. Julien is my best bet to getting there.

"Julien, hey!" I find him standing by the open backyard door, smoking a joint and staring into space. He grins at me, his eyes glazed, and reaches forward to kiss me on each cheek before I can pull back. Guess he still hasn't gotten the memo that Americans don't do cheek kisses.

"What are you, uh, up to?" I ask, shoving my hands into my pockets and smiling back awkwardly. It's clear to anyone with eyes what he's doing, but I'm hoping he humors me. How else am I supposed to start a conversation at a party? I didn't read *High School Partying for Dummies*.

Julien raises the joint to his lips and exhales a puff of smoke. "I am enjoying the simple pleasures of living on beautiful Earth," he says dreamily. "Food. Beer. Pot. Making love." He gestures to the party at large. "What more could I want out of this one life I have been granted?"

"Uh." I shuffle my feet and laugh. "Coffee?"

His lips curve into another smile, his straight teeth bright against his dark skin. Why *hasn't* Lucy fallen for him yet? He looks like a model straight out of Paris Fashion Week. "Yes, coffee," he agrees, and it's only then that he seems to take a closer look at me. "But look at you, you are empty-handed! We must get you a beer."

"I don't actually drink—" I start, but he's already taking me by the hand to the kitchen. While he's rummaging through a cooler for a beer, I tap Sushant on the shoulder. "Hey there, neighbor."

As soon as I say it, I cringe internally. Who says that? But Sushant only beams at me. He excuses himself from the beer pong game and leans against the kitchen counter, his strong arms folded. "Hiiii, favorite n-neighbor," he says, his words slurring a little. "Why is this the first time I'm seeing you at a party?"

Because I'm a nobody and I've never been invited to one before? Saying that would only make him pity me, so I shrug and accept a bottle of beer from Julien. When in Rome . . .

"I'm very selective with my social life." I take my first sip—the beer tastes like piss, but it warms me from the tips of my ears to the depths of my belly—and add, "You should be honored that you get to talk to me right now, Sushant Khera."

Sushant's mouth quirks, and he taps his thumb against the side of my drink, then pinches my cheek with cold fingers. "Meera Rao-George, I like you even more all relaxed," he replies, before returning to his friends.

I try not to squeal out loud as I tremble in my sneakers. If he likes me more after one sip of alcohol, that means he already likes me a certain amount. I drink some more of the beer and walk around the room with Julien, who's talking about the beauty in every leaf on the trees of Madre Maria or some philosophical bullshit like that. Someone passes by with a tray of clear shots, and I down one. *Gah!* It tastes like something foul from the Chemistry lab—vodka, perhaps? I splutter and chug the beer until the bitter chemical flavor leaves my mouth.

"Another drink?" Julien asks when I set the empty bottle down on a nearby table. He doesn't wait for me to answer; he just heads back to the kitchen, whistling.

"Sure, why not?" I call out after him. The corners of my vision shimmer like someone's put an Instagram filter over it. Every inch of me feels radiant, warm, soothed. Is this what alcohol does to people? No wonder everyone in school drinks. This is some magic potion shit.

Julien brings back a cocktail he made with tequila and orange juice. His father is a bartender in Paris—and a good one at that, as it turns out. I savor every sip of the sugary, citrusy elixir.

I'm teetering on the edge of the backyard door, eyes closed, smiling as Julien talks about the miracle of human life, when someone enters our comfortable nook. "There you are!" Natalie grabs hold of Julien's hands and tugs him toward the center of the room, where everyone's dancing. "Dance with me like one of your French girls," she jokes, and he laughs before spinning her around.

Damn it. I groan out loud, but the party's so noisy, no one hears me. How can I sic him on Lucy when her own best friend is gunning for him? Lucy would never steal—

I stiffen, my teeth grinding into one another. What am I saying? Of course Lucy would make a move on the guy her best friend likes. Isn't that what she did with me and Sushant?

I can still remember waiting for Lucy in the parking lot that first day of junior year, excited to see the car her mom had gotten her right before she left for summer camp.

And then she'd driven to school in a new Honda, sunglasses perched atop her straightened hair, makeup hiding those adorable freckles on her cheeks, with some girl sitting in the front seat beside her. Her name was Natalie Something. I recalled that she was the one with the vegan cat. Confusion crept up the back of my neck, snaking around my face like a vine. Since when were they friends? Had they met at camp? Was this why Lucy hadn't texted me for weeks? No, there was probably no cell service at camp. Lucy would never replace me with someone else. This was just a weird misunderstanding. It had to be.

Lucy pulled into a shady parking spot and got out of the car with Natalie. Her dress sense hadn't changed—bright, floral, colorful; the opposite of my all-black wardrobe—but she looked different with those sky-high heels and the purse dangling from her wrist. Designer-wardrobe different. Like she'd fit right in at the cheerleaders' table.

They both started toward the school building, so I raced ahead to block their path. "Lucy!" I exclaimed in a huff, desperate to talk to my best friend. "I love the car!"

Natalie shuffled beside her uncomfortably. I couldn't understand what was going on. Lucy bit her bright pink lip, then jutted out her chin. "Thanks. Bye, Meera." She sidestepped around me and walked ahead.

I grabbed the side of her arm and pulled her back, exhaling

softly. "What is going on?" I asked, lowering my voice. "Why are you being weird?"

Lucy didn't seem like she wanted to keep this private. "Look, Meera," she said loudly, and the other students in the now-scattering crowd looked our way. "I've honestly outgrown our friendship. It's best if we don't talk anymore."

"Wait, what?" I stared at her through misting eyes. A tear fell down my cheek. What the fuck? I never cried. I wiped it hastily and stepped in front of her as she moved to leave. "Lucy, we're best friends."

"We *were* best friends," she corrected me. A painful emotion clouded her eyes—to this day, I don't know what it was—but it couldn't compare to the gaping, bleeding hole in my heart, the knife stabbed and twisted into my back. "Goodbye, Meera."

Three periods later, I spotted her kissing Sushant by his locker, and that cemented the death of our friendship.

That fucking bitch.

Now, as I take in the musty, hazy party with the loud music thumping through the base of my skull, I let out an exhale. Julien and Natalie are grinding against each other. Probably seconds away from making out. And Lucy's nowhere to be seen. For the Plan to work, I have to put aside my loathing for her and pretend to make amends.

Did she even show up to the party? I need liquid strength if I want to get through tonight. I stumble over to the couch, down another shot from a tray on the coffee table, and resume searching the living room. I apologize as I bump into people—some who greet me politely, having recognized me as the Café Kismat girl, perhaps; others who ignore me and continue talking to their friends. Finally, I head down the hallway. She's got to be here somewhere. She's the head cheerleader. She needs to show up, right?

When my phone buzzes, blinking with a text from Valeria, my stomach churns. It's our group chat. I bailed on the movie marathon and told my friends my parents needed me tonight, and they thankfully bought the excuse. I didn't have a choice—who knows when I'll get another party invite? Bringing them along with me here was not an option. Not until I have more sway with the popular crowd.

Valeria:

You're missing out on the greatest rom-com movie of the century, Meera

Ron is typing . . .

Ron:

And by that she means "overly cheesy snoozefest." What you up to?

I bite my lip, type out, Still helping Dad with chores, y'all have fun, then mute my phone and shove it into my pocket. I don't like lying to them, but I can't admit the truth now. I have more pressing matters at hand.

I push open the door to what seems like a study, and as I nearly fall into the room, the smell of Lucy's flowery perfume hits me right in my nostrils. Bookshelves line every inch of the walls, a poufy lounge chair sits beside the cozy electric fireplace, and Lucy stands in the center of it all, her back to me. She's looking through the titles on the shelves, one open book already in her hand. Her red hair is swept to one side of her neck, and she's wearing a short black dress and bright pink heels. It's jarring to see her looking so good in black. She hates that color.

"Lucy?" I call out. It comes out as "Lusssy," like I'm slurring or something. Weird. I thought you had to drink a lot more for that.

She jumps a foot in the air, slams her book shut, and spins around. Her eyes narrow. "Meera? What are you doing *here*?"

I put my hands inside the pockets of my baggy blue jeans and walk over to her. "I was invited, remember? After the book club meeting?"

She frowns, returning the book to the shelf. "I mean here in Seth's parents' library."

The words slip out before I can decide if they're sensible or not. "Oh, I was looking for you."

Lucy blinks and steps back, her hip colliding against a bookshelf. She clears her throat, her head lifting an inch like it does when she's calling on her inner cheerleader bitch. Even after all this time, I can read her like a book. "You've been bothering me a lot more than usual lately," she says.

I bite the inside of my cheek to stop myself from retorting. Something swirls in my belly—is it anger? Resentment? Whatever it is, I have to hold it back.

"I should get back to the party," Lucy says, when I continue my silence. She gulps and takes a step forward, then adds, "Sushant is probably wondering where I am."

Look at her, mentioning the boy I love in front of me. The nerve. I walk closer to her, my nostrils flaring, but when I open my mouth to tell her how much I despise her, words don't come out.

Vomit does. Right where Lucy's standing.

Lucy

Having anxiety means you're jumpy at the smallest of things and your body reacts to keep you safe before you can even think about what's happening. Which is helpful in times like right now, because I instinctively push back against the bookshelf, and the puke narrowly misses the front of the designer heels I found at the thrift store. Not that I've told anyone that.

Meera finishes retching and stands up straight, teetering slightly as she wipes her mouth with the back of her shaking hand. Eyes wide, she steps backward and lets out a nervous chuckle. "I'm so sorry. How expensive are those shoes?"

In all the years of our friendship, and now nonfriendship, I've only lied to Meera a few times. "I got them from Goodwill," I blurt out, carefully hopping to the side of the puke. "But they are real designer shoes. Just . . . secondhand."

Pink dusts Meera's cheeks. I bet she can tell I'm embarrassed, and she actually feels bad about it. "Oh. Well, at least I didn't puke right on them."

I nod slowly. "Yeah. Thanks a lot."

She stares at me like she's trying to figure out if I'm being sarcastic, then looks around the room. "I should—I should clean this up." As she turns, a guttural sound escapes her lips. She clamps a hand over her mouth and runs out of the library.

I pause, deliberating, then stomp over to the nearest bathroom. I can't in good conscience desert her, and I doubt her friends got invited to the party. She must be all alone.

My phone buzzes as I look around the hallway. *Dad*, the caller ID says. I roll my eyes and hit the reject button. I don't need anything else fueling my anxiety today, thanks.

When I swing the unlocked bathroom door open, there she is, heaving over the toilet. I gently pull her black hair away from her face, careful not to let my touch linger over the soft skin on the back of her neck. God, she smells incredible, the puke notwithstanding. Guess she never switched her coconut shampoo.

I help her up after she flushes and give her the bottle of mouthwash from the medicine cabinet. "I didn't know you started drinking," I say, leaning my weight against the wall and crossing my arms over my chest.

Meera spits out the mouthwash. She stares at my reflection in the mirror and grips both edges of the sink with her hands. Her black nail polish is chipping. She never did like any other color. "There's a first time for everything," she answers, scowling. Then she turns to me, and a radiant smile lights up her face. "You know what this reminds me of?"

I know the exact memory she's thinking about, but I feign confusion. "What?"

"*Your* first time drinking." Meera puts a hand to her mouth. I wonder if she needs to puke again, but it's only to contain her laughter. "Freshman year. We crashed Brittney's party, and you were in the bathroom for twenty minutes, throwing up. I held back your hair, made you coffee, and helped you sneak into your house without your mom figuring out you were drunk."

That had been a fun night. The next morning, not so much, although I did wake up to an Advil and a glass of water on my bedside table. I remember every minute of that night, right down to Meera's fingers brushing mine when she handed me the coffee mug. I didn't know back then why I felt shivers at her touch. I know now.

Meera was so good to me. I never deserved her friendship, especially not after how I broke it—and broke her heart too. My throat closes, and I exhale out a lie. "I can't seem to remember that."

Her lips part, and she frowns. Then she shakes her head, smiles, and reaches for the doorknob. As she walks out, she says, "It's nice to see you wearing my favorite color for a change."

The door slams shut. I stay back for a few minutes, holding

in my tears and running my hands over my black dress. She noticed what I'm wearing. She said I look nice. She—she's being kind.

Don't, Lucy. Don't you dare. I splash water on my face, careful not to wash off my makeup, and walk back into the loud, aggravating party to distract myself, so I can go back to thinking straight. Literally.

CHAPTER TWELVE

"I Like Me Better"

by Lauv

Lucy

I haven't spoken to Sushant in person since I ran out of his bedroom earlier today. He texted me to check in, and I said we could talk at the party. But I've been avoiding him. I don't know if he spotted me sneaking off to the library, but he hasn't tried to find me. Maybe he wants to give me more space.

But space isn't going to help me forget the coconutty scent of Meera's shampoo, which refuses to leave my nostrils. So I clear my throat, down a shot from the tray on the coffee table, and waltz over to the kitchen island, where Sushant stands.

The open kitchen is terribly crowded and smells of beer, sour cream dip, and, well, sweat. The beer pong game must have ended, because the guys on the football, swim, and hockey teams are just sipping their drinks. Seth is making obscene gestures with his hand while everyone laughs, Sushant included.

"Hey, babe," I greet him.

His whole face lights up as he sets his cup down. He reaches forward to kiss me, then excuses himself from the guys and walks us over to a slightly isolated corner. Before I can ask him if he wants another drink, Sushant puts his arms around my waist and tugs me to his chest, lifting my feet off the ground. "I missed you," he whispers. "I'm sorry about earlier."

I breathe in the smell of him—cinnamon spice and the laundry detergent his mom buys from the Indian grocery store—and sigh loudly. "I'm sorry too. I should have told you I'm not ready yet."

Sushant sets me down on my feet again and groans into his hands. "I should have asked you first. I can't believe I was such an ass."

"Hey." I pull on his T-shirt, and he bends so I can reach his face. I kiss him once on the nose, twice on the cheeks, and thrice on the lips, and by the time we break apart, he has the widest dimpled smile on his face.

"I love you so much," he whispers, thumping his hand against his chest. "How did I get so lucky?"

"I love you too." I press my cheek against his shoulder, promising myself that I'm worthy of Sushant's love, that my feelings for him are true now, even if they weren't once upon a time. But today has been . . . a lot, and fatigue is seeping into my bones. I pull away and say, "I'm tired. Can we go home?"

Sushant laughs. "Someday, when you say that, it'll mean *our* home. In New York." He cups my cheeks in his hands and adds, "NYU is sending out acceptances soon. And Coach said we should be hearing back from Syracuse about the scholarship any day now."

Yes. I grin and kiss him hard, pushing him against the wall, and a moan escapes his lips as his hands find my hips. The sooner New York is set in stone, the sooner I can embrace Sushant in every way possible and let go of Madre Maria . . . and Meera. And then everything will be perfect.

"My God, get a room." We break apart at Natalie's giggle. She looks drunk—her cheeks are flushed, and she's sweaty from all the dancing. "Has either of you seen Julien? We were dancing, and then I lost him."

"I think I saw him go down the hallway a while ago." Sushant looks around, frowning. "There's a library and another bathroom over there."

Natalie blows a kiss at us. "Thanks! See you in school on Monday, Lucy." As she walks away, I catch sight of Meera talking to one of the cheerleaders who attended the book club. I bite the inside of my cheek. Do *not* tell me they're starting to like her. I won't be able to deal with Meera showing up to our lunch table and being weirdly nice like she has been all month.

"Shall we?" Sushant holds his arm out, and I wind mine through it, looking away from Meera just as she turns toward us.

We've both had a little to drink, and we didn't bring our cars, anyway, so we walk down the street, hand in hand, talking about going to Central Park someday and the New

York Public Library, of course, and which neighborhood we might be able to afford when we move there. After we kiss goodbye, I unlock my front door and find Mom standing in the living room, dressed in a silk nightgown, yelling into the phone.

"No, goddamn it, we don't want you here or any of your filthy family money. I wouldn't take it even if we needed it, you motherf—" She whirls around at the sound of the door closing, and her jaw drops when she sees me. "I'll call you later," she mumbles, and throws her phone on the couch beside her.

"Hi, Mom," I say cautiously, stepping inside, my eyes on her phone. *Filthy family money*? I recall Mom telling me about Grandpa's death and the large sum he left my father. "Were you just talking to Dad? Did he call again?"

Mom laughs shrilly, but her voice cracks in between. "It's nothing to worry about, sweetheart. He'll stop bothering us soon enough. Why don't you go to bed?"

I look from the phone to my mother. Was Dad calling me earlier to ask if he could support me through college? Natalie thought it would be a good idea, and maybe she isn't wrong. If Dad wants to make amends by paying for my tuition, I could let him. It doesn't mean I have to forgive him. He owes me at least this much for not bothering to fight for me during the divorce. What kind of father does that?

Maybe it's the alcohol or how much she's been around me lately, but the one thing I ask myself before speaking is this: *What would Meera Rao-George do*? I hold out my hand and tap my heel against the tiled flooring. "Give me your phone, Mom."

Her face darkens even as her brow lifts up. "Lucy, go to bed."

"Mom." I step forward, licking my lips, still eyeing her phone. "I know you have my college fund, but if Dad's offering to support me with Grandpa's money, let him. A New York lifestyle isn't cheap. Sushant doesn't come from money, either."

She grabs her phone and hides it behind her back. Her chest is heaving; her eyes are wet. "Go to bed."

"No," I say. The courage coursing through my veins feels alien, like I've put on someone else's personality. Meera's, perhaps. "I'm almost eighteen, and he's my father. Taking his money doesn't have to mean we forgive him. It'll make our lives easier, which is the least he could do, honestly."

She looks up to the ceiling as though she's talking to God in her head, then takes out her phone and waves it in my face. "Yes. It was him on the phone. But you know what, Lucy? He doesn't get to support you or make your life easier, because he's not your father anymore. We're all the family each other's got, you get me?"

"But—"

Mom plants a fake, watery smile on her face and waves her fingers at me, and it breaks my heart to see her crying. "I'm going to bed. Good night, Lucy."

I lower my head and nod. "Good night, Mom." She pads up

the stairs to her room without looking back. So much for embodying my inner Meera Rao-George.

Meera

On Monday, I'm waiting for Sushant by the bus stop after an especially heavy breakfast of uthappam topped with shredded coconut, tomatoes, and onions—Appa's family recipe, which I mastered years ago. The bus is coming any minute, but Sushant is nowhere to be found.

Is he unwell? Maybe he had too much beer at the party and had a raging hangover just like I did. I'd thought throwing up right after drinking would help, but I had a blinding headache all day yesterday anyway.

Thank goodness Appa and Dad didn't suspect anything. I stayed in my room, played Gryffin songs on loop, and read the first few chapters of the desi young adult romance Lucy picked for the book club meeting next month. Ron and Valeria didn't reply to my texts asking what they're up to, which is weird, but I'll see them at school. Besides, I spent all of yesterday figuring out how to tell them about the party and apologize for lying to them. I'll wait for the right time—maybe during lunch, when neither of them is cranky or hangry.

"WOOOO!"

I nearly jump out of my skin as Sushant runs out of his house, arms raised to the sky, a big grin breaking out across his face.

"What happened?" I ask, staring as he chucks his backpack onto the ground and does a very famous Bollywood song-and-dance sequence from the early 2000s, popularized by Hrithik Roshan well before we were born. If it weren't seven a.m. on a weekday, I'd think he was high.

Sushant dances for a few more seconds, singing the iconic Hindi song loudly, and finally grabs his backpack and wipes his forehead with a whoosh of breath. Then he smiles at me. "Meera, guess what? I got into Syracuse on a football scholarship!"

I freeze. Syracuse. In New York. Which has always been Lucy's dream. And now Sushant's going there too. For real. A beat passes; then I force myself to gasp and jump up and down. "Oh my God, Sushant, that's great news!"

He beams at me. "Isn't it? Coach is psyched too. Oh, and I'm telling Lucy when I see her, so keep your lips sealed." He puts his fingers near my mouth and mimes zipping it shut.

"I promise." I ignore the heat radiating from his fingers and give him a thumbs-up. "I haven't spoken to Lucy since the party anyway."

"Oh, you ran into her there?" Sushant raises a brow just as the bus stops in front of us. We climb in and take our usual seats in the middle, and he adds, "I didn't see her until the beer pong game ended."

"She was in the library." I grab my earphones, set my bag by my feet, and push the window open, breathing in the cool breeze and soaking in the bright sunlight that washes over my face.

When Sushant doesn't respond, I turn around in my seat. His eyebrows are arched, and he looks like he's trying to piece something together.

"What's wrong?" I ask.

He grimaces rather nervously. "Nothing. Never mind."

I bite the inside of my cheek, then nod, although I'm so desperately wishing he'd tell me what he's thinking. "Okay."

A few minutes later, the bus lurches to a stop. Sushant leans away from the aisle as more people climb in, his gaze fixed on me. When I tug one earphone out and frown at him, he asks, "Lucy was in the library? For how long?"

I shrug. "I don't know. Why?"

Sushant shuffles in place, shadows falling over his brown skin. "I don't know. It's just . . . I thought Julien was hiding out there after he had another joint. He gets very literary when he's high. Seth found him asleep with his head in a book after the party ended and he was cleaning up."

Wait a minute. Is Sushant . . . jealous? I can't seem too eager, or he'll get suspicious. However, I do need to egg him on, ask him if he thinks there's anything between the two of them. But when I open my mouth to add fuel to the fire, only the truth comes out. "Julien wasn't in the library when Lucy was."

Fuck. Why the hell did I say that?

The relief on Sushant's face is almost palpable. "Really?" He sinks back into his seat and closes his eyes. "Thank goodness. I was scared because she was upset with me and—"

"Why was she upset?" I ask.

He turns to me and rakes a hand through his hair, smiling awkwardly. "That's kind of a private matter, Meera."

"Right, of course." I put my earphone in again, cringing. Only Gryffin can save me from this embarrassment. The electronic beats pound in my ears, and Sushant heads to the back to talk to other people who take the bus with us. I rest my head against the window as we pass by Lucy's house. Ms. Miller, dressed in a pin-striped jumpsuit, is finally mowing the overgrown lawn.

The Plan is working so far. After I left the bathroom, I spoke to at least five people at the party who wouldn't have otherwise given me the time of day. Sushant is having doubts about his relationship with Lucy. And as for Lucy . . . she doesn't have a clue what I'm doing.

But my stomach churns, and a sheen of sweat breaks out on my chest at the possibility of my getting everything I've ever wanted, and I can't figure out if it's excitement, anticipation, or a sign from the Universe telling me to stop before it's too late.

CHAPTER THIRTEEN

"Bad Blood (Taylor's Version)"

by Taylor Swift feat. Kendrick Lamar

Meera

Ron and Valeria are mumbling to each other when I catch up to them. Leaning against my locker, I hold out a homemade energy bar for Valeria to take. "Sorry I missed the movie marathon. Was it fun?"

They exchange wordless glances; then Ron slams his locker shut and nods. "Yeah. And how about you? How was the party at Seth's?"

"Oh my God, it was so cool—" I freeze. My blood turns to ice as I stare at my friends, my jaw dropping. *Shit.* They beat me to it. "Wait, how did you find out?"

"That's your way of apologizing?" Valeria rolls her eyes and yanks the energy bar from my fingers. She takes the first bite and adds, "We saw you in the background of someone's Instagram Story from the party. Why didn't you take us along?"

I look from Valeria to Ron, frowning. "Because this was my first party invite. I couldn't bring people with me! That's against, like, party rules."

Ron runs his fingers through his shaggy hair, staring at me head-on. "Yeah, and I'm sure a bunch of underage-drinking, pot-smoking teenagers care about rules."

"Come on, I'm sorry. Don't be mad. Don't be mad. Don't be mad." I tug on Ron's baggy T-shirt until he relents and smiles.

"You're a dumbass," he says. He tucks his books under his arm, mumbles, "Bye," and heads down the hallway to class.

Valeria's still studying me as I take my stuff out from my locker, her eyes sad.

"What?" I ask.

She exhales loudly and shakes her head. "Just don't lose yourself in this whole Plan thing, Meera. Because then you'll lose us too." With that, she walks away without looking back at me, the half-eaten energy bar clenched tight in her fist.

Ugh. I don't get her and Appa's obsession over this losing-myself bullshit. You can't lose a nobody, and that's what I am. A stinking nobody. I grumble under my breath and head to homeroom.

It's only during third period, PE, that I notice people milling around the track, discussing NYU acceptances. They must have come in last night or sometime today. I didn't apply to NYU or anywhere else because, well, my parents don't have the funds to pay for college, and there's no way for me to get a scholarship with my poor grades and complete lack of athletic ability. My Indian grandparents are upset I won't get an Ivy education, but they don't have much money to contribute, either. Community college it is. I don't care too much about that decision; I'd rather help out at the café for as long as I can until eventually taking over the business. Madre Maria and Café Kismat are home and always will be.

A bunch of people didn't get into NYU, and they're all commiserating with one another like a pseudo support group while the ones who did get in are dancing around instead of doing their stretches.

Coach Lauv instructs us to run a few laps after our warm-up. I don't share third period with Ron or Val, so I look around for someone to talk to while I stretch. I grab my ankle and pull it up to my butt with a pained groan, pausing in my scan when I see Lucy. She's wearing the pink-and-yellow PE uniform like the rest of us, her short shorts and tank top showing off her toned figure.

She stands with her arms by her side, looking at the crowd of girls screaming with joy about their friends getting into NYU, and her eyes are red rimmed.

"Hey," I say, walking over to her. She makes a small strangled noise when she notices me, and her body twitches. Gosh, she's been jumpy lately. I stretch my left hamstring and add, "So? Did you hear from NYU?"

Lucy holds my gaze for a second before her head lifts and she sneers, "None of your business, Meera." Then she dashes ahead along the track, and I stay behind, knowing she's too fast for me to keep up with her.

I watch her run, her ponytail swishing around like a red-hot flame, and a sickly sensation spreads across my limbs:

anxiety. She doesn't want to talk about NYU. Instead of showing off like the others, she's staying silent. Does that mean she got—

Lucy

Wait-listed.

As I run my first lap around the track as fast as I can, desperate to leave Meera and the others behind, the W-word is the only thing on my mind. I got wait-listed at NYU. Me. Those debate team students with their B-minuses got in, and I didn't? How is that possible?

A burning ache shoots up along my feet inside my sneakers. Years of working out ensure I don't need to stop to catch my breath, so I keep going. Coach Lauv cheers as I streak past him, leaving nothing but dust in my wake.

The faster I run, the faster my thoughts catch up to me. Sushant was so happy this morning when he spun me around and kissed me in front of everyone. We're supposed to go out to dinner tonight at his favorite pizza place (the only one in town that makes pizzas with real cheese). It's a double date with Julien and Natalie to celebrate his Syracuse scholarship. "And we can celebrate your NYU acceptance too," he told me, kissing my cheek while I giggled. "There's no way you won't get in."

Wait-listed.

I finally pause midway through my second lap, resting my hands above my knees. My lungs burn, refusing to take in oxygen, and I know the running has nothing to do with this wave of nausea plaguing me. *Inhale and exhale, Lucy,* I remind myself. *That's all you have to do.*

I catch my breath for a minute until Coach Lauv blows his whistle, and off I run again. I have a straight-A average. I'm captain of the cheer squad. I was the star of the track team last year. Three of my teachers wrote me glowing letters of recommendation.

The only thing that could have hurt my application is my essay. I'm a good writer; my English teacher's told me that enough times. But maybe the problem is what I wrote, not how I wrote it. The essay topic was "Reflect on your most impactful relationship. What lessons has it taught you? What realizations have you had because of this person?"

When I saw the topic, my brain instinctually thought of Meera. Headstrong, stubborn, does-what-she-decides Meera. My first love. She taught me so much about love and spirituality and friendship . . . and myself. She sparked the biggest realization I could have ever had about who I truly am. But I've never said *that word*—the one Julien said during the museum trip—about myself in my head or out loud, forget writing it down in an official college essay.

So I wrote about my dad and my parents' separation, how it taught me the fragility of relationships. If Dad had agreed to see the Christian counselor Mom had suggested instead of filing for divorce, I might still have a whole family. I wrote about how my parents' marriage ending unexpectedly after twenty years together taught me that if you love someone, you have to do the work and keep holding on even when things seem rough. You hold on together. You love hard, you love forever.

Maybe the teenaged-girl-from-a-broken-family thing made my application too mainstream, and that's why I got wait-listed. Fair enough. I finally stop running and lean my weight against a pole, thinking. Funny how I don't take my own advice. Holding on to Meera would have meant letting go of the girl I've been for all these years. And I can't let that girl go—not just yet. Maybe not ever.

"Hey, Lucy." Brittney, the girl I beat to become cheer captain earlier this year, smiles scathingly at me. She holds her phone in her hand and wiggles it in my face. "I got into NYU. And Stanford. And Berkeley."

I force myself to smile back, lifting my face to look her in the eye. "Congrats, Brittney."

"Rumor has it that you didn't get into NYU, though." She walks forward, tutting in Mean Girl fashion. "I'm so sorry they couldn't see how precious and practically perfect you are."

"Thanks," I say out of the corner of my mouth. I'm stretching my calves when Brittney the witch speaks up again.

"Guess you're not gonna get to go to New York with your himbo boyfriend after all."

Something in me snaps. I raise my gaze, my eyes stormy, as my chest heaves with the knowledge that even if I do follow

Sushant to New York, my dream of working in publishing will be on hold for a whole year. Because would a publishing house offer so much as an internship to someone who didn't even go to college?

"Did I hit a nerve?" Brittney purses her lips as a few boys jog past us. "You stole cheer captain from me. Maybe this is the Universe's version of payback."

The word "Universe" makes me think of Meera, which brings up the question *What would Meera Rao-George do?* in my head. Instead of overthinking my own instincts like always, I let the fury build in my veins and explode. I move forward and shove Brittney onto the ground.

"Ow!" she exclaims, rubbing her elbow. "That's gonna leave a bruise!"

"Oh, I'm gonna leave a lot more than just a bruise," I shoot back, lunging for her just as she gingerly stands. Before I can reach her, someone grabs me by the waist and pulls me away. I kick and yell, and we both tumble down. I get onto my knees and crawl around. It's Julien, breathing hard as he shakes his head at me.

"What is going on here?" Coach Lauv walks over to us and surveys the scene. "Why are you kids on the ground?"

"Lucy pushed me!" Brittney squeals, showing Coach the barely-there bruises on her elbows. "I don't know what made her do it. I was just telling her about my college acceptances, and"—she sobs exaggeratedly—"she must have gotten jealous!"

Coach Lauv glares down at Julien. "And why are *you* sitting down, Mr. Perrin?"

"I was breaking up the fight." He stands and extends a hand to me, and I take it.

"You're supposed to be playing field hockey with the other boys," Coach says to Julien, his voice stern. He crosses his arms and looks toward Brittney, who cries out in pain again. *Oh, for heaven's sake.*

"Detention," Coach finally says, turning to Julien and me. "After school today."

Julien and I both open our mouths in protest, but Coach Lauv shushes us. "If you argue with me, I'll make it a whole week. Now get back on the field!" He marches ahead to check on some other students.

"I'll see you this afternoon, then," I say to Julien, sighing. "I'm sorry."

"Do not be sorry," he says, teeth gritted. "American coaches are— Oh, merde. Forget it. I'll see you later." He speeds off toward the field hockey game.

I leave Brittney and the crowd of girls sympathizing with her so-called bruises and run into Meera. I guess she's been watching the commotion play out. "What?" I ask her, my voice elevating. "What do you want from me? Why do you appear everywhere I go?"

"Sorry," she mumbles, a pinch between her eyebrows. "I just hope you're okay."

"You shouldn't care if I'm okay," I tell her, stepping backward, "since you're supposed to hate me! So just let me be."

"I don't hate you."

That makes me stop. "What?"

"Well." Meera flicks the end of her braid, not meeting my eyes. "Not as much as I used to, at least." She exhales, then runs ahead, her pace considerably slower than mine.

Try as I might, I can't get my heart to stop hammering in my chest. I put a hand over it, hoping I can somehow magic it into slowing down, but all that does is make me aware of the blood rushing into my ears and all the oxygen that can't make its way to my lungs. Because Meera Rao-George doesn't hate me.

The question is: Why not?

CHAPTER FOURTEEN

"Stand By You"
by Rachel Platten

Meera

As I scrub the underside of one of the café's tables vigorously with a plastic fork, wishing hell on the customer who couldn't be bothered to throw their bubble gum into the trash, the door swings open, bringing in a whoosh of warm, sunshiny afternoon air, and Sushant's voice fills the café. "Hey, Meera."

My heart almost explodes with joy. Lucy's not here and Sushant hates coffee, so he must have come to see me. Me! But in the game of love, playing it cool is everything. So I grunt out a hello without looking up.

"What are you doing?" Sushant comes over to where I'm standing and bends down to examine the days-old bubble gum that refuses to peel off the table. "That's gross. Do you have ice?"

"Ice? Yeah, ask Dad for some." My eyebrows furrow as I focus on the gum. It's stringy now and sticking to the plastic fork. *Eww.* I try not to gag.

Sushant's footsteps fade only to reappear a minute later. He steers me away from the table, squats down, and presses a bag of ice against the gum. "Once the gum is cold and frozen, you can get it off easily," he explains.

He's right. Barely three minutes later, the gum is at the bottom of the trash can. "How did you know this?" I ask, grinning as I wipe my washed hands on my apron. "I didn't peg you for a home economics kinda guy."

Laughing, Sushant grabs a chair and sits down, then gestures for me to join him.

I look around, biting my lip. The café's been fairly busy since the book club launched, but Danny and Dad are both at the counter. No one will miss me if I take a quick break. I sit beside Sushant and wait for him to answer my question.

"Growing up, I was obsessed with this one brand of Indian bubble gum," he says with a chuckle, his fingers tapping the side of the table. "My granddad used to bring back a whole box of Boomer from Delhi every time he visited his family there. And like any bratty kid, I'd stick gum all over the furniture. It drove Mom nuts until she searched online for this ice trick."

I smile, wondering what Delhi must be like, whether Sushant has ever returned to his roots, his culture. Might as well ask. "Have you ever been there? Delhi?"

His fingers are still fidgeting, and although he nods, his feet start swinging too, like he's restless. "Once, a few years ago. Trust me, the Indian street food you get here sucks compared to actual Delhi chaat."

"I'd love to visit India someday. Bangalore, especially, where my grandparents are from, although they now live—"

"Hey, Meera?" Sushant averts his gaze, his tongue against

the inside of his cheek. He finally stops moving his limbs. "Can I . . . can I ask you something?"

I muster as much playing-it-cool energy as possible, running a hand along my messy braid and shrugging. On the inside, though, my heart might beat its way out of my chest. "Sure, what's up?"

His eyes show concern as he says, "Do you think there could be something between Lucy and Julien?"

Thank goodness I have resting bitch face and robotic features. Because if I had expressive features brimming with emotion, like Lucy does, then there'd be no way I could hide the celebratory cheers raging in my head—the kind of cheers that erupt from Appa's mouth only when India wins the Cricket World Cup. "Lucy and . . . Julien?" I frown. "I don't know, why?"

Sushant blows out a breath. "She's been distant lately. And I think it started after Julien moved here. I get that she had to show him around for school when he first started, but he's been here for weeks, and he still never leaves her side."

I hesitate, then put my hand on his, which is clenched into a warm fist. "What brought this on? Because they both got detention today?"

He nods, but his body doesn't loosen up, and he shifts his hand away from mine to interlock his fingers behind his head. "I didn't even get to see her before football practice."

"So"—I raise my eyebrow—"what are you gonna do about this?"

"We have a double date tonight with Julien and Natalie. I think I'm going to talk to them and see what's going on." Sushant's face darkens more than usual. "If he's trying to steal my girl, I'll kill him."

Whoa. I didn't think Sushant was this protective of Lucy. And also, I'm quite sure there's nothing between her and Julien, so if he outright asks them, my Plan will go nowhere. "Hey." I nudge him. "Don't get too hotheaded. Try to be calm and observe them for signs. Don't ask them anything, or they'll just deny it."

Finally, he cracks a small smile and playfully punches the side of my shoulder. "Thanks for listening, Meera. You're a good friend." Then he adds, his words tentative, "Will you be working tonight?"

I look around. "Uh, I might have to. We've had so many people rediscover their love for nonvegan food since the book club that we're launching a new menu tonight. I've been working on it for weeks."

He smacks his hand against the table, and I jump in place. "Perfect!" he exclaims. "I'll bring everyone here for our double date. You can gather intel on Lucy and Julien from the counter."

My eyes have probably never been wider. "Sushant, you're joking, right?" I put my trembling hands under the table so he won't notice. It's working. The Plan is working!

"Please, you have to do this. For me."

Inside, my mind is cheering knowing that Step 3, becoming Sushant's confidante, is officially a success—in fact, I'm more than his confidante now; I'm his partner in crime. But on the outside, all I do is exhale loudly, pretend to consider this, and then finally say, "All right. You owe me one, okay?"

Before Sushant can say anything, Danny walks over to us, his lips pursed. "Meera, I know you're the bosses' kid, but you're not on a break right now. We have, like, a billion customers waiting."

I bite my lip. "Sorry, Danny. Be right there."

Sushant actually hugs me—me!—before heading out. As I return to the counter to help Dad and Danny, I catch Appa's eye from the tarot corner. He raises his brow and mouths the words "What was that about?" He must have overheard parts of our conversation.

I give him a quick shrug and turn to the next customer, someone from the high school debate team, as my smile refuses to leave my face. "Hi, welcome to Café Kismat. What can I get you today?"

Lucy

"American detention is evil," Julien grumbles. He pauses, resting his mop along the wall, and wipes sweat off his forehead. "We did nothing wrong, and here we are, cleaning classrooms that are used by messy, disgusting American teenagers." His narrowed eyes go to the trash, where we disposed of five or six pieces of chewing gum already, and he gags.

I smile kindly at him. "You'll get used to it. But honestly? This is my first time getting detention in, well, forever."

Julien chuckles. "I wouldn't expect anything else from you, Lucy. I bet you'll get all the votes for Most Likely to Succeed."

Instead of replying, I continue focusing on the graffiti someone scrawled on the chairs and desks. If you asked me two days ago, I'd have said nobody could win Most Likely to Succeed except me. But now I probably won't be going to my dream college next year. I'm in detention instead of cheer practice. Brittney must be turning all the other cheerleaders against me. Meera's confusing words of kindness are making me think and feel things I vowed never to think and feel again.

And then there's the question of Mr. Rao's prediction. The Tower card has finally announced its presence in my life. I had my doubts earlier, despite knowing how psychic Mr. Rao is, and with the way life has been lately, I believe things are only going to go downhill from here.

"Do you believe in spirituality, Julien?" I stop scrubbing marker stains off a desk and turn to him for his response.

He mulls over my question silently as he dips the mop in the bucket of water, then speaks. "Well, I believe in a higher power. What that higher power is, I am unsure."

"And do you believe in tarot cards?"

"I do not know anything about tarot, no."

"Well, I do. And a few weeks ago"—I swallow hard, averting my gaze to the random words scribbled on the wood—"Mr. Rao pulled the Tower card for me."

I look up at the sound of the mop being set aside. Julien walks over to me, concern in his eyes. "What does that card mean?"

"Destruction. Ending. Unexpected change." I squeeze the sponge in my tense hand and add, "Mr. Rao's readings always come true. And now, with the way things are going for me, I have no doubt he's right this time too." I put the sponge away and clutch the edges of the desk, breathing heavily with my eyes shut.

"I am sorry life has been so hard for you lately." Julien pries my fingers from the desk and takes them in his palms. "Not everyone gets into every college they apply to, and nobody can be calm and quiet all the time when someone treats them badly."

"But I can," I insist, "and I have. At least, I thought so."

He frowns at me, scanning how my shoulders shake and my legs tremble. "Lucy," he asks, pulling out a chair for me, "is there something you wish to share with me? I do not think school stuff is all that is troubling you."

I settle into the chair, and he grabs one for himself, facing me. "Something's been on my mind for years now," I admit. I can't bring myself to look him in the eye, the one person in Madre Maria who might actually understand how I'm feeling, so I lower my gaze to the blue-inked heart someone's drawn onto the desk's wood. "But I don't know how to say the words."

He nods in my peripheral vision, then takes my hand again. "If you need a listening ear, I am here for you."

The words slip out before I can decide to end this conversation. "Julien, how did you know you're . . . pansexual?"

The corners of Julien's lips turn up, and he leans his head back against his crisscrossed arms like it's his favorite thing to talk about. Maybe it is. "I was fifteen," he replies, his smile widening. "There was a boy living next door to my family in Paris. We became fast friends, then lovers. It was the best four months of my life. He moved to Marseille that summer and we stayed in touch for a while, but I suppose it wasn't meant to be."

"But—but—" I'm searching for the right way to ask him this. "How did you go from friends to lovers? How did you realize you liked him that way?"

"Because I ached to touch him. All the time." His face contorts into a half smile and a half grimace, like the memory is painful in the best way. "One day, I couldn't hold it in any longer, and I kissed him. He returned the kiss. I was on top of the world." Julien looks up when a tear splashes onto my desk. "Lucy, are you asking yourself the question you asked me?"

It's hard to say it. So I let my sobs do the talking. Julien moves his chair closer to mine and envelops me in a tight hug, and I cry on his shoulder until the tears dry and my body stops shaking. I resurface and nod at him. "Julien, I—I think I'm pansexual too."

He smiles and wipes the only tear still in the corner of my

eye. "You're pansexual, Lucy. And you're wonderful and brave and beautiful."

I can't believe I ever disliked him. I hold my arms out for another hug, and he obliges. A few seconds later, I pull away and look at the time on my phone. "We should get back to cleaning. I don't want to stay here all night."

"Same," Julien agrees, his cheeks burning red. "We have our double date, and I have to look my best. For Natalie."

"Aw." I shove him with my elbow until he laughs. "Someone's blushing."

"Tais-toi," he mumbles as the flush deepens. I know enough French to understand that, so I shut up, and we finish cleaning the rest of the classroom in silence, wide grins on both our faces.

"Hey, Julien," I say after we put the cleaning supplies back, wash our hands, and head out to the parking lot. "Don't tell Sushant or Natalie or anyone else about our talk, okay?" I wring my hands, biting my lip. "Nobody knows except for you."

He smiles at me and bows his head. "I will take it to the grave, Lucy."

CHAPTER FIFTEEN

"Just For A Moment"

by Gryffin feat. Iselin

Lucy

Almost as soon as I get into Sushant's car and lean over to peck him on the lips, he pulls back, his lips widening into a forced smile. Under his seat, his leg jiggles, which only happens when he's anxious.

I frown. "What's wrong?"

"Uh." He scratches the base of his neck. "Change of plans. We're not going to Gianni's for dinner."

My forehead crinkles in confusion. Sushant drags me to Gianni's literally every time we go out to eat because he thinks they have the best pizza in the world. And he was talking Julien's ear off at lunch about their Chicago-style deep-dish pepperoni.

After a beat, Sushant carefully adds, "We're going to Café Kismat."

"Why?" I throw my head back against the car seat and groan loudly. "Sushant, caffeine already flows through my veins instead of blood. It's nighttime. I don't want more coffee."

"Yeah, but—"

"Besides, they have such a limited menu for meals. It's a grab-a-quick-bite kind of place, not a double-date-night kind of place."

"They . . . are . . . adding new things to the menu," he explains, his words slow and deliberate, "and Julien hasn't been to Café Kismat yet. I already told him, and he's excited to see it."

I don't say anything. Instead, I strap on my seat belt and gesture for Sushant to start the engine. My mind is racing as we pull out of the driveway; my thoughts are garbled and jumbled and make no sense, much like this situation. It's one thing for Meera to accidentally be everywhere I go; it's a whole other thing for my boyfriend to force me to be around her.

Julien hasn't been to Gianni's, either, but I suppose showing him Café Kismat is more important than making him try the pizza Sushant likes to have four times a week. However, I say none of this. I simply fold my arms and play a Spotify-recommended mix from my phone. The first song is by Gryffin, of course. God is out to get me. I roll my eyes, and I'm about to skip to the next song when Sushant stops me with a hand on my knee.

"Hey, nice song. Who is it by?"

"I thought music is just white noise to you," I quip, then add, "It's Gryffin and Iselin."

"Gryffin—that's Meera's favorite artist." He glances at me once before returning his gaze to the road. "And yours too, right? You have that 'MSG' playlist on our Spotify."

It's "MRG," but I don't want him to know whose initials those are, so I shrug. "He makes good music, but I'm not obsessed with him like I am with Taylor—"

"Are you excited about the double date?" he asks. His fingers tremble as their positions shift on the steering wheel. "It'll be nice to see Natalie and Julien."

"Yeah, it will be." Julien. The name automatically makes me smile. A month and a half ago, I found his personality exhausting, his words a waste of breath. And now, he's the one person I've trusted with my secret. *He's my confidant*, I realize. I've missed having one. The only other confidante I've ever had was Meera.

Sushant quirks an eyebrow at my smile but says nothing. We get to our destination and spend five minutes finding parking because Café Kismat seems to be packed. I sigh inwardly in relief. Maybe there won't be any tables available, and we can go to Gianni's instead.

Unfortunately, Julien's rental car is parked across from ours. When we walk into Café Kismat, the scents of jasmine essential oil, coffee, and incense aren't all that greet us; Natalie and Julien do too. They've found a table for four right opposite the counter, where Meera is brewing coffee, wearing her apron over a black tank top she bought when we went shopping together years ago. Her eyes are done up in black eyeliner today—"kajal" is what she always called it—and she's biting down on her lower lip as she pours coffee beans into the grinder.

I tear my eyes away from her mouth just as she glances up.

"Hi!" Natalie squeals, throwing her arms around me. She's wearing a red velvet wraparound dress and simple black flats. After we pull apart, she adds, "Our first double date!" She hasn't seriously dated anyone since we became best friends, and it makes me grin to see her this excited about someone.

While Sushant greets Natalie, Julien leans over and pecks me on both cheeks, very French of him. It doesn't bother me anymore. I return the gesture and notice he's wearing a gray button-down and black pants with a red tie. "Did you match Natalie's outfit on purpose?" I tease.

Julien beams at me. "You see right through me, Lucy."

Sushant gestures for us to sit down, and he splays his arm around my seat, his fingers curling over my shoulder almost protectively. "What do you ladies want? Julien and I can order."

There are two laminated one-page menus on the table already. Judging by the font and colors, it must have been made by Meera on Canva. I steal another glance at her over the top of Julien's head. The all-black look doesn't usually intrigue me, but on her—

"Lucy?" Sushant nudges my hand. "What do you want?"

I read out the first dish I see on the menu. "A sourdough chicken tikka sandwich sounds good."

"It does," he agrees, then casts a sideways look at Julien before adding, "Babe, do you want to split a rasmalai sundae for dessert?"

"Sure."

The boys head to the long queue at the counter to place our orders, and I grin at Natalie once they're out of earshot, making sure to lower my voice when I ask, "So? How's it going with him?"

Natalie squeals softly and cups her head with her hands. "We finally kissed. In his car. Oh my God, Lucy, he's so perfect for me."

I coax her hands away from her face and squeeze them tightly. "You deserve perfect."

"Look at this." She shows me some pictures on her phone. The first few showcase Julien dressed in the same button-down and black pants, a grin on his face as he drives. Even with just a phone camera, Natalie's captured the radiant glow of his dark skin and the texture of his curls.

I swipe to the next photo. This one of Natalie covering her face with one hand and reaching her other arm forward, presumably to stop Julien from taking the photo, is slightly blurry. Her soft blush and wide smile are visible underneath her fingers anyway. "This is so cute!" I gush.

She pouts. "Yeah, but he'll go back to Paris right after prom. And then that'll be it, unless he stays or I go."

I've only dated two boys, neither of whom lived anywhere but Madre Maria, and I can't imagine how hard it must be for Natalie when she's already so confused about what the future holds for her. This is just another part of her life she can't be sure of.

Before I can speak, her eyes widen. "God, remember Mr. Rao's tarot prediction? The Star? What if meeting Julien is how I discover my destiny? Maybe I'm meant to go to Paris too!"

My smile wavers, but I try not to show it. The Star is one

of the most favorable cards in the deck, according to Mr. Rao. And, well, I love Natalie and Julien together, but they've known each other less than two months. It would be silly of her to want to uproot her life and move to France just for the sake of their budding relationship. "Let's see what happens," I say, shrugging. "Like Mr. Rao said, you'll figure everything out soon enough."

Natalie nods and then turns back to study the counter, where Sushant and Julien are still third in line. "Look at all the people here," she mumbles. "You sure made the café a success, Lucy."

Meera walks over to take Danny's place at the cash register. Our eyes meet before she looks ahead at the next customer. "Well, I had some help," I say, cracking a grin.

Meera

By the time I get home from my dinner shift, about an hour after Sushant and the others finished their date, there are three messages on my phone from him. Squealing, I sit cross-legged on my bed and look at them.

Sushant (9:47 p.m.):

Just dropped Lucy home.
You still working??

Sushant (10:11 p.m.):

Call me. What did you think???

The last one is from mere minutes ago.

Sushant (10:24 p.m.):

Hellooooooo?????

I grin widely and let my finger hover over the call button for a moment before I press it. He picks up within seconds. "Hey!" His voice is eager and dripping with excitement. "So? What are your thoughts, Agent Rao-George?"

I grin, cross over to the window to peel my curtains back, and spot Sushant lounging in his bed against the wall, wearing Captain America boxers and a bright yellow T-shirt. His phone is resting beside him on the pillow, and he's tossing and catching a baseball in his hands. "For one, I didn't take you for a Captain America fan, Agent Khera," I say.

He shoots out of bed with a jerk and looks around until he spots me through his window. Eyes widening, he makes a face at me and closes his red curtains. I hear a rustle; then his voice comes through the phone, lighthearted and easy. "And I didn't take you for a stalker."

"I was simply enjoying the cool breeze and the view," I reply. "It's not my fault I have such a great view."

Silence.

I clap my hand over my mouth. *Shit.* Did I . . . did I just say the view of Sushant in his boxers is a great view? I mean, yeah, it is, but he's not supposed to know that. I can't be flirting with him yet—he's a taken man, and that's wrong.

"I meant the pink flowers in the tree next to my window," I hastily explain, running a finger along my curtains. "I didn't mean anything else."

"But what did you think?" he says, seemingly unconcerned about my slipup. "About Julien and Lucy? Did you notice anything off about them?"

I let my hand fall back to my side and purse my lips. There were a few things I did notice. Lucy was chatty for a change. Completely at ease, her face lit up, and not just because of her flawless makeup. Multiple moments when she and Julien burst out laughing in tandem surface in my mind. Not to mention the many times she looked my way and almost smiled. *Almost.*

She hasn't done that in months.

The annoyance I spotted in her gaze toward Julien weeks ago? It's not there anymore. The weird energy between them from the museum is gone too. The only thing in its place is . . . friendship.

"Meera?" Sushant prods. His voice is small, like he knows I'm mulling over the situation at hand.

"Yeah, um . . ." My mind urges me to say the words that will propel Step 4 into action. *They seemed very comfortable and happy. Didn't you think they were laughing too much? Isn't it weird how they seem so fond of each other already?*

All true but inconclusive, because this can be said about

friends too. That's how Lucy and I were before she betrayed me. And we were just friends. Obviously.

Regardless, I should let Sushant make his own conclusions. Let him think Julien and Lucy are in love. Let him think she's a cheater. Let him loathe her the way I did—no, the way I *do*.

"They seem like they've gotten very close," I start. I need to follow it up with something more leading, something that'll cement doubt in his brain, no questions asked. But at the last moment, I fumble and say, "As friends."

Sushant is quiet for a second before he exhales. Loudly. "You know, I thought the same." The relief is evident in his voice. "I didn't feel a romantic vibe between them. Maybe Lucy's just warmed up to him now that he's dating Natalie?"

My stomach flips. How can I be *this* bad at being a Mean Girl? "Yeah. I'm sure that's all there is," I assure him, biting on the side of my thumbnail. *Shit. I screwed up again.*

"Good night, Meera. And . . . thank you."

"Of course, Sushant. Sleep tight."

He hangs up. I head to the shower, strip off my clothes, and decide to try to drown myself in the hot water raining down upon me. Fuming, I grit my teeth and punch the tiled wall with my fist. Step 4 was in my reach. It was so close, I could touch it; I could feel it. And I failed. Again.

Why, though? Why couldn't I just say, *Yeah, they're definitely hooking up behind your back*? Lucy stole Sushant when she knew I loved him, and then she dumped *me.* She's certainly capable of destroying relationships and breaking people's hearts.

But . . . maybe I'm not.

And I hate myself for it.

CHAPTER SIXTEEN

"Iktara"

by Amit Trivedi, Kavita Seth, and Amitabh Bhattacharya

Lucy

When I asked Meera to lead the second book club session, I did it because the desi young adult romance I picked out deserves to be shared with the club members with the support of an Indian voice. And given our not-so-diverse small-town community, that meant either Sushant, who hasn't read a book for fun in his life . . . or Meera.

Honestly, as I now claim my spot beside her in the circle at Café Kismat, holding a copy of the book, I half expect her to back out, hand me the reins, and resign herself to chiming in whenever I say something she agrees with.

But once everyone is seated, Meera starts talking right away about the author, the book, and the themes of belonging, acceptance, and culture that are so prevalent throughout the story. "I thought our school is pretty welcoming for people of color," Meera says, frowning, "but it was only after reading this book that I became aware of all the microaggressions I've faced from teachers and peers over the years."

Sushant, the only other Indian in the club, raises his hand, and Meera gestures for him to speak up. "Full disclosure: I skimmed through the book," he says, eliciting laughs from others, "and I've gotta say, I loved what I read. And I still don't believe in astrology or destiny." He shoots Mr. Rao an apologetic look, then slumps in his seat. "But it made me think about how I've pushed away so much of my culture simply because it didn't feel 'cool' to me."

I open my mouth to thank him for his perspective, but Meera gets there first. "Exactly!" She's on the edge of her seat, fingers clasped together, her teeth tugging on her bottom lip. "Thanks for sharing, Sushant. What did everyone else think?"

Some people raise their hands, and Meera gives them a chance to discuss turn by turn. Others make some valid points, and by the end of the hour, everyone manages to get a word in. People get up, thanking Meera and me for sparking such an interesting conversation, and a couple Muslim students—sophomores, I think—come over to us to suggest a Muslim thriller for next time.

"Absolutely." Meera smiles at the two girls. "We'll announce the next book soon."

"Thanks once again," they say, before heading to the counter for more coffee.

Meera turns and nearly bumps into me. She shuffles behind, hands in her pockets, and mumbles a soft apology. Her face is still flushed from the excitement of the past hour. "Sorry. It was a good session, don't you think?"

I nod. "You did a great job, Meera."

She smirks, taking a tentative step forward, and folds her arms across her chest. Then she cocks an eyebrow. "Bet I surprised you."

My face flushes. She did surprise me, but I'm not ready to admit that to her and bridge the distance I've so carefully built between us over the last year and a half.

An opportunity to get away from Meera presents itself when Mr. Rao calls out my name from his tarot corner. "Lucy, putta, get in here. Let me do a reading for you!"

But I grimace. Our usual weekly readings have halted since Mr. Rao pulled the Tower card for me. Natalie still gets her fortune told, but I'm wary. Who knows what other darkness lies before me? Living in denial seems safer than facing the inevitable truth.

"I'll join you," Meera says enthusiastically. She takes my hand in hers—a jolt shoots up my elbow—and starts leading me to Mr. Rao. Midway through, I spot movement across the street from behind the café's glass windows, and I halt in my steps.

A man has just gotten out of his Range Rover and is walking toward the café. Toward me. It's been years since I last saw him, but I would recognize that gray hoodie and the cowlick on his sparse head of hair any day.

Meera's gaze follows, and she blinks twice. "Isn't that your—"

"Run," I say.

"Wait, what? Lucy—" Meera nearly screams as I yank her hand and drag her into the supply closet beside the kitchen. Seconds later, a man's heavy footsteps thud inside the café.

I close the door behind us, lean against a large, hopefully clean broom, and take in gasps of stuffy air in the cramped space. "Fuck," I whisper. "Fuck, fuck, fuck, fuck."

Even in the darkness, Meera's brown eyes are visibly wide. "Lucy Hughson, did you just say the f-word your mother taught you never to say?"

If I weren't having trouble breathing, I would have laughed. "Mom's not here, and besides"—I inhale, trying to get oxygen into my lungs—"I think this situation warrants a string of expletives."

There is hardly any room in the supply closet—empty buckets, mops, brooms, and rags litter the shelves—but Meera closes the gap between us anyway, concern etched in her sharp features. "Hey," she says, ducking her head. "Are you okay?"

Ten seconds ago, the answer was *I'm not sure.* But now that the sparse air around me smells like coconut and jasmine, not to mention Meera's sweet breath, I think I might actually collapse. All I want to do is stay here with her, feel the overwhelming familiarity her presence always brings, but I can't do that. I could never do that. Not just for Sushant's sake, but for mine too. So instead, I shake my head.

Thankfully, Meera backs up to the wall behind her. She looks around, then lifts a hand to open the door. "We should get out of here," she says. "I think you're having a panic attack. Lucy? Lucy, say something."

I'm down on my knees now, my breaths erratic, my palms over my eyes. It's like someone's lodged something in my windpipe, making it impossible for any air to escape or enter. My eyes sting with tears. He's back in town after all these years. To see me? Isn't it clear I want nothing to do with him? Does Mom know? Does he know I got wait-listed at NYU? Did Mom tell him? Have they talked since the night of Seth's party?

Something plasticky clatters to the floor, and I feel Meera pushing it away and crouching down beside me. "Lucy." She doesn't peel my hands from my face. She just puts both her hands on my shoulders and squeezes. "Hey. Just try to breathe, okay? Can I count with you?"

Slowly, I nod.

"Inhale . . . two . . . three . . . four. Exhale . . . two . . . three . . . four." Meera guides me through a series of deep breaths, her fingers drawing soft circles on my skin. Her scent is all over me now in this tiny room, tantalizing and heady, but I breathe it all in. I soak in her touch, my eyes shut, my chest rising and falling, and focus on her words and the numbers she's counting.

A minute later, when my senses can register nothing but oxygen and coconut and Meera's skin on mine, my eyes fly open, and I pull my hands away from my face. Standing up, I exhale loudly. "We shouldn't be in the closet together," I say. The irony hits me. There's no "together" when it comes to Meera and me. Least of all in the closet.

"Yeah, you need fresh air." Meera pries the door open, and we step out into the bright lighting of the café. Her scent dissipates, and I take in a huge gulp of caffeinated air.

The man in the gray hoodie catches my eye from the table he's seated at. He stiffens, perhaps trying to reconcile my face with the face of the daughter he deserted eight years ago. Then he stands up and rushes to me, his arms outstretched. When I don't move, his hands drop, and he clears his throat. "Lucy. It's—it's good to see you."

I wipe my shaky palms on my dress and hold my chin up. "Hi, Dad."

Meera

I stand back as Lucy and her father greet each other awkwardly. A barrage of questions hurtles through my mind. She hasn't seen him in, what, eight years—since her parents got divorced? Why is he back now? Have they been in touch at all since she and I stopped being friends? We grew close shortly after her dad left, when Appa and Dad quit their jobs to open Café Kismat, and she never talked about him much . . .

Wait, why do I even care? Lucy's not my best friend anymore. I don't need to be worried on her behalf.

So I push my unwarranted concern down and smile politely when Mr. Hughson turns to me. "And who is this? One of your friends, Lucy?"

"This is Meera," Lucy says, grabbing my hand with a jerk. "We were just about to head out for, um, Froyo. Weren't we?" She turns to me with an eyebrow raised, and I nod hastily.

Her hand is cold but so . . . soft, sending a flurry of memories through me of Bollywood dance parties and running through sprinklers in the hot summers of our friendship. I blink them away. What magic lotion does she use?

Mr. Hughson hangs his head. "I'm sorry if I caught you at a bad time, but I was really hoping we could talk. You weren't picking up your phone, so I thought I'd show up in person."

Her eyes narrow. "Does Mom know?"

Mr. Hughson nods. "I went by the house earlier, but she wouldn't tell me where you'd be. I looked all over for you, and finally, some kid from your school said I could find you here."

Lucy blinks back tears at that. I open my mouth, wondering if I should make up an excuse and get the hell out of here, but then Mr. Hughson speaks. "Hey, why don't I take you both to the Froyo place?"

The last thing I want to do is spend time with my sworn enemy and her estranged dad, but knowing Lucy's complete inability to fight back in the face of confrontation, I reluctantly accept that I'm going to have to play along without any choice in the matter.

Sure enough, ten minutes later, Mr. Hughson drops us in front of the vegan Froyo store and leaves to find parking. Lucy and I head inside toward the counter. I refuse to look at her; my arms are crossed over my chest, and I'm focusing on the different flavors and topping combinations I might like. That being said, this is vegan Froyo. It's probably going to taste like shit.

"I'm sorry," Lucy mumbles next to me as the door behind us opens with a swing. "I didn't know what to tell him. You can leave if you want to."

"What are we having, kids?" Mr. Hughson puts one hand on each of our shoulders and peers curiously at the flavors on display. "Lucy, you love strawberry, right?"

She bites her lip, her shoulders slumping. "Um, yeah, when I was nine."

Mr. Hughson's face falls. "I just thought . . . Well, whatever you want now, it's on me, all right? You too, Meera." He pats me on the back and pulls out his wallet.

Lucy looks like she's on the verge of tears, her body so sunken and small that even my inner Mean Girl can't make me walk out of here. So I put on a weak smile and turn to the employee at the counter. "I'll have the Tahitian vanilla with rainbow sprinkles and some marshmallows, please."

Lucy takes a deep breath, juts her chin out, and follows my lead. Mr. Hughson gets a strawberry oat-milk milkshake for himself, and once we have our orders, we get a table by the window, and I pretend like it's totally natural for me to be sitting here with Lucy and her father.

"So, Lucy, you look so pretty, all grown up," Mr. Hughson says, pushing his shake aside. I can't figure out if he got something strawberry to appease nine-year-old Lucy or if he just likes that horrible pink color.

Lucy stares at him from above her cup of matcha Froyo and licks a chocolate chip off her spoon. Her face is blank, nonchalant, but the trembling of her shoulders tells me she's terrified.

"Yeah," I chime in, turning to Mr. Hughson, "most people grow up a lot in eight years. Lucy just had the advantage of growing up pretty." As soon as I say that, my face burns red.

Mr. Hughson laughs, but Lucy's gaze flies to me, and she sucks in a breath. I return to my yogurt, shoveling the frozen dessert into my mouth. I'll take brain freeze over saying the wrong thing any day.

"How's everything at school?" he goes on, seemingly unaware of how confusing this all must be to Lucy. "How are your grades? Do you play any sports? Catch me up on everything."

She nods meekly, staring at her half-empty cup. "I have straight A's. I'm the cheer captain. I did track last year." There's a smidgen of green Froyo on her lip. I'm about to tell her when her tongue darts out to lick at it. I look away just as she catches my eye.

"That's fantastic, Lucy." Mr. Hughson is all smiles. "And is there anyone special in your life?"

We sit in silence for a few seconds. Lucy is still staring at me, her mouth moving without any words coming out. Just as I start to answer his question for her, she turns to him. "Why are you here, Dad?"

"Oh, well . . ." Mr. Hughson shifts in his seat, and the leather cushion makes a fart-like noise. If this were any other moment, if I were with absolutely anybody else, I would have laughed.

"Well?" Lucy says, voice elevated.

"You haven't answered my calls, and your mother's too angry to have even a polite phone conversation," he finally says, slapping a hand to his face.

"And she has every right to be angry," Lucy points out, her fists clenching. "You dumped her after twenty years together. You were all she had. All *we* had."

Mr. Hughson's voice trembles. "I'm sorry. I know I was wrong to give up custody of you, but I miss you, Lucy. I've been trying to make amends for so many years."

"You mean the past couple of years," Lucy says. "Where were you before that?"

I shrink in my seat. Shit, I shouldn't be here. I should *not* be here. *Fuck.*

"I moved to LA for work. I kept asking your mother if I could see you, but she told me to stay away." Mr. Hughson looks close to tears. "She didn't want you to see me after how everything turned out between us."

Lucy is slack-jawed for a second before she speaks. "How what turned out, Dad? I was nine when you left, and Mom never talks about you or what happened, except that you fell in love with someone who wasn't your doting wife and the mother of your child. And she gets to be furious, honestly. A good man would never do what you did, and you know it."

Oh shit, this is going into emotional-family-secrets territory. I need to get out of here. As I'm about to get up, Lucy puts an ice-cold hand on my wrist and shakes her head. I sigh and sit down again.

Mr. Hughson breathes out sharply. "I admit, I was . . . emotionally unfaithful to your mother. It was a mistake I never intended to make—"

"But you did." Lucy's words are quiet, her gaze solemn. "Dad, I don't want to talk to you without Mom knowing. It's unfair to her. Why don't you give her a call, and we'll set a time to talk? All three of us? You can say your part, and then you can leave."

"But I don't want to leave so soon—" he starts to protest, then bows his head. "All right. I'll call her again and tell her we met. Can I at least drop you off at home?"

Lucy stands up and dumps her half-eaten Froyo in the trash. *There's that inner cheerleader bitch.* "I'll walk."

She's almost out the door when I realize I should get up too. "Nice meeting you, Mr. Hughson," I say, and rush out, following her. I yell her name until she stops at the next intersection. When she turns, her tear-stricken face is red. "Lucy, I'm so sorry—"

The force with which she hugs me nearly sends me stumbling back, but I regain my footing just in time. I wrap one arm around her and pat the top of her head, not saying a word. I have no idea how to offer words of comfort to her, not just because we haven't been friends in a long time, but because I don't want to say the wrong thing and hurt her more. This doesn't seem like the time for positivity or advice; I should just let her cry.

She resurfaces a minute later and wipes her eyes with the back of her hand. "Thank you for that. Seriously."

I shrug, hands now in my pockets. "I hope you'll be okay soon."

"Me too," she mumbles. "Can you . . . walk me home?"

I hesitate, but I know she needs someone right now. Even if it has to be me, of all people. "So . . . did you know he's back in town?" I ask as she leads the way.

Lucy lowers her gaze to the cracks in the sidewalk. "I didn't. He's called a few times over the years. I never picked up. Why should I?"

I nod, falling into step beside her. "He's been a bad father. He doesn't get to see you thrive anymore."

She lets out a sarcastic laugh. "I'm not thriving. Far from it."

Oh. I blink. Is this about NYU or something else? I heard she'd gotten wait-listed. Maybe my Plan is working better than expected. Somehow the thought makes my head ache. My inner Mean Girl needs to get a hold of herself.

"Do you think your mom will—"

"Can we talk about something else?" she asks, exhaling. "Like, um, do you have any birthday plans?"

My head jerks back. I turn eighteen next week, right before spring break. I don't want to think about why she still remembers her ex-bestie-turned-enemy's birthday, so I answer honestly. "I haven't thought about it. With how busy Café Kismat has been lately, I might just end up working all day."

What she says next surprises me, especially when she chuckles as she says it. "Remember when you wanted to throw a big party the year your birthday was the same weekend as Holi, but your parents said no?"

I do remember. Holi, the Indian festival of colors, usually happens between March and April, depending on the Hindu lunar calendar. This year, the festival already happened three weeks ago, but now that more people know my name, maybe a late Holi birthday party wouldn't be the worst idea to solidify the success of the Plan. I'm so close to winning, I can feel it, even though my last few attempts have backfired.

"Should I ask my parents if I can do that this year?" I muse aloud as we reach her house. "I'm older now, and they wouldn't even have to be around to supervise."

She smiles at me—a real Lucy Hughson smile, one that warms me down to the tips of my toes. "You should. It would make a great party. Your friends would love it."

As she unlocks her front door and waves goodbye, I hesitate, my hand halfway up to wave back. "Lucy, wait." I bite my lip and say the words I never thought I'd say again, unsure why I'm even saying them: "If the party happens, I'd really like it if you came too."

Her expression shifts from joy to confusion to something almost bittersweet in the matter of a split second, and she slowly nods. "I'll try to make it. See you. And . . . thanks again." She shuts the door, and I continue on my way home, my head swaying with the weirdness of today and what it might mean for the Plan. What it might mean for *me*.

CHAPTER SEVENTEEN

"Serenade"
by BANNERS

Lucy

It's rare that our four-seater dining table is ever completely occupied, but that's not even the most surprising thing about tonight. It's that Mom is being nice. To Dad, of all people. She passes the bowl of rice to him with a smile, and he accepts gratefully.

"Alice, this chicken korma is delicious," Sushant says, taking yet another bite of the very mediocre Indian dish my mom prepared specially for him. "It's just like what I have back home."

She beams at him, and I squeeze Sushant's free hand under the table. Mom always puts on a good front for my boyfriend, and that applies even when her archnemesis, aka her ex-husband, is sitting beside her. It was a good idea inviting Sushant to this dinner. He's obviously lying about the authenticity of the chicken korma to keep the peace. He must really love me. I've had his Dadima's chicken korma, and for one, it didn't have raw onions, raisins, or peanuts. God knows where Mom got this recipe.

After dinner, we put our dishes in the sink and sit down again with some ice cream. Mom clears her throat, a fake smile plastered on her face. "So, Ken, to what do we owe the pleasure? What brought you here?"

Finally. I close my eyes briefly, then open them. The moment of truth. Beside me, Sushant nudges his leg closer to mine, his way of saying, *I've got you, babe.*

Dad sets his spoon down and looks my way. "Lucy will be off to college soon. It's a new chapter, and a big one at that. Let's just say, I don't want to miss it. Your mother said you're still waiting to hear from NYU?"

So he knows. They've talked in detail since that phone call when she swore at him. I lower my gaze to my melting ice cream. There hasn't been an update on the status of my wait-listed application. I'll probably only know next month, when final acceptance letters are sent out.

"She's also applied to schools around here, so NYU isn't set in stone," Mom says, lifting the spoon of chocolate ice cream to her lips. "New York is so far away from California."

Dad reaches across the table to take my hand in his sweaty palm while he's still talking to Mom. "I told you this earlier, Alice, that I want to help pay for Lucy's tuition. It's the right thing to do. Will you let me?"

Mom looks from me to Sushant, her lips pressed into a thin line. She doesn't want to say no in front of him, though that's her final answer. But it isn't her decision. It's mine. If Dad was okay deserting us—me—for eight years and he wants to win me back by paying for my life in New York, then let him. It's the least he can do.

So I answer on Mom's behalf. "Yes, Dad, you can help. But"—I exhale—"that doesn't mean I forgive you for what you did to Mom and me. That doesn't mean you get to come back into my life now or ever. You can't fix everything with money. Certainly not leaving us for another woman."

Dad's face darkens, and he whips his head to stare at Mom. "You didn't tell her?"

"Tell me what?" I ask, my eyebrows knitting together.

"Lucy said nothing wrong," Mom answers, still smiling tightly. She pushes her chair back and stands. "Well, Sushant's parents must be wondering where he is. It's almost ten!"

"Don't worry, Alice," Sushant starts, just as I open my mouth to protest. "My curfew isn't until midnight—"

"I didn't leave your mother for another woman." Dad's voice is quiet but solid. A tear shines in the corner of his eye. "I fell in love with someone while I was still married, and I will always regret hurting Alice, but I will not tolerate disrespect for my partner."

Sushant and I exchange confused glances. "Partner"? Is Dad—

He takes out his wallet and shows me the two pictures inside it. One is my childhood yearbook photo from a year before Dad left. The other is a picture of Dad and someone else, their cheeks pressed together. They're both dressed in tuxes. "This is Jade," he says, pointing to the other person, "my nonbinary partner. We got together shortly after your mother and I filed for divorce. They are not a woman, and they are the love of my life."

I blink as I process this. Dad is queer. That's what Mom has shielded me from all these years. She always said he met someone else but never gave any details about who they were. I guess she didn't want me to know the full truth. Blood rushes into my ears, and my mouth opens and closes wordlessly. "Oh," I mumble finally. "Dad, that's . . ."

He lowers his gaze and gulps, as though he's afraid of what I might say.

"That's great," I finish, my lips twitching into a small smile. His betrayal still stings, but somehow it doesn't feel as heavy. Dad is queer. Just . . . just like me. "I hope you're both happy."

Dad cracks a grin and wipes a tear that's fallen midway down his cheek, chuckling softly, like he can't believe I'm being supportive. "We are."

"We should call it a night." Mom's mouth is set in a thin line. She grabs my bowl of melting ice cream and heads to the kitchen, huffing loudly.

A few minutes later, Sushant kisses me in our usual fashion at the front door, his eyes worried. "You okay?" he asks, pressing a warm hand to my cheek.

I settle my face into his grip and shrug. "I don't know. I have so many more questions than answers."

His fingers move to my shoulder, giving it a comforting squeeze. "Do you wanna talk about it?"

My body stiffens. How do I tell him the full extent of what I feel about Dad's revelation and how much I relate to it? How do I bare my thoughts without revealing everything I've hidden from him for months?

Maybe he gets the message, because his grip loosens. "I'll be fine," I reply quickly, shifting my gaze to my feet. "I'll see you tomorrow?"

"Yeah. Sure." Sushant gets into his car and then pulls out of the driveway. "I love you!" he yells as he turns into the street, and I wave, somehow unable to repeat those words to him.

After he disappears from my line of sight, I don't go back inside. I sit down on the steps of the front porch, resting my elbows on my knees, thinking back to my parents' divorce. All these years, I'd made assumptions about my father. Mom never answered my questions about Dad except to say he'd left us for someone else. I had my fair share of guesses—maybe a work colleague or a drunken one-night stand he'd ended up falling for. But every time I imagined Dad with his new partner, I pictured a woman. There was never any room for speculation. Why? Why did his being with another woman have to be the obvious assumption?

"Hey." Dad taps the top of my head and sits down beside me. "You doing okay?"

I nod. "Yeah. I just . . . I'm sorry, Dad. I shouldn't have assumed anything about who you're with."

Dad whooshes out a breath. "I wish your mother had told

you, but maybe she didn't know how to talk about it. Most people don't. Not even my parents."

I stare up at him and lower my voice. The front door is ajar. "How long have you known you're . . . queer?"

"Since I was about your age, when I fell for a boy the summer after high school graduation. That's why your grandparents cut off all ties with me. I . . ." He sighs. "Soon after, I met your mother at the local church near my college, and we got married a few months later. I wanted to be happy with her—and I really did love her—but I know now that I rushed into it to hide that part of me from the world. When you grow up in the church like I did, you get used to living in denial about anything that isn't the norm."

"Did she know the truth when you got married?"

He shakes his head. "I couldn't tell her until our marriage was crumbling and I fell for Jade. Then I came clean and asked for a divorce."

I shift in place, wondering if I even want to know the answer to my next question. "Why didn't you ever want custody of me, Dad?"

"Your mother insisted on full custody. She said I owed her that much, at the very least, especially because everyone in church was talking about us behind our backs." He shuts his eyes and grimaces. "She was also scared I'd . . . influence you to go down the wrong path."

My throat fills with sobs. *The wrong path.* I knew it. Mom will never be okay with my sexuality. Nor will she understand it. "I'm sorry," I choke out.

"Don't be." Dad shrugs, his shoulder jostling mine. "It is what it is."

I cross my fingers. "Has Mom spoken to them? Jade?"

"No, and I don't think I want to make that introduction." He laughs, then puts a tentative hand on my upper back. "But I'd love for you to meet them. They know all about you."

I shoot him a funny look. "Dad, we haven't spoken in years. *You* don't even know all about me. How could they know?"

"Well, then"—Dad stands up and offers his hand to me, and I take it—"I promise I'll try to change that, starting now. If you'll let me."

"I'll think about it," I say, biting the inside of my cheek.

Dad hesitates, then says, "Sushant seems like a nice kid. Where is he going to college?"

"Syracuse." I force myself to smile. "So here's hoping I get into NYU."

"Listen, kiddo." Dad smiles. "If there's anything else I can do to help—"

Dishes clatter from inside the kitchen. It's Mom's way of reminding us that this dinner is over. "I'll see you soon, Lucy." Dad steps forward for a hug, but then sticks his hand out instead. We shake hands. A laugh bubbles out of me, and then he's gone.

I wish Mom good night—she answers stiffly, her focus still on the dishes—and go upstairs to my room. Then I text Julien. He's the only one I can talk to about this. So I had dinner with my dad today. After like 8 years.

I change into my pajamas, crawl under the sheets, and wait for his reply. It comes minutes later. Oh waouh! How did it go?

Lucy:

Turns out, Dad is queer and has a nonbinary partner. Mom never told me, so I'm guessing she doesn't "approve"

Julien:

Oh . . . are you ok?

Tears spring into the corners of my vision as I text him back. I bet she'd hate me if she ever found out I'm . . .

I stop just short of typing out that word, "pansexual," and hit send.

Julien:

You don't have to tell her until you're ready Lucy 😊

Lucy:

What if I'm never ready?

Julien:

That is ok too. I am here for you

I know, I type back, smiling through the salt water trickling down my face. Good night. Thanks for listening

Julien:

I put my phone aside and lie back in bed, thinking. I've come to terms with my sexuality, but as much as I respect Dad and Julien for owning their truths, I doubt I could ever truly do it. It would change how people see me. How Mom sees me. It might even affect my relationship with Sushant, make our New York plans go awry.

No. Coming out is not an option. Not right now, and maybe not ever.

Meera

I look around my backyard, arms folded, appraising the space. Next to me, Sushant stands tall, with his calloused fingers stroking his chin. "I think this should work," he says. "It'll be a little cramped, but you definitely can't do a Holi party indoors."

"Yeah." I walk over to the fence that separates our backyards. "We could put a table here with the supplies. Colored powder, water balloons, hoses. And on that end"—I point to the other side—"we could keep the drinks and maybe some snacks?"

It still blows my mind that Sushant offered, unprompted, to help me plan my Holi birthday party when I told him about it earlier this week. Appa and Dad were surprisingly cool about it, with the caveat that it has to be a daytime event with no alcohol, of course. I doubt people from school will stop by if there's no alcohol involved, but I've invited everyone I know on a first-name basis anyway. Worst-case scenario, it's just me, Ron, Valeria, and Sushant drinking thandai, the special Holi cold drink made of milk, sugar, rose, spices, and nuts. Which is still better than not having a birthday party at all.

"Sounds good," Sushant agrees. He has a weird grin on his face as he asks, "And what will the drinks be?"

Groaning, I explain the no-alcohol rule to him, then add, "Dad looked up a recipe for dairy-free thandai since half this town is vegan."

"Thandai, huh?" He leans closer to me and whispers conspiratorially, "Care to crank it up a notch?"

My eyebrows rise a fraction. "Um, how so?"

He takes out his phone and shows me a photo of what looks like . . . pot? I can't be too sure. Recreational marijuana has never been my thing. What does pot have to do with my party, though?

And then it clicks. I stare at him, my lips widening in a smile. "You don't mean—"

"Bhaang, baby!" Sushant yells, then whips his head to my back door, his eyes wide. "Hope your folks didn't hear that."

I sit on one of the two chairs in the backyard, still grinning. "Don't worry, they aren't home. But Appa will kill me if he finds out. We're underage."

Bhaang is basically the marijuana version of thandai. You add the paste of cannabis seeds and leaves to the drink, and *bam*! Your Holi party becomes ten times more fun. I've grown up watching Indians drink bhaang in Bollywood Holi scenes, but pulling it off with potentially so many people in attendance is going to be difficult. And . . . possibly illegal?

Sushant sits down on the chair beside me and nudges my toe with his foot. "Then it'll have to be a secret."

I expect myself to break out into goose bumps like I usually do as I return the gesture. The boy I like is being playful with me. Dare I say flirty? No, he has a girlfriend. He wouldn't intentionally flirt with me, not just yet. But I'm his confidante, his co-conspirator. And *he's touching me.*

But I only sense his touch on my skin. My heart doesn't race. My skin doesn't heat up. And I feel nothing more than excitement for the party and the bhaang plan.

Weird.

"So, how are things with Lucy?" I ask, though I don't know if he'll open up. Last time I tried prying, he told me it was personal. But that was long before we became confidants.

"Uh, good," Sushant answers. He fiddles with his fingers, his face darkening. "I'm not worried about Julien anymore, but things have been hard since Lucy got wait-listed."

I try to pry a little more. "Are you scared you won't go to college together?"

"Honestly? A little. But I love that girl, and she loves me." He smiles hesitantly. "I'm hoping our love will be enough to get through anything, even long-distance."

I lick my suddenly dry lips. I've hit all stages of the Plan except the last one: Break them up. And with the way he's talking about their relationship, it'll take something drastic to make that happen. *Fuck.*

We talk about our favorite Bollywood Holi scenes until my phone chimes. It's my group chat with Ron and Valeria. I ignore the notification, then unlock my phone again, deciding I might as well read it. Apart from hanging out with them in school, I haven't really spent much time with them. The Plan has kept me busier than I'd thought.

Ron:

Meera I don't care what you're doing. Get your ass to your front door

Valeria:

SPONTANEOUS MOVIE MARATHON!!! You pick 😊😊😊

Sighing, I stand up. They're trying to stick around, even though I've been an avoidant friend occupied with her own thing. I should be grateful, not just guilty. "Well, my friends are here."

"You seem upset about that." Sushant quirks a brow. "Why?"

I wave away his concerns. "Nah, I'm just tired. See you in school?"

"Cool."

I lead the way back inside, since our fences are too high for Sushant to go back that way. As he fist-bumps me goodbye on the porch, Ron and Valeria walk up to us. "Hey," Ron says warily, while Valeria blinks in surprise.

Sushant leaves, whistling the tune to a Bollywood song. Once he's out of sight, Ron scratches the side of his nose and says, "Uh, I didn't realize he's started hanging out with you at your place."

I push open the front door and nudge my head back inside, but they stay rooted in place. So I put my hands in my pockets and shrug. "He was just helping me organize the Holi party."

"Huh," Valeria snorts, her arms folded. "The party you told us you don't need help organizing?"

Shit, she's right. That's what I told them in school earlier this week. "I'm just making sure the Plan is still on track," I explain hastily. "There's not much time to go before we graduate."

"Cool." Ron looks down at his feet. "Are we still on for the movie marathon, or . . . ?"

"Of course," I say. My eyes go to Valeria, who looks close to tears. With a jolt, I realize I don't know anything about what they've been up to lately. How they're feeling. How they're doing. "How about Val gets to pick?"

A small smile graces her lips. "All right. Get ready to watch that shirtless Shah Rukh Khan movie for the hundredth time." She walks past me inside the house. Ron follows, grumbling about the movie selection, but his shoulders have loosened.

They put on Netflix while I microwave some buttered

popcorn. As I wait, my phone lights up with a text. It's from Sushant. Told my boys on the football team about the bhaang and they're IN! PARTY TIME YEAHHHHH

"The movie's starting!" Valeria yells from the living room.

I slide my phone into my back pocket and carry the two bowls of popcorn to the couch. My fingers itch to reply to Sushant, but I know my only priority right now should be my friends. Things feel iffy between us, but hopefully the Holi party—and the bhaang—cools us all off. Three more days. I can't wait.

CHAPTER EIGHTEEN

"Good Things Fall Apart"
by ILLENIUM and Jon Bellion

Meera

The next day on the bus, I'm swiping through Instagram Stories while Sushant catches up on the replay of a college football game he missed. I get to Sushant's latest Story, and my eyebrows rise. It's a photo of him and Lucy posing in front of his car—she looks breathtakingly beautiful, as always—and the text reads **Who knew Mr. Hughson was so good with a camera?**

I poke him in the shoulder with my finger, and he grunts "Hmm?" and takes one AirPod out, still focused on his phone.

"You met Lucy's dad?" I ask.

At that, he pauses the video and turns his attention wholly to me, grinning. "Yeah, twice so far. He's in town for a few more days before he goes back to LA. He's pretty cool."

"Oh." My stomach tightens. I know Sushant is Lucy's boyfriend and everything, but after her dad dropped by without notice and she brought me with them to the Froyo shop, I thought it would be an experience Lucy would only share with me. She trusted me that day, more than she has in over a year, and I thought it meant something. To both of us.

But who am I kidding? Of course Sushant has met her father too. She and I aren't best friends anymore. We're not *anything* anymore. She doesn't owe me a thing. For all I know, Natalie's met Lucy's dad too, and she's been introduced to him as Lucy's best friend.

And that's fine. I won't let it bother me. I mean, it doesn't bother me. Why would it? We're nearing school, so I unlock my phone to put it on silent and see a new IG notification:

@lucy_hughson started following you.

Oh my God.

I don't have a chance to think about it because the bus has stopped and people are getting off. Sushant makes a beeline for Lucy's parked car, where she waits for him every day. She gives me a small smile and a wave before jumping into Sushant's arms.

I duck into the building before my subconscious does something stupid like smile back.

Ron and Valeria greet me at our adjoining lockers, and I mumble back a hello. I lean against my locker and stare at the "Follow back" button on Lucy's Instagram profile. What's gotten into me? Why am I even considering this? The only reason I let myself get this close to Lucy was so that the Plan would work. Not because I want to be her friend again. God, no. She doesn't deserve another chance after what she did to me.

"Uh, Meera?"

I blink out of my thoughts and return to my friends. I must have missed something they said, because they both frown at me in silence, save for the sound of Valeria munching on potato chips.

"Sorry, I didn't get that," I say. "What are we talking about?"

Ron shuffles his feet, not meeting my gaze. "What were you looking at on your phone?"

I turn the screen toward them and lower my voice to a whisper. "Lucy followed me on Instagram. Should I follow her back?"

Valeria crumples the empty packet of chips in her fist and exhales, not bothering to keep her voice down even though the hallway is crowded. "Do you realize that all we talk about whenever we hang out is Lucy? Or your stupid Plan?"

I shush her, but she only shakes her head. "And do you have any idea what we've been up to this past month while you've been working on that Plan of yours?"

"No, but—"

"After a point, we started to wonder if you even care." Ron blows a strand of his shaggy hair out of his eyes and folds his arms across his scrawny chest. "Or if the only person who lives rent-free in your head is Lucy fucking Hughson."

I put my hands on my head and exhale. "Look, I've had a lot going on—"

"So have we," Valeria says, teeth gritted. "Prom is coming up, so Ron—"

"Oh my God!" My eyes widen as I cheer internally. "Are you finally together?"

"What?" Valeria exclaims. "No! Ron finally mustered up the courage to ask Brenda to prom, and she said yes."

I look from her to Ron, whose lips are pursed. "Who's Brenda?"

"Brenda Tran, the girl from Chemistry I've been crushing on for the past month. The girl I would have told you about if you even cared."

My back hits my locker as I process this turn of events. I always thought Ron and Valeria had a thing for each other. That all their oblivious flirting was based on mutual attraction. Was I wrong?

"I'm sorry," I start. "I . . . I just assumed because you two are always flirting—" Then I clamp my mouth shut. That's not going to help this situation.

"Flirting? We don't flirt." Valeria's nostrils flare. "Ron, tell her."

Ron rakes a hand through his hair. His freckles are flaming red. "I mean, I kinda thought we do. Or, at least, used to. But that's all in the past."

Valeria stares at Ron, her chest heaving. "Wait, so did you really have feelings for me?"

Silence.

Shit. A bead of sweat rolls down my back under my black tee.

"Ron?" she presses.

"Well." Ron scratches the back of his neck and looks down

at his sneakers. "I did. But I didn't think you felt the same way, so I moved on."

"Oh." She exhales, her eyes closing for a brief moment. "I don't feel the same way. So . . . I'm glad you found Brenda."

Ron might be going to prom with Brenda, but I sense that Valeria's rejection still stings. He steps back and rubs his forehead with one hand. "Um, thanks."

You could cut the awkward tension with a knife. Goddamn it. I open my locker, take out my books, and nod at my friends. "See you at lunch?"

They exchange glances, seemingly having a telepathic conversation. Then Valeria's jaw clenches. "No," she says. "I need a break from you, Meera."

My mouth falls open. "Val—"

Ron's face is slowly turning purple. He tugs on his collar. "Correction: *We* need a break from you."

The first bell rings. They grab their things from their lockers and walk away in unison, not even turning back when I call out their names. *Fuck, fuck, fuck.* I blink back tears as I head to homeroom, texting rapidly in our group chat.

Meera:

Y'all are still coming to my Holi party, right???

Ron is typing . . .

Valeria is typing . . .

Ron is typing . . .

Valeria:

I don't know

Ron:

Same

I slump against the classroom wall and wipe my face with the back of my hand. *Fuck.* The thing Val said a long time ago floats into the front of my mind. *Just don't lose yourself in this whole Plan thing, Meera. Because then you'll lose us too.*

But instead of making me feel guilty, the memory only eggs me on more. I open Instagram and follow Lucy back, fuming. Valeria and Ron want to leave me too? Fine. Let them. All I need is for the Plan to work, and then everything will be as it's meant to be. Who needs friends anyway?

Lucy

By all means, this has been a great week. Dad took me and Sushant out to dinner last night, and although Mom was passive aggressive and snarky about it this morning while she made coffee, she didn't say anything outright rude. I considered asking her why she never told me about Jade, but then let it be. I already know the answer, and my heart can't take any more proof that Mom will never accept me for who *I* am.

Things did feel a bit awkward when Dad asked Sushant about Syracuse. He asked us if we'll do long-distance on the off chance NYU doesn't work out for me. I thought it was understood that's what we'd do, but I caught the hesitation in Sushant's smile as he said yes.

As I walk over to the gym for cheer practice after school, I check my phone. Meera followed me back on Instagram. A warmth settles in my belly, and I bite the inside of my cheek to avoid grinning. She's been so nice the past couple months. I know what I felt for her was real, but I also know my love for Sushant is just as real, although it's more affectionate than passionate. The more I avoid Meera, the stronger my so-called attraction to her grows. Maybe facing her head-on is the way out of my feelings now that I've accepted that I'm pansexual. And maybe . . . just maybe . . . Meera and I can be friends again. If she'll have me.

When I get out of the locker room, dressed in my cheerleader uniform, Coach Michaels flags me down. "Lucy, let's have a chat real quick," she says, ushering me over to a corner.

I follow her, turning back once to wave at my cheer squad. Only one or two of them return the greeting. Brittney, I notice, is smiling wide. She took two weeks off after our fight during PE, claiming she was hurt. I don't believe for a second that she actually bruised her elbows, but that was her excuse, and everyone bought it.

"This isn't an easy conversation to have," Coach Michaels starts when we're a considerable distance away from the rest of the squad, "but the cheerleaders have decided you might not be the best person to lead the team anymore."

I suck in a breath as her words sink in. "You're making me step down as cheer captain?"

"Lucy, after that, um, altercation you had with Brittney, there's been a serious lack of morale and team spirit in the squad." Coach bows her head. "She and some of the other girls had a chat with me and the vice principal, and we think they're right."

A ringing sound pierces my ears, but I grit my teeth and try to stay in the present moment. "So, what happens now? What about the routine for the final game of the year?"

Coach checks her clipboard. "We could go with the routine you choreographed. Brittney's picked it up well, and she can lead. But let's have the entire team vote on it."

I open my mouth to protest, then close it and nod. "All right. I understand." I'm not going to give Brittney the satisfaction of seeing me pissed off. I can deal with this in a mature manner.

Which, of course, means running up the stairs to my bedroom after practice and screaming into a pillow. Once my throat is hoarse, I go downstairs for a glass of water. Mom's office door is ajar. She's on another Zoom call. "Annie, I know exactly how you feel. My ex-husband also ended up—"

I don't want to listen to this conversation. I head into the backyard, sit on the swing, and cry in silence, staring up at the blue sky and bright yellow sunshine through my tears. One crow caws in the distance while others flap their wings and take off in flight. I almost mistake the chiming of my email inbox for birdsong. Then I snap to my senses and open the email.

My hands shake. Oh my God. It's from UCLA.

Dear Lucy,

Congratulations! It is our great pleasure to offer you . . .

Wait. What? I skim through the rest of the email, then let my eyes rest on that first sentence again. *I got in. I got in. I got in!* Relief floods through my veins—at least I got an acceptance from somewhere—but my pulse thrums with the reminder that I still haven't heard from NYU. That Sushant is still going to Syracuse in the fall. That if I don't go too, our relationship might end. The look on his face from last night flashes before my eyes. He's scared for us . . . and so am I.

Focus on the present moment, Lucy, I remind myself. I wipe my eyes and read through the entire email again, then text Natalie, Sushant, and Julien. Just got my acceptance email from UCLA!!!

I'm tempted to head inside to tell Mom too, but she's probably still talking to Annie Something and being bigoted. I gulp, then call Dad. The line rings for a few seconds before he picks up. "Hello? Lucy?"

"Hey, Dad," I say. There's a buzzing of people and phones

ringing in the background. He must be at his company's local office here in town. "Are you free to talk?"

"Give me a moment." A door closes, and then his voice grows louder. "How are you?"

"I got into UCLA."

For a moment, Dad is silent, like the words are still sinking in. Then he exclaims, "Lucy, that's incredible! You'd be so close to Jade and me! I don't believe this!"

"Dad—"

"We have to celebrate. Why don't you visit LA over spring break? Jade and I can show you around. They've already made a list of places they want to take—"

"Dad," I repeat, louder this time. "I'm still waiting to hear from NYU."

Dad exhales. "I get that NYU is your dream college. But UCLA is a great school too. It's close to home. To both your mom and me."

I bite the side of my nail. "I might take a gap year and move to New York anyway. Sushant and I love each other, and—"

"He's a great boy," Dad agrees. "But I hope you'll consider all the factors before deciding something that could impact your entire future—"

My phone buzzes. Natalie's calling me. My shoulders sink in relief, and I tell Dad I'll talk to him later. As soon as I answer her call, Natalie's excited shriek nearly ruptures my eardrums. "Lucy! I'm so proud of you! How are you feeling?"

"I don't know." I grip the chain handle of the swing with one hand, resting my head against it. "Bittersweet?"

"I get that." Natalie exhales. "How did Sushant react?"

My eyes water. She knows me so well. Our friendship might have started off as a lie, at least on my end, but she's become a true friend through and through. "He hasn't replied yet. But Dad's happy for me."

"Your dad is really trying to make up for lost time, isn't he?"

"He is." I raise my gaze to the blue sky. "Maybe I need to leave the past behind. You only get one dad, after all."

Natalie chuckles. "Unless you're Meera. Hey, are you going to her birthday party?"

I smile. Meera's invited half the school, and given how successful the book club—and the café—has become, I'm guessing her backyard's going to be packed. "I'll be there," I finally answer. "Sushant's helping her plan it, and she and I are kind of . . . reconnecting? And I don't totally hate it."

"I'm happy to hear that." I can hear the joy in Natalie's voice. "Calling a truce is way more important than whatever went down between you two."

"Yeah, I—" I pause to look at a new text message from Sushant. Woohoo congrats babe! Any word from NYU? "I need to talk to Sushant now," I mumble into the phone. "He just texted me."

Natalie exhales. "Good luck."

I hang up and press the phone to my heart. Sushant already turned down the Berkeley scholarship and accepted

Syracuse's offer, so there's no chance he can go to school in California. If I don't get into NYU . . . would we be able to make long-distance work? Dad's words run through my mind. He wants me to be closer to home and go to college somewhere, even if it isn't in New York. But New York would also mean distance from Madre Maria, which is what I've always wanted, and the possibility of a new life with the boy I love. I could get my foot in the door with publishing somehow, network my way up the ladder.

But wouldn't it be easier to study English at UCLA and move to New York with more skills on my résumé than just waitressing and babysitting during my gap year? To save money and give myself the gift of more time to plan?

My phone alerts me to another text from Sushant. Free to talk now?

Gulping, I call him, ignoring the thumping of my heartbeat.

"Congrats, babe!" is the first thing he says when he picks up the phone, genuine pride in his voice. "They'd be lucky to have you."

I curl one hand around the cold metal chain of the swing and force myself to smile. "Thanks. And, um, about NYU . . . no updates yet."

Sushant chuckles softly. "You'll get in, I just know it. You're perfect, after all."

What did I do to deserve this wonderful boy? I look down at my flip-flops and try to swallow back my anxious thoughts, but they slip out in a whisper anyway. "What if I don't get in?"

There's silence on the other end for barely two seconds before Sushant says, his voice shaky, "Uh, I'm sure it'll be fine. We'll figure it out when we have to."

"Okay," I mumble, rubbing my temples. "Anyway, what are you up to?"

"Funny you should ask," Sushant says, clearing his throat. "My folks are gonna be out for a few hours. Do you wanna come over and watch a movie?"

My stomach squirms as my mind recounts the last time we were alone in his room. I know Sushant doesn't mean it like a booty call and he would never rush me, but what if I feel ready for it in the moment, things do end up progressing, and then my panic attacks get the best of me once more? No. Not . . . not today.

"Babe?" Sushant asks.

"I—" A kitchen cabinet opens inside the house, and I look up to see movement near the counter. Mom must have finished her client call. "I'd better go tell Mom the good news," I say, then add, "I love you."

"Right. Yeah. Love you too," he says before hanging up, and for the first time in our entire relationship, those words sound the slightest bit emotionless.

CHAPTER NINETEEN

"Tujh Mein Rab Dikhta Hai"

by Roop Kumar Rathod

Lucy

My gaze remains steady out the window of Sushant's car while he drives us to Meera's house, since Mom took the car this morning for a life coaching conference outside of town. The afternoon sunshine is warm, and the sweet-smelling air signals the arrival of spring. A rap song plays on the radio, but all I can hear is the stifling silence between me and my boyfriend.

Things have been weird between us since I got into UCLA two days ago. Sushant is happy for me, of course, but I get the feeling he's afraid of the three thousand miles that will separate us if my NYU acceptance letter doesn't arrive soon.

I don't blame him—I am too. I thought about it, and Dad's right—if NYU doesn't work out, a gap year doesn't make sense when I already have UCLA welcoming me with open arms. I can't let go of this opportunity.

Is love really enough to make a long-distance relationship work? We haven't even had sex yet. I'm not entirely sure I'm ready for it. The suffocating guilt of having lied to Sushant this whole time about the origin of our relationship, which held me back when he tried to initiate sex, still weighs heavy on my heart.

To distract myself, I look down at Meera's gift-wrapped present clutched tightly between my hands. I don't know how she'll react to it, if she'll be surprised, but I've wanted to gift her this for years. Now that we're so close to graduation and I'm so close to possibly leaving Madre Maria—forever—it's my last chance to give her this.

"You excited?" Sushant asks, and I snap my gaze back to him. He's dressed in a white cotton kurta, the sleeves bunched up at his elbows. Apparently, wearing white is custom at these Holi parties so that the bright colors streaking your clothing stand out more.

I nod, wiping my hands on my own white dress. "I am. Thanks for driving me."

"Of course." Sushant's Adam's apple bobs, a telltale crease appearing between his brows. He's aware of it too, how the energy of It Couple Sushant and Lucy has shifted. Everything I've looked forward to in our combined future feels like it hinges on my getting into NYU—and with every passing day, I'm wondering if this relationship, born out of a lie, was ever real at all.

No. It was real. It *is* real. How can it not be?

We pull into Sushant's garage, and he parks neatly in his spot. I dimly register Bollywood music booming from Meera's backyard next door, the excited buzz and laughter of guests who have already arrived.

Sushant switches off the engine and faces me, one hand undoing his seat belt. He licks his lips, bringing his face closer to mine, and whispers, his breath on my skin, "We're okay, right?"

My mouth parts. I don't know how to answer him. But I force myself to smile and nod, planting a quick kiss on his lips. "Of course. I love you."

As we get out of the car and head to the party, I spot familiar faces from the swim team and the football team, book club regulars, and Meera herself. She's grinning as she shows Seth everything she's set up on the two tables: food, drinks, colored powder, water balloons . . . but all I really notice is her. She looks radiant in a white flared tunic and light blue cutoff denim shorts, so unlike her usual getup. Black suits her, but so does white.

"Meera, happy birthday!" Sushant waves to her eagerly, and I snap out of my daze, plastering on a smile when the birthday girl approaches us. "The backyard looks so great," Sushant adds, after giving her a one-armed hug.

"Well, you helped." She beams at him, returning the hug. "And don't worry, Appa and Dad have no idea about the bhaang."

Sushant punches the air with his fist. "Yes! Let's get high, baby." He rubs the side of my cheek with a warm hand and jogs over to the table where Seth is standing.

It's only then that Meera smiles at me rather nervously. "Thanks for coming, Lucy. I wasn't sure if— Wait, is that a present for me?"

"Happy birthday." I smile back and hand her the present

wrapped in black paper. "Open it later," I add when she weighs the paper-thin present in her hands. "Not . . . not here."

Meera's eyes widen with curiosity, but she nods and excuses herself to set it on another table, where two gift-wrapped packages are already stacked.

Natalie, hand in hand with Julien, runs over to me. "You came!" she exclaims. "I'm so excited. I've never played Holi before."

Julien simply smiles at me, his eyes crinkling at the edges. We haven't talked about my dad or anything related to our last text conversation since it happened, but all it takes is his mere presence to comfort me. Despite once being the reason for my annoyance, the French exchange student is now my safe space.

Within minutes, the party begins, and the backyard fills up with bodies dancing to the beat of the Bollywood dance music blaring from the Bluetooth speakers. Meera's parents aren't around to chaperone since it's a daytime event and the café probably needs their attention. Which means Sushant eagerly hands everyone a glass of the cool, fragrant dairy-free drink he calls bhaang. Apparently, it's laced with . . . pot?

"Thanks," I say as I take the glass from him, but he's already moved on to the next person. Frowning, I take a small sip, letting the flavors of rose, almond, and cardamom mingle in the back of my throat.

Everyone's had some of the bhaang now, but Sushant still

isn't giving me a second glance as he dances with his jock friends and my fellow cheerleaders, pausing every few seconds to dab colored powder on their faces and hands.

My stomach knots. God, what's happened to us? I hesitate, then gulp down the rest of the drink in one go. I wipe my mouth with the back of my hand, walk into the crowd, and join them, twirling in my dress and forcing out a giggle as one of the cheerleaders rubs red powder onto my cheeks.

I grab some blue powder and turn to throw it in Sushant's direction, but he's already walked over to where Meera is. His laughter booms across the space between us. He pulls on her arm, spinning her around as she smiles, then finishes his glass of bhaang and sets it aside.

"Happy Holi!" Natalie shrieks behind me, rubbing green powder on my bare shoulders. I put the blue powder in my hands on her instead of my boyfriend, then give in as she pulls me in to dance with her and Julien. The bhaang is slowly coursing its way through my veins, reassuring me that Sushant and I will be okay once again. That the Tower card won't take everything away from me, that I won't let it.

Someone turns up the volume, and people pass around more steel tumblers filled to the brim with bhaang. I bring my hands up and let loose, allowing the song and dance and drink to take control. In my peripheral vision, I see Sushant still dancing with Meera. He hasn't left her side in over twenty minutes. Part of me is certain he's just having harmless fun, that he loves me and would never look at anyone else that way, forget Meera, the girl he knows I have bad blood with. But the doubt pooling in my gut forces me to turn and watch them.

My heart lurches.

Sushant's brightly colored hands are cupping Meera's face, trailing their way down her neck and shoulders while he grins and sings along at the top of his lungs to the Bollywood song that's playing. She mumbles something, stepping out of his grasp, and starts to flick her hair out of her face, but his fingers get there first.

And then stay there. *What is happening?*

Meera looks over his shoulder and steps away just as Marvin from the football team points the hose at Sushant. He laughs, falling to the ground while drenched in water, still jamming to the music.

My eyes lock onto Meera's. Her lips part as her gaze takes me in—the shades of red, green, blue, and yellow coating my body and clothes; my wet hair, which sits on one shoulder, probably limp from the humidity and sweat. Then the widest grin spreads over her face, and she grabs a magenta-colored water balloon from the table and aims it at me.

I can't help the laugh that escapes my lips. "Meera Rao-George, don't you dare—" Before I can finish my sentence, the balloon smacks me right in the chest, and my white dress turns every shade of red.

"Too late." She doubles over, laughing. It's the most musical sound in the world.

And despite my fears about her, Sushant, us, the Tower card, NYU, and all the things that are threatening to destroy my picture-perfect life one frame at a time, I let myself enjoy this moment.

Meera

Two hours into the party, we run out of bhaang and Holi supplies, so everyone reluctantly calls it a day, their clothes dripping and their faces beaming with both sweat and joy. I smile and hug everyone, handing them towels to dry off with before they head home.

Sushant wishes me a happy birthday again and leaves hand in hand with Lucy. She gives me one last look, her brows pinching together, then walks back to his place. Maybe she noticed his overly friendly behavior toward me. I blink the thought away. No, I can't think just yet about how differently he was acting—first, I need to figure out what I feel or, rather . . . what I *didn't* feel.

When the backyard clears, I check my phone. With the high of the party and the bhaang slowly fading, the loneliness of not having my friends around hits me. Forget the fact that they didn't show up today—they're mad at me, I get that. But they've ignored all my calls and messages and haven't even greeted me on my eighteenth birthday, of all days.

This time last year, when the wound of losing Lucy had been only seven months new, Ron and Valeria took me out to a concert to cheer me up, despite neither of them liking EDM or any of the featured artists. Sadly, Gryffin wasn't performing, but it was still the best birthday party I'd had in a long time. It was fun because I spent it with two people who didn't care that I was unpopular, only ever wore black, and hadn't had my first kiss yet.

I type out a text in our group chat again—my fourth one of the day—and hit send before I can regret it. A minute later, the "Read" status appears for them both, but they don't respond.

Sighing, I head to the table in the backyard and take my three birthday gifts inside the house. Dad and Appa are both at the café, so I have all the privacy to open my presents without their curious eyes on me.

I sprawl on the floor and go through my presents. If I sit on the couch with my clothes in this condition, Dad will come home and have a heart attack. Raj makes himself comfortable beside me, his tongue wagging, as I rip open wrapping paper. Seth got me a fifty-dollar gift card to Target, which was sweet of him, considering we've barely talked. Julien got me his favorite Pablo Neruda poetry collection that he personally annotated. Cute. As for Lucy . . .

I frown when the black packaging gives way to a Polaroid-style photograph with a QR code on the back, as well as a piece of paper listing ten of Gryffin's songs in Lucy's neat handwriting. The picture, taken by Lucy during our sophomore year, is of me wearing my black Gryffin merch T-shirt, my hands in the finger-guns pose. When I scan the code with my phone, it redirects to a Spotify playlist titled "MRG" with those same songs. I scan the handwritten list next. Beside the title of each song is a small message from Lucy, ranging from "Remember when you streamed this on loop every day for three straight months?" and "When this plays on the radio, all I see is you dancing to it in your living room" to "This song used to remind me of us." A shaky breath escapes me. That final song is undoubtedly my favorite Gryffin song of all time . . . about friends falling in love. I know she doesn't mean it that way, but it's sweet nonetheless.

Why would Lucy do this for me if she hates me so much? Or, at least, used to hate me? Thanks to the Plan, we're as close to friends as we'll ever get. But this must have taken her hours to put together. It's not a last-minute present. And the name, "MRG" . . . those are my initials. Is this the Gryffin playlist from Sushant and Lucy's shared Spotify, the one he told me about during the museum trip?

"What does this mean?" I say out loud, scratching Raj under his chin as he barks. I guess it's time to confront all the weirdness that's gone down today.

I pick Raj up in my arms and take the stairs to my room. I head into the shower while he waits outside, whining softly. I scrub the colors off my body, grateful for the oil I applied beforehand that makes every stain come off. The hot water rains down on me, and I close my eyes, finally replaying what happened at the party over and over in my head. The "moment"

Sushant and I shared, the one that would have made Ron and Valeria promise me that the Plan is working—if they were still talking to me, that is.

My mind drifts to the way Sushant, high on bhaang, didn't take his eyes off me while he put color on me: my face, my neck, my shoulders. The way he brushed my hair off my cheek. The way his hand lingered before one of his friends hosed him down and he fell to the ground, laughing.

The way I didn't feel . . . *anything.*

Raj stops pawing on the bathroom door when I get out of the shower, wrapped in my fluffy gray bathrobe. I sigh and ignore him, so he runs across my room and settles himself in a corner, where sunlight is streaming through the window. I pull my damp hair to one side and lie back in bed, putting a hand to my head.

What is wrong with me? I've loved Sushant since I can remember. He's the first and only boy I've ever wanted to kiss. Everything I've done this year has been to make something happen between us. But now that it feels like the Plan just might work, despite all the screwups, all I feel is . . . nothing.

I should be thinking about how warm his rough and calloused hand felt on my cheek, the way his hip was pressed up against mine. But I'm not, because I'm thinking about Lucy's giggle seconds before I hit her with the water balloon, how the colors spun in the air around her, suspended for a second before settling on the wet white dress that clung to every inch of her athletic body. After having a moment with the boy I love, the only person on my mind is the girl I hate—the one who gave me the most thoughtful birthday present in the world.

What does that mean?

"Knock, knock." Appa pokes his head into my room. He smells like incense; he must have come home on his break from the café. "Want to talk?"

I can't get over how psychic Appa is. I nod and make space for him on my bed. Appa sits beside my feet, and I clutch a spare pillow against my chest and turn to him, still lying down.

Appa looks at me with fondness. "How was the party, putta? Did you have fun?"

It takes me a few moments to figure out what I want to know from him. He waits patiently, his eyes laced with concern, until I speak. "How did you know you loved Dad?"

Appa throws his head back and laughs. "I must have told you this story a hundred times. It was love at first sight, really."

"No." My voice is low, frustrated. "How did you know he was *it* for you? Your twin flame, your soulmate, the One?"

"Oh." Appa twirls his mustache, thinking. "I didn't know that right away. Or maybe I did, but I was afraid to believe it because the feeling was so strong. It scared me at first."

"What changed?"

He smiles, his eyes misting. He must be going back in time—at least twenty-five years—in his mind. They met in high school, after all. "I saw something in his aura that I'd never seen in anyone before. At first, it was soft, murky, foggy. But the more time we spent together, the clearer the aura got.

It sparkled; it shone and shimmered. And my soul lit up every time I saw it. Every time I saw him."

I sit up and peer at him. "What did you see?"

"The Universe."

I try not to laugh. That sounds like a line straight out of a Shah Rukh Khan movie. "You're being so silly, Appa."

He doesn't look amused, and his eyes narrow. "It's not silly. It's more like . . . being around him feels holy. Our relationship is a divine connection. I know, because he is in every cell of my being, and I am in every cell of his being. Just like my relationship with the Universe and my Angels."

Somehow this conversation is frustrating me. "But what does that mean?" I ask desperately, gesturing with my hands. "You're just saying words. Random spiritual words."

"You won't understand me now, but you will when you feel that way about someone, putta. You'll know it to your very core when you feel this connection with someone."

"What if . . ." I pause. "What if I thought I loved someone, but I'm not so sure anymore?"

Appa's face crinkles into a soft smile. "Soul unions never end, and love often gets put on hold, even if it's with your soulmate. But no matter what, some emotion will always tie you to your twin flame—whether it's love, hate, anger, or bitterness. The only emotion you will never, ever feel for them is indifference."

My eyes widen. That's literally how I felt when Sushant touched me. Indifferent.

Appa pats my damp cheek before getting up from my bed

with a grunt. "Give it some thought. And remember, everything always works out in divine timing the way it's meant to."

"Thanks, Appa," I mumble.

He stops by the window to bend down and scratch Raj's belly before closing the door behind him. Once he's gone, I let out a loud groan and press my face into my pillow as I replay Appa's wise words in my head. Even though not everything he said made sense, one thing is clear: Sushant doesn't belong with me after all.

So does he really belong with Lucy? And if so, has my Plan been working against the Universe?

Am I, not Lucy, the villain in all this?

CHAPTER TWENTY

"sometimes"
by Chelsea Cutler

Lucy

I don't speak the entire ride back until Sushant slows the car to a halt outside my house. It's only then that I undo my seat belt, mumble a "bye" to my boyfriend, and get out of his car.

"Lucy, wait. What's up?" Sushant scrambles to get closer to me. I'm seconds away from slamming the front door in his face, but he squeezes into my living room before I can do that. "What's wrong?" he asks, his lips turning downward. It's a cute look on him. If I could stop replaying his interactions with Meera at the party in my head, I'd kiss him.

Instead, I glare at him, arms folded. "You ignored me the entire party, and now you're mad I'm doing the same to you?"

He runs a hand through his hair. "I wasn't ignoring you on purpose. It was Meera's birthday, so I thought I'd hang out with her—"

"You could have included me." My voice is borderline pleading. "But every time I tried to get close to you, you walked away."

Sushant doesn't have an excuse, evidently, because he hangs

his head low. "I'm sorry. I might have gotten a little carried away with the bhaang, the music, and wanting to have some fun. I'm just so anxious about everything between us that I needed a break from it all."

Thud. Thud. Thud. My heartbeat pounds in my ears. "You—you needed a break from us?" I say, my voice a loud whisper. "Like an actual let's-not-be-with-each-other break?"

"No! God, no, just from the situation—" he starts when my email pings with a notification.

I open the Gmail app, and my pulse only grows more erratic. "Shit. It's from NYU."

Sushant sucks in a breath. "Oh," he says.

"Should I . . . should I open it?" I hate the way my voice cracks at the end of that question, the way it's trembling—no, it's not just my voice. My whole body is shaking.

Sushant notices. He puts his arms around my waist and pecks the top of my head. "Want me to read it for you?"

I nod silently, give him the phone, and step away, rubbing the sides of my arms. Goose bumps sprout along my skin, so I force myself to look away from Sushant as he taps on the screen.

A few seconds of silence later, I raise my face. My stomach turns. Sushant's breathing is unsteady, his chest rising and falling as he stares at my phone. There's no sign of a smile on his face. Not even in his eyes.

"Sushant?" I ask.

He hands me the phone and envelops me in a hug. "I'm sorry," he says.

I hug him back, my eyes welling up, and skim through the email. Words like "it is with regret" and "unable to offer you admission to NYU" jump out at me right away. I hold back a sob and pull away from my boyfriend. "What now?" I ask.

Sushant hangs his head, putting his hands in the pockets of his jeans. "I don't know."

"Do we . . . ?" My unspoken words hang in the air. Do we try long-distance across three thousand miles, or do we break up?

He exhales. Wiping the side of his face, caked with colors, he says, "I don't want to lose you, Lucy. You've been my person for so long, I—" He claps a hand to his mouth and spins around. Maybe he doesn't want me to see him cry.

I curl my fingers around his bicep and pull him toward me again. "I don't want us to end, either," I say. "But there's so much distance between New York and LA—"

"It's not just that." He shrugs. "I love you, but I feel like you've been pulling away from me on purpose. Like that day at my place or this morning, when you barely let me kiss you."

"I have a lot going on in here." I tap the side of my head. "I'm not ready yet."

"I get it, and I don't want to pressure you. I just don't know if it's because of things with your dad, the cheer squad, or . . ." He swallows. "Or because there's something you're not telling me."

I gulp, and his eyes flick down to my throat at the movement. There are so many things I haven't told Sushant. The fact that I'm pansexual. That I used him to make Meera hate me. That as much as I love him, I don't know if I can love him in the same way I loved her. That I used to be so terrified to accept who I am. That I'm not afraid anymore.

His eyes darken. "What aren't you telling me, Lucy?"

But I *am* afraid of other people finding out. I'd rather pick a fight now than admit to my boyfriend that I'm pansexual and change the way he sees me, maybe even the way he loves me. After all, I've read about this countless times on social media. People find out their partners are queer and stop trusting them—or, worse, stop loving them.

So I pivot.

"I know there's something going on between you and Meera."

Sushant literally backs away, his mouth falling open. "Wait, what?"

I narrow my eyes. "You spent the entire party with her—"

"Lucy, it's her birthday!"

"Birthday or not, you were standing a little too close to her," I point out.

"I'm sorry about that. I was in my head about us, and that's why I—" He sighs. "I feel nothing for her, Lucy. I promise. How could I?"

"Don't lie to me." I hold a hand out. "You're always with her lately."

Sushant scoffs, raking a hand through his hair. "Oh yeah? I could say the same about you and Julien. But I won't, because I'm not an asshole making up bullshit."

It breaks my heart to play along, to distract him from my

secret on purpose. But I don't have a choice. "Julien is my friend. And he's dating Natalie. How can you accuse me of—"

Sushant shakes his head and pushes past me to the front door. "I'm out of here."

"Sushant—"

He swings the door open, then turns around, one hand around the knob. "I was wrong earlier. Maybe a break from the situation isn't enough."

I stare at him as my knees nearly give way. "What are you saying?"

Sushant's frown deepens. "Maybe we need a break from our relationship, after all."

Before I can protest, the door slams shut behind him, and I let my boyfriend walk away from me, tears streaming down my face.

Meera

Spring break is supposed to be a time to relax, have fun, and party. That's what I'm trying to do as I get dressed for a beachside party Seth invited me to, although it started hours ago. My mind is in the mood to self-sabotage and isn't letting me do anything except spiral into a cloud of gloomy thoughts. The past two days since my birthday, all I've been able to think about is my stupid Plan and how I was wrong all along.

Part of me doesn't want Sushant anymore. It doesn't want him to be my first kiss. Maybe it's all of me that doesn't want him. Maybe I was just so caught up in the idea of being with the unattainable hot jock who lives right next door to me and has always seen me as a friend, nothing more.

"So what now?" I whisper to my reflection in the mirror. Sighing, I grab a flannel shirt from my closet, roll the sleeves up, and head downstairs.

"Big party tonight?" Dad says from the reclining leather chair. He's reading a book while Appa's made himself comfortable on the couch, watching his favorite Kannada movie on Netflix.

"Just a casual get-together with friends," I lie, bending down to give Raj a belly rub. Then I grab my flip-flops from the shoe rack. "I'll be home by midnight."

"No drinking!" Appa yells as the front door swings closed behind me.

The beach is only a twenty-minute walk from home. I stroll down the street, hands in my pockets, a heaviness in my chest. What have I done, and where has it gotten me?

I selfishly tried to sabotage my ex–best friend's relationship. For all I know, Sushant and Lucy are soulmates. And, worse still, my friends hate me because I ignored them for the sake of the Plan. No texts, no calls—Ron and Val didn't even like my last few Instagram posts or Stories.

Appa was right. I've fucked everything up, the fuckup that I am.

The sun is dipping into the horizon, turning the ocean all

shades of orange and pink and blue, by the time I get to the party. I go straight to a tray of Jell-O shots and down one, then grab a beer from the cooler. Most people from school are here. Seth and a few jocks are playing volleyball—shirts and skins, by the looks of it. I glance at Sushant's bare, muscular upper body, forcing myself to feel something, anything, the way I used to when I'd see him shirtless at the beach, so that this Plan wasn't for naught. But . . . nothing.

I exhale, walking around. Some kids from book club nod at me; others wave or say hello. I'm smiling back at them when I spot Valeria and Ron with another girl by the ocean in the distance. Ron is splashing water on the girl while Valeria clicks pictures on her iPhone, laughing. The girl kicks water back at Ron, a blush tinting her fair cheeks. Then she puts her arms around him and kisses him on the lips.

A jolt shoots through me. This must be Brenda, the girl Ron has a crush on. Looks like it worked out for him. It's a bittersweet feeling. Ron hasn't had a serious relationship since freshman year, long before we went from locker neighbors to close friends. He deserves to be loved. But why can't I be included in that joy? I still care about Ron and Val. Of course I do. I just . . . haven't been the best at showing it.

I swallow my sadness and chug my beer, purposefully making my way toward the ocean, an apology on my lips. Brenda spots me and frowns, then mutters something indistinct to my friends. They turn to glance at me, scoff, and walk away, back into the crowd. My shoulders slump, but I decide I won't give up so easily. I'll find them later tonight. I'll fix this. I have to. I've been a horrible, selfish friend to everyone in my life. I can't let that define me anymore.

"Meera!" Julien greets me by kissing me on each cheek. He's wearing a dress shirt, and his hair is gelled back like always. "How are you?"

I give a noncommittal shake of the head. "I'm, well, alive."

He throws his head back and laughs. There's a bottle in his hand—rose kombucha? "What a time to be alive, isn't it? A fun party with wonderful friends. It is a beautiful night."

"I guess," I mumble. My eyes search the beach for my friends and Brenda, but there are so many people here, it's hard to pick out three faces from among the crowd.

"It cannot compare to your party, though." The smile blooming across his face reaches his eyes. "I must introduce Holi to my friends back home in Paris."

I finally turn to him. "You're leaving after prom, right?"

Julien nods, his eyes misty. "I will miss all of you. Especially Natalie." He coughs and sips his kombucha. "Have you seen her, by the way?"

"Speak of the devil." I use my bottle to point. "She's walking over here."

Natalie jogs to us, slightly out of breath. Her dark skin is flushed, her coily black hair tied back into a ponytail. "I need your help," she says, taking Julien's hands in hers.

I step aside, deciding to give them some privacy, but what she says next piques my curiosity. "Lucy's wallowing in self-pity by the end of the beach. She's refusing to come out here and join us. I'm worried about her. I asked Sushant to help too, but he won't talk to me, and—"

"What happened?" I ask.

Natalie hesitates, dropping her eyes to the sandy ground. "I'm not sure I can say."

Julien looks from her to me and clears his throat. "Meera, let's talk soon?"

I nod, although this feels like a sucker punch to the gut. Natalie replaced me a long time ago in Lucy's heart. Soon, someone else will replace me as Ron and Valeria's best friend. But there is still something I can do, something kind and selfless and wonderful, to make up for at least part of my bad karma.

"See you," I say out of the corner of my mouth before I sprint toward the last stretch of the beach, hoping Lucy's still there—and that she'll let me in.

CHAPTER TWENTY-ONE

"Still Falling For You"
by Ellie Goulding

Meera

I find Lucy sitting on the sand by the shore, her legs crossed underneath her skirt. Her red hair is flying around in the wind like a raging flame, but even from the short distance between us, I can tell her eyes are wet.

"Hey," I say, sitting down beside her. "You okay?"

Lucy turns her head the other way and wipes her nose with a dainty, shaky finger. "Yep. All good."

"You don't seem that good," I mumble, spotting three empty beer bottles on the sand beside her.

"Very observant of you, Meera." She pulls on a strand of her hair and blows air out through her mouth, then leans back. "I'll be fine soon."

I mimic her and rest my weight against my forearms. The waves run up to the shore of the beach, almost reaching the tips of our toes in our flip-flops before retreating into the ocean. Lucy's toes are painted a bright neon pink. Mine are bare and cracked around the corners, in desperate need of a pedicure. I laugh, and her head finally spins to regard me. "What?" she says.

"Nothing." I nudge her toe with mine, and she visibly shivers. Then, tentatively, I add, "About that birthday present you got me . . ."

Lucy's body stiffens. She looks away, frowning, and whispers, "Did you hate it? Was it too much?"

I grin. "I loved it. I can't believe you'd do that for me. Thank you."

She doesn't reply, but I catch the small smile resting on her lips before her eyebrows thread together again, and she exhales, shoulders sinking.

"Hey," I say. "Tell me why you're upset."

"No."

"Tell me." Even as I repeat myself, I'm not sure why I care. This is what I'd wanted all along, right? For Lucy to sink deeper and deeper, as far away from Sushant and success as possible, so I could rise up and get my revenge.

But, shit, seeing those damp green ocean eyes makes something inside me break. And I don't like being broken.

I'm sure she doesn't, either.

Lucy sits up and faces me, and I do the same. Her tears have dried now, leaving small dark trails of mascara down her cheeks. They're pink from the cool breeze blowing around us. I have the weirdest urge to touch my fingers to those cheeks, to see if they're as soft as my mind promises me they are.

I must be *really* drunk.

"I didn't get into NYU." Lucy says each word slowly,

measurably, as though she's weighing it on her tongue before letting it slip out. She grits her teeth and looks back to the water.

"Oh shit." I duck my head and wait for the relief to come. Sushant's going to New York. But now Lucy isn't. This probably means their future together is at risk. I should be glad, gleeful, ecstatic. The old me would have been.

But I'm . . . not. And I know why after the Holi party. Because Sushant isn't mine to keep. He never was.

"I should have applied to more than one school in New York," Lucy says. She lifts her chin up and rubs her nose on the back of her hand. "My mistake was thinking everything would work out for me. It always used to. But not anymore, clearly."

"Don't say that—" I start, but she shoots me a fierce look that makes me shut up.

"It's true, Meera. I had to step down as cheer captain, Sushant and I are probably over, and"—she cups her face with her hands and breaks down—"and now I don't even have a reason to get away from Madre Maria, as far as I can. I'll have to settle for going to LA."

"Why do you want to get away?" I ask softly.

She raises an eyebrow. "What?"

"Madre Maria's great. It's home. Why would you ever want to leave?"

Lucy avoids my gaze. She finds a stick lying a few feet away and swirls it around, making random shapes until she starts writing her name over and over again in the sand in her cutesy cursive handwriting. *Lucy. Lucy. Lucy.*

I'm about to repeat my question when she answers in

her quiet voice, "Home isn't a place. It's a feeling. Of warmth and—and safety. And I don't feel safe here. I don't feel like I can be myself all the time. Not even most of the time."

"Oh." The word leaves my mouth slowly. I can't relate. I've never felt safer than when I'm with Appa and Dad, with Valeria and Ron, with Sushant, roaming the streets of our little town, not a care in the world.

"I'm sorry," I say. I scoot closer to Lucy, and she sets her head on my shoulder. Her hair smells like roses and lilies—a combination that takes me back in time to ninth grade dance parties and Bollywood movie marathons when we'd fall asleep on the couch in front of the TV, right beside each other. I guess she never switched shampoos.

Some things never change.

I notice she's shivering slightly, so I take off my flannel shirt and wrap it around her slender frame. She mutters a soft thank-you before leaning her head on my shoulder again.

"Maybe the next book club will cheer you up," I say. "The week before prom."

Lucy shrugs. "I haven't even started reading it yet. I've been so busy being anxious and depressed and feeling like somebody else."

"When was the last time you felt like you could be yourself?" I ask.

Lucy stares down at our sandy knees pressed together and radiating warmth between them. She raises her head and shifts so we're no longer touching, then exhales shakily. "Right now."

I look at her and grin. "That's a good thing, right?"

She blinks back more tears as a weird shadow dawns on her face. "I—I should go."

"Wait, Lucy!" I pull her down as she stands. She stumbles and falls into my lap. Her head bumps against mine, and we both jerk up, unable to stop the giggles bursting out from us.

But she doesn't move away. Instead, she smiles at me, only inches between us. Her breath smells beery and yet sweet . . . delicious. "I've missed you, Meera."

"I've missed you too." My hand moves of its own accord to cup her face. Her skin is even softer than I thought. I tap on the side of her cheekbone, sharp and yet so smooth, and her face melts into a wide grin. For the first time tonight, she looks like she feels safe.

With me.

Her eyes fall to my mouth, and she runs her tongue over her perfect lips. The smile fades. She swallows and starts to pull back, but before she can put even an inch of distance between us, I wrap my arms around her waist and tug her closer.

And then I kiss her.

Lucy

The second our lips touch, I jerk away. Not because it feels scary, or confusing, or awkward. But because the zap of electricity surging between our mouths is too much to handle.

Despite that . . . I need more. I need her.

Meera gasps, her eyes wide and apologetic. "Fuck, Lucy, I am so—" She shuts up when our lips meet again, and the sound that comes from the back of her throat—a cross between a groan and a purr—makes my insides clench with sheer joy. Her hand weaves into my hair, her fingers skimming my scalp with just the right amount of pressure, while I dip my fingers into the loops of her shorts and pull her even more flush against me.

So this is what it feels like to kiss Meera Rao-George. This is what it feels like to let myself fall and be caught by the hands of someone I truly and unconditionally lo—

"Oh my God."

The voice that carries over the wind makes us spring apart, but Sushant has already seen us. I don't know how long he's been standing there for. Even from a few feet away, his brown face looks an unpleasant shade of green and purple.

Meera opens her mouth to speak, but I launch up from her lap and race toward him. "Sushant, let me explain—"

There's a hardness in his gaze. He breathes in and out deeply, his eyes flitting behind me to Meera and then back to me. "So this is why you were so fixated on Meera and me."

I lower my head, wondering how to explain this to him. Hell, I can't even explain this to myself. "I didn't expect us to—"

"Not here." Sushant glares, then hooks a thumb behind him and gestures for me to follow him to the other side of the beach, where the party's happening. I cast a glance at Meera before I follow Sushant. Her head is in her hands, and I think she might be crying.

My heart aches, wishing I could kiss away her tears. But reality is sinking in. I'm Lucy, daughter of the very queer-phobic Alice Miller and girlfriend of the sweetest guy in the world. There's no way I could end up with a girl.

Sushant stops only when we're standing in one corner of the party. It's crowded enough that no one will notice us but still secluded, with no eavesdroppers. "Talk," he says, his tone accusatory. "Now."

I let the tears cascade down my face as I grip his fingers in mine. Thankfully, he lets me hold his hand. "I think I've been in love with Meera for years. I was just too scared to admit it. I wanted out of those feelings. I wanted to not be in that situation, because I was so terrified of what it might mean for me."

Sushant's fingers clench around my hand tensely. "So that's why you two had a falling-out?"

"Yeah."

He gasps. "And that's why you started dating me. Because you needed a beard. Someone to hide the fact that you're, what? Gay? Bi?" He whispers the last two words, perhaps so no one at the party overhears.

I shift my eyes, thinking back to my conversation with Julien. "I guess I'm . . . pansexual."

Sushant lets go of my hand to put his fingers in his pockets. "Did you ever love me?"

I nod, aching for his touch again. "I did love you, Sushant. I do love you. In every way. But it's just not—"

"It's just not like it is with her."

Slowly, I nod my head in a yes. "I'm sorry."

Sushant stares into the distance, scratching his jaw. "I thought you were it for me, Lucy. The One, my soulmate, or whatever they call it in those romance novels you read."

"I wanted that too," I say, "and I tried my best to love you the way you love me—"

"No, stop." He holds up a hand and steps away. "Don't make me feel worse about this than I already do."

"I'm so sorry." I reach for him, my eyes squinting from the tears blurring my vision. "Maybe not all soulmates are romantic."

"I wish *we* were." A small but sad smile tugs at his lips. "Looks like the big promposal I was planning will have to be canceled."

"I'm sorry, Sushant," I say again as my heart sinks, thinking of how we're both nominated for prom king and queen. And now . . . I've ruined it all.

He pulls me in for a hug and exhales as his grip finds my waist over Meera's flannel shirt. I nestle into his warmth, into his spicy scent that I know like the back of my hand, for the very last time. "Take care, Lucy. I only want the best for you."

"You too," I murmur, kissing the side of his neck.

He pulls back with a grimace and walks away, his hands

gripping fistfuls of his hair. I'm sure he's crying too. But I can't comfort him anymore. I've lost that right.

I rub my eyes with the flannel shirt's sleeves and return to where we left Meera, but she's not there anymore. In her place is a message with the stick I was using to write my name in the sand.

This was a mistake. I'm sorry.

CHAPTER TWENTY-TWO

"you broke me first"
by Tate McRae

Meera

It's only when I wipe the tears streaming down my cheeks with the back of my hand that I remember Lucy still has my flannel shirt. There's a chilly breeze tonight as I walk down the street, away from the beach and the party and Sushant and Lucy and everyone, and I have to wrap my arms around my body to keep from shivering.

In Madre Maria, broken hearts feel like a blizzard.

How did I let this happen? How did the Universe let this happen? I put a hand to my forehead and stare at the heavens—or whatever heavens-equivalent my Angels reside in—trying to make sense of this situation. The Plan was always to date Sushant and dethrone Lucy. I don't want to date Sushant anymore. My conversation with Appa led to the epiphany that Sushant's not the one for me.

But where does that leave things with Lucy? Why do I want to . . . kiss her? My mind is eager to replay that minute-long kiss when nothing mattered except Lucy and her perfect skin and perfect mouth, but I tell my mind to go fuck itself. That was a foolish thing to do.

I scoff out loud. The streets are empty, and I kick a pebble out of my path, my hands in the pockets of my jeans as I walk faster, desperate to outrun my mind. The sooner I get home, face-plant into bed, and fall asleep, the sooner I'll get the alcohol out of my system and start to think clearly.

Because I kissed Lucy. And I . . . liked it. And that is the *opposite* of thinking clearly.

Am I not straight? I thought I loved Sushant. Why, then, would I want to kiss his girlfriend, aka my sworn enemy?

Someone's car honks behind me, and I cross over to the sidewalk. I've been walking in the middle of the street. But they honk again and come to a stop beside me.

"Hi," Julien says from the driver's seat. As soon as he sees my face, his own face falls.

I squint at him—his headlights are really bright, not to mention his teeth, which practically glow in the dark. "Julien? What are you doing here?"

"Driving back from the party after dropping Natalie off at home. Are you okay, Meera?"

I look down at my flip-flops and laugh. "Is there a point to lying and telling you I'm fine? I'm an ugly crier, after all."

"I would never call you ugly," Julien replies, chuckling, "but, yes, I can tell you've been crying." He leans to the side and opens the passenger door for me. "Let me drop you off at home."

He doesn't look drunk and he was sipping kombucha at

the party, but he could have had alcohol before that. I narrow my eyes and ask, "How much have you had to drink?"

"Not a drop." His grin widens. "I'm doing an alcohol detox. I feel so good!"

I try not to roll my eyes as I get into his car. When the door slams shut, I buckle myself in, then lean back and groan loudly, smacking my head against the soft leather headrest.

Julien gives me a funny look as he resumes driving. "What are you doing?"

"It's an American technique that prevents hangovers," I say as I bump my head against the headrest again.

He raises an eyebrow and puts his left blinker on. "Really? I must try it the next time I drink after my detox. How long does one do it for?"

That gets a laugh out of me. "I was being sarcastic, Julien. I didn't have the best night, and I screwed up in the most screwed-up way possible."

He brakes and hands me his phone. "Put in your address in Maps and tell me what happened. You're confusing me, and I do not drive well when I am confused."

That's the second time he's made me smile since I got into his car. Someone should give him an award. I type my address into the app and let out a breath. Nobody knows the whole story except Valeria and Ron, but maybe I need an unbiased perspective to make sense of all this. "Julien, what I tell you can never leave this car. You can't tell anyone—not even Natalie. Especially not Natalie."

"I promise." He parks the car and turns in his seat toward me, waiting patiently.

Sighing, I fill him in on everything. My former friendship with Lucy, the Plan, all the sabotage I pulled Julien into, my realization that I don't love Sushant, and . . . the kiss.

"And then Sushant saw us, and Lucy bolted after him—"

"He saw you kissing?" Julien claps a hand to his mouth. "Oh mon dieu, he's like the hair in the soup!"

I squint. "What?"

He thinks for a moment. "It's the French way of saying . . . How do I say it? That he showed up at the worst time."

"Well, yeah." I shift in place, then add out of the corner of my mouth, "I'm sorry I tried to use you to break them up."

Julien snorts with laughter. It's jarring to see someone so French and posh make that noise. "Meera, the Plan didn't work anyway. You don't have to apologize."

"Thanks." I play with the strap of my seat belt. "I don't know why I did it."

"Why you did the Plan?" He thinks for a moment. "Because you wanted revenge."

"No, not that. Why I . . ." It's hard to even think the words, let alone say them. Every time I think of what happened, my heart flutters and my stomach lurches in both the best and worst ways possible.

Understanding flashes across Julien's face. "Ah. Why you kissed Lucy."

Slowly, I nod. A tear falls down my cheek.

"Here. Your nose is leaking too." Julien gives me a handkerchief that smells like men's cologne. I'm hesitant, but he puts it in my hand, so I thank him and blow my nose on it, making an ungodly noise.

"I know why you kissed Lucy," he says when I surface from the handkerchief. "You have feelings for her."

"But I hate her!" I exclaim. "And—and I'm supposed to be straight."

His eyes narrow. "According to whom? Who says you are supposed to be this or that?"

"Julien—"

"No, really. Why can't your heart decide who you want to love? Why does your love have to fit into that one label you assigned to yourself years ago?"

I exhale slowly as my eyes shut. "You're right. I guess . . . I'm not straight."

"And that's okay," he assures me, putting a hand on my knee.

"I know. I have two dads, after all." Another tear falls down my cheek. "But maybe I just liked kissing Lucy. It doesn't necessarily mean I have feelings for her."

Julien moves his hand from my knee to my shoulder, and I open my eyes to look at him. He's smiling. "What is it you say in English? 'There is a thin line between love and hate'?"

"That's not the case here," I insist, teeth gritted. "It can't be."

"Meera, maybe you created the Plan not to get revenge but to get close to her again. Because maybe you loved her all this while without knowing it."

It dawns on me as he says those words that he's probably right.

That my constant fixation on Lucy ever since the abrupt death of our friendship means more than just resentment or hatred.

It means that I haven't been able to stop thinking about her, missing her.

It means I'm in love with her.

But after the way her life has crumbled to pieces, though it wasn't all due to my efforts, it's selfish to say what I feel for her is love. Because when you love someone, you don't consciously or knowingly hurt them or even try to. Ever.

"If I did *this* out of love, then I loathe myself," I say finally. My eyes are foggy with fresh tears. "I shouldn't be allowed to love someone ever again."

Julien starts the car with a purr and shrugs. "I think you need to sleep on all this. It has been a long night for you."

I rest my head against the window. "It really has."

We don't talk for the next few minutes, until he pulls up in front of my house. The living room lights are on, which means my parents are still up. I put a hand out in front of my mouth and exhale, then wrinkle my nose. The kiss seems to have sobered me up, but my breath still smells like vodka and beer.

Julien rummages in the glove compartment and hands me a mint. "Voilà."

I pop the mint into my mouth as I get out of the car; then I lean my arms against the open window and smile. "Thanks, Julien. For listening, and for promising not to tell."

He mimes zipping his lips shut. "I will take it to the grave." Once he drives away, I force myself to take a long, deep breath and unlock my front door.

Dad is sitting on the reclining leather chair in the living room, eyes closed, with the same book on his lap. When I take off my flip-flops and close the shoe rack, he rouses at the sound. "Oh, hey." He stifles a yawn. "How was the party?"

"Good," I answer, avoiding his gaze. I might not be that close with Dad, and he definitely isn't psychic like Appa, but he's still my father. One glance exchanged, and he'll know something's going on.

Somehow Dad figures it out anyway. "You okay?" he asks, standing and cracking his back. He pushes his glasses up his nose and quirks an eyebrow at me.

"I'm fine," I answer quickly, faking a yawn. "I'm going to sleep."

He looks at me, frowning, then sighs and gestures for me to go upstairs. "Good night."

"Good night, Dad."

The second my bedroom door shuts behind me, I crawl into bed, still in my shorts, and bury my face into the pillow, drenching it only moments later. When I raise my head to wipe my tears, my eyes land on the whiteboard with the name of the Plan in block letters and the four bullet points I made.

Right. I should erase that.

I stand, but before I can reach for the eraser, a pebble hits my window. I yelp, then look back at the closed door, hoping Dad's asleep by now and didn't hear that. There's only one person it could be—Lucy. She saw my message in the sand, and she wants to talk. And although there are so many unresolved questions in my head, I can't do this right now. I can't face my feelings tonight. Maybe not ever. Especially not with what's written on this whiteboard.

All I can do is tell Lucy I'm about to sleep and we'll talk later. I race to the window, open it, and look down, but no one's there. Sushant stands by his window across from my bedroom, though, muscled arms folded, glaring at me. In his hand is his cell phone. He holds it up.

I take out my phone from my back pocket and look at the screen. There's a text from him from five minutes ago.

Sushant:

We should talk. Come over

I shake my head at him and reply, It's late

There's no way I'm ready to talk to the boy I used to love, who spotted me kissing his girlfriend, whose life I tried to destroy. Nope. Not happening. No fucking way.

Sushant:

If you're not coming over, I am

I hesitate, then text back, I don't think our folks would be ok with us meeting this late. Talk tomorrow?

Sushant:

Our windows are only a few feet apart.
Climb in

A laugh escapes my mouth, loud enough to carry over the wind. He laughs right back—although his is more sarcastic—and waits, arms still folded. He looks pissed. Rightfully so.

Licking my lips, I look back at my closed door. Appa's most definitely already asleep, and Dad seemed to have only been waiting up for me. There's no way they'd come to my room to check on me.

So I whoosh air out of my mouth and climb out to the tree that stands between our windows. I don't look down even once. It's not that high up, but it's still a fucking tree. If I fall, I'll break a bone, but more than that, I'll wake my parents. And that's a scarier thought.

Sushant helps me into his room, grabbing my hands and stepping away as soon as I'm on my feet, pausing only to close the window. I guess I deserve this. My phone buzzes in my pocket, but I ignore it.

Sushant sits down in his revolving desk chair while I continue to stand by the window. Then he crosses one leg over the other. "Explain, Meera."

And so I do.

Lucy

The tears I shed over Meera's message in the sand have dried on my cheeks, leaving nothing but mascara stains in their wake. I touch up my makeup with what's in my compact and then ring the bell to the side of the Rao-Georges' front door.

I have never been good at confrontation. It's not easy to be good at it when the front you show the world is a façade and nothing more. But I can't stop thinking about our kiss. I can't stop clutching the sides of Meera's flannel shirt in my hands, and I can't ignore the fact that I know what her lips taste like, what they feel like pressed against mine.

Sushant and I are done, and there's no way to undo that. I thought Meera and I were over for good by my doing, but she's wormed her way back into my life—into my heart—and I can't let this be the end of us, not even if she won't answer my calls. Because I think she might love me like I love—

"Lucy?" Mr. Rao opens the door, stifling a yawn with one hand and scratching the base of his neck with the other. He wears a faded pajama set, his eyes bleary. "What are you doing here so late?"

I fumble with the sleeves of Meera's shirt. "I need to return Meera's shirt. And also, I need to talk to her."

Mr. Rao steps back to let me in, a curious expression on his face as I take off my flip-flops at the door. "Have you been crying, putta? Is everything okay?"

Forcing myself to smile, I nod. "Yes. Can I go up to Meera's room? She asked me to come over." The lie falls out of my mouth before I can stop it. Hopefully, he'll buy it.

He holds up a hand and climbs the stairs barefoot, pausing outside her door. "Well," he says once he comes back down, "her lights are still on. She's definitely awake. Go ahead."

The hammering of my heart mimics the knock that sounds on Meera's door. There's no response, but I can't turn back now. Slowly, I try the knob. The door swings open, and I walk inside and shut it behind me. "Meera, I—"

Wait. The room is empty. The comforter has fallen off one side of the bed, the sheets are wrinkly, and cool air blows through the open window. In the distance, I can hear two people arguing in soft voices. And I'd recognize those voices anywhere, though I can't make out the words.

I step closer to the window, careful not to be spotted by Meera and Sushant. They're both standing near his desk. Sushant's head is hung, his gaze averted, while Meera is making a pleading gesture with her hands. She's crying.

What is going on? I move back, confused. Why is Meera in Sushant's bedroom this late at night? Did he want to talk to her about our kiss? Is she asking for his forgiveness?

I shouldn't be here. I should not be spying on the girl I'm in love with and the boy who has always loved me. I take off the flannel shirt, fold it, and set it on the foot of the bed, then walk over to the door. Just as I'm about to leave, I take one final look at Meera's room. I haven't been here in nearly two years. It still looks the same: barely-there lighting, midnight-blue walls, her tarot and crystal collections on the light-brown desk, the whiteboard full of Bollywood quotes—

Except there isn't a single movie quote on it this time. I clap a hand over my mouth and walk over to the whiteboard, which has the words *THE PLAN: DATE SUSHANT & DETHRONE LUCY* at the very top. Below is a bullet-point list that says *Step 1:*

Keep your enemies closer—book club, Step 2: Inner circle—get invited to parties, Step 3: Become Sushant's confidante, and finally—

My breath stalls in my throat. Tears burn my eyes for the fourth time tonight. Because the final item on the list is *Step 4: Break them up.*

No, no, no, this can't be happening. This—this is—I can't—

I shake my head and bolt down the stairs. Mr. Rao hastens from the kitchen when he hears me, a glass of turmeric milk in his hand. "Lucy?"

"Good night, Mr. Rao," I yelp as I put my flip-flops back on and run into the street. Mr. Rao calls out my name in a hushed whisper, but I don't stop until I'm at my house.

I lean against the front door and cradle my head in my hands, trying to breathe. *Inhale* . . . Meera was only nice to me so she could dethrone me and date my boyfriend . . . *Exhale. Inhale* . . . She kissed me so Sushant would see us and break up with me for good . . . *Exhale. Inhale* . . . She doesn't love me, and this was all just for show . . .

At the final exhale, I wipe my eyes and go upstairs to my room, to thc comfort of my bed. I put my head between my knees, breathing in and out for ten counts before sitting back upright and jutting my chin out.

Meera may have succeeded in breaking up my relationship, and she may have gotten under my skin and broken down my defenses for the second time.

But she will not get to break *me* down. I'm Lucy fucking Hughson for a reason.

She will never hurt me again.

CHAPTER TWENTY-THREE

"Someone You Hate"
by Sasha Alex Sloan

Meera

Telling Sushant the truth is not an option. How can I, someone he considers a close friend, admit my past feelings for him and also say in that same breath that I tried to tear him and his now ex-girlfriend apart?

And clearly, I succeeded at it, despite having given that part of the Plan up. Because if I hadn't kissed Lucy, they would have gotten back together eventually. They'd have figured out what to do about New York. They'd have ended up together, even if it were long-distance.

So I pad the truth with even more truths that I wish were lies—that I never found closure after my friendship with Lucy ended; that maybe there were always feelings there; that I didn't mean to hurt him, ever; that kissing his girlfriend was a mistake. That I hope he'll forgive me.

When I'm done talking and crying, I sit down on his bed with a thud and a gulp, pressing a pillow to my chest. It smells like him, notes of cinnamon and spice. All I can think about, though, is how different Lucy's perfume is—fragrant and flowery. How it's a hundred times more intoxicating than the scent of this pillow.

I look up. Sushant hasn't spoken since I started explaining my half-truths. "Can you say something?" I mumble weakly, scratching the side of my ear. "Please?"

"Do you love her?" Sushant asks carefully. His left eye twitches as he rakes a hand through his dark hair.

"I'm not sure." Yet another truth I can't seem to believe. "I don't want to love her, if it's any consolation," I add, tugging on my lower lip. "You two are such a wonderful couple. Lucy was just drunk and sad. And I made the first move. It didn't mean anything to her."

He sits beside me and exhales, rubbing the side of my shoulder. The gesture is warm, affectionate. Why? He should hate me. "If you love her, you love her," he says. "You don't have to pretend for my sake. Besides"—he sighs—"she and I are done."

"No," I hiss. Water pools in my eyes again. The Plan has ruined not just Lucy's life but Sushant's too. I never even thought of that. "Don't break up with her just because of me. You're supposed to go to New York together. You belong with her."

He starts to speak, then shakes his head as a tear slides down his cheek. He doesn't bother wiping it away. "I think you should speak with her tomorrow. It might give you more than just closure."

"Sushant—"

He pushes the window open and gestures for me to leave. "Good night, Meera."

My heart sinks. I'm such a horrible person. In my quest for love, all I've done is break hearts and end relationships. "Good night," I whisper. I climb back in through my window without looking back; then I shut the curtains and change into pajama pants and a T-shirt before turning off the lights and hoping tomorrow never comes.

I get into bed and pull the comforter over me when something falls to the floor, beneath the bed, with a soft plop. I squint in the dark, fumbling for the light switch, and then get down on my knees and look under the bed. There's something there—a shirt?

The flannel shirt wrinkles in my clutch. It's the one I was wearing today, the one I gave to Lucy because she was cold. How did it get here? I stand up and look around. Goose bumps sprout along my arms and neck. There's an ominous air about my small room, some sort of tension that my senses pick up on. Appa might be the psychic in the family, but I have a connection with the divine too.

And then I get a whiff of it—Lucy's perfume. It hangs in the air like a delicate aroma by the door to my bedroom. And directly opposite the door is the wall showcasing my whiteboard.

My vision blurs. Lucy was here. Lucy was in my bedroom. Lucy must have seen the Plan. *Fuck.*

I race toward the whiteboard, grab the eraser, and scrub away every trace of the Plan that, in the end, has ruined me. My hands fumble when I sit on my bed and dial Lucy's number.

She doesn't pick up, although I see a few missed calls from her from before. I don't need to leave a voicemail, because seconds later, my phone chimes with a text.

Lucy:

Hope you got your shirt back.
I left it on your bed

I don't know how to respond to that. Is there a chance she never saw the whiteboard? That she missed it?

And then another text pops up on the screen.

Lucy:

Also? Stay the hell away from me

The phone slips from my hand and falls onto my sheets. Whether she knows the truth or not, she loathes me. Maybe it's because I kissed her and ended her relationship. Maybe it's because she saw the Plan. But it doesn't matter, because I deserve every bit of that loathing.

Lucy

My alarm rings at six the next morning, the same as every day so I can go for my morning jog, but I turn it off and shove my face into the pillow, damp from my tears, cocooning myself in my fluffy white comforter. If I don't get up, I don't have to face the consequences of what happened last night: losing Sushant, losing Meera . . . almost losing myself.

So I fall back asleep, and it's only when someone's soothing hand touches my forehead that I rouse. As I open my eyes, Julien pulls his fingers away and studies me. "Hmm. No fever," he says.

I look from him to Natalie, who is seated at the foot of my bed, concern etched onto both their features. "What—what are you two doing here?" I mumble, rubbing the back of my neck to loosen the stress knots there.

"You disappeared from the party, didn't check your phone all night, and when I called your mom, she said you were *still* sleeping!" Natalie's voice is shrill as she wraps her arms around me. "You never sleep in past nine a.m."

I dazedly return the hug, then stifle a yawn. "What time is it?"

Julien taps on his wristwatch and holds it up. "It's almost noon."

"Ugh." I slump back into the pillow. "Can I get a rain check on having to wake up and face the day?"

Natalie stands up and pouts, her arms crossed against her chest. "What happened last night, Lucy? What's wrong?"

Beside her, Julien coughs and shifts in place. Confused, I turn toward him, and his Adam's apple bobs, a flush creeping down his dark skin. My eyes widen. He's hiding something. I quirk a brow at Julien. "You know, don't you?"

He puts his hands in his pockets and exhales roughly. "It is not my business. But, yes, I spoke to Meera, and she told me what happened."

"Wait." Natalie tugs on his arm, frowning. "What are you two talking about?"

Julien looks to me, and I nod.

I guess it's time to hear Meera's fake, two-faced side of the story. I rest my head on my hand, listening as Julien tells Natalie about the kiss and everything that followed. Apparently, he dropped Meera off at home, and she told him she's had feelings for me all along, presumably to cover up her real intentions. He makes no mention of the Plan on her whiteboard. Of course he doesn't know—Meera wouldn't want him to see her as the bad guy.

Natalie sits down beside my feet with a thump. "You and Sushant broke up? And—and you didn't—"

I put my head in my hands in an attempt to hold back my tears. "I'm sorry I didn't tell you. I just wanted to be left alone."

She shakes her head, squeezing my ankle over the comforter. "That's not what I was going to say. You broke up with him, and you didn't push Meera away when she kissed you. Does that mean you're . . . gay?"

As she waits for me to speak, Julien's gaze flits to mine, his eyes telling me, *You've got this.* I smile softly at him, hold my head up, and say, "Actually, I'm pansexual."

Natalie is silent for a second before she pulls both me and Julien into a half hug. "Oh my God!" she shrieks. "Both my favorite people are pansexual! How cool is this?"

Laughing, I hug her back. "Keep your voice down," I add once they pull away. "Mom doesn't know, and I . . . don't think I'm ready for her to find out."

Natalie tucks a lock of my hair behind my ear and nods. "It's your decision."

"I love you both so much." My face crumples into tears. I might have had the worst night of my life yesterday, but I have the best friends in the world—and that counts for a lot.

"And we love you too," Julien says fondly. "I will give you both some space." He heads downstairs, whistling a song I don't know under his breath.

When his footsteps recede down the stairs, Natalie speaks. "Are you okay, Lucy?"

I sigh. "Not really. I . . . Something else happened last night."

She leans closer to me, holding my hand in hers. "Want to talk about it?"

My voice trembles as I tell her everything: why I ended my friendship with Meera and started dating Sushant, how I finally felt like myself when she kissed me, and the moment I stumbled upon the Plan on her whiteboard.

A stream of tears is trickling down Natalie's face by the time I'm done. She puts a hand to her mouth, her eyes wide. "Oh, Lucy. I'm so sorry. I can't believe this."

Julien walks in through the ajar door, holding three mugs of coffee with just two hands, not a drop spilled. I raise a brow. He'd do pretty well as a barista. "Who wants coffee?" he asks, then does a double take when he sees us both crying. He sets the mugs down on my bedside table and joins us. "Oh là là, what happened?"

Natalie brings up the Plan, and Julien coughs again. That's his tell, isn't it? "I already know of this," he admits, tracing a line along my bedsheet. "Meera told me. I promised her I wouldn't tell anyone."

Well, at least he's proven himself trustworthy. He's kept so many secrets in the few short months he's been in Madre Maria. I shake my head. "I need a break from Meera, from this town, from . . . everything."

Julien hands me a coffee mug. "Drink. You need it."

I take a sip. It's delicious—gingery, milky, frothy, just the way I like it. Julien really is great at everything, huh? "I think I'm going to go visit my dad in LA until spring break ends," I say slowly. "Maybe UCLA is the right school for me after all."

"We can meet each other every weekend if you go there!" Natalie squeals. Then she hands Julien a mug, grabs her own, and holds it up. "A toast: To never letting go of us. No matter what."

"Cheers," we all say, touching our mugs to one another's. And for the first time since that kiss, I smile.

CHAPTER TWENTY-FOUR

"Need Your Love"

by Gryffin and Seven Lions feat. Noah Kahan

Lucy

Dad's LA house is huge—four bedrooms, five bathrooms, warm wooden flooring, a backyard that leads directly to the beach—and it's hard for me not to feel a twinge of resentment. Sure, Mom got our house in the divorce—plus custody of me—but Dad made a whole new life here that's a hundred times more full than what he had with us. And now he has Grandpa's money.

If Dad hadn't complied with Mom's requests, if he'd only tried to fight for me, this could have been my life too.

I shake that thought away as the backyard door opens and Jade sits down across from me on the second lounge chair. After breakfast, they changed out of their pajamas and into a crisp white dress shirt and cutoff jeans, and their short salt-and-pepper hair is slicked back with some gel. They hand me a cup of coffee with a smile that I return. We haven't talked much since I drove here last night, but the only other queer people I know are Meera's parents, Dad, and Julien, so I'm eager to broaden that circle.

"How's spring break going so far?" they ask.

I sip my coffee—warm and creamy, but nothing like the iced ginger turmeric chai latte from Café Kismat—and wonder how to answer that question. *Honesty works,* I tell myself. "It's been crap."

Jade nearly spits out their sip of coffee. "And here I thought spring break was all about parties and hooking up." They pause. "Don't tell your father I said that."

I hold back a chuckle and rest my head against the back of the lounge chair. "Well, my boyfriend and I decided to break up. Or, rather, he decided to break up with me because I broke his heart."

A crinkle appears between their brows. "I'm not quite sure I understand, Lucy."

I hesitate, then speak. "I haven't told Dad this yet, but I . . . I fell in love with a girl." It's surprising how easily the words slip out. I guess confiding in virtual strangers is less intimidating than admitting the truth to people who've known me forever.

Jade's lips broaden in a grin. "Tell me about her."

As much as I hate myself for it, my heart somersaults in my chest when I tell Jade all about Meera. Her dusky beauty, her all-black wardrobe, her snarky comments, her "bitch, fight me" attitude . . . and her unrelenting, loyal friendship. Until now, that is. I pause midway and exhale. "But she doesn't feel that way about me. She just used me to get to Sushant."

"I'm so sorry, Lucy." They reach out and squeeze my knee with a warm hand, their forehead wrinkled. The gesture is so protective, so gentle, that my eyes dampen.

"It's fine." I push my chin out. "I'm done with her, and Madre Maria, and my old life. Maybe NYU isn't where I'm meant to be yet, but I'll make LA my new home until I can find my way to New York."

Jade shoots up from their chair, gasping. "So you're going to UCLA?"

I nod. "I think I am."

"Oh, your father is going to be so thrilled! Ken!" Jade runs back inside the house, calling for my dad.

Dad whoops and screams excitedly when we share the news with him, and he twirls me around for a few seconds before putting me down. He's old; his back probably wore him out, and the last time he lifted me up was eight years ago. "I'm taking the next two days off from work," he decides. "Let's see if we can arrange a tour of the UCLA campus. Oh, and we should go to Disneyland! I used to take you to Disneyland all the time when you were younger, remember?"

And then you walked out on Mom and me forever, a voice in my head whispers. But I force myself to smile. "I remember. That sounds nice, Dad."

"Lucy, your birthday's coming up next month," Jade says, putting one arm each around me and Dad, leading us back outside to the lounge chairs. "What do you want as a present?"

"Hmm." I gaze up at Dad's eager face and whoosh out a breath. "How about a Pride flag for me to hang up in my dorm at UCLA?"

Dad stiffens in place. He looks from me to Jade, then mumbles, "You're queer?"

"Pansexual," I say proudly.

He grins before his eyes darken. "Does your mother know?"

My face falls. "No. As much as she loves me, I don't think she'd be happy about this."

Sighing, Dad puts his hands in his pockets. "You don't owe anybody any information about who you are and who you love. If you ever do get around to telling Alice, it's on her to make her peace with it."

"I know." I sit down and grab my now-cold cup of coffee from the small wicker table. "So, Disneyland. Will you ride the roller coasters with me, or . . . ?"

"No." Dad visibly shivers as Jade laughs aloud. "I'm not as brave as you, Lucy."

I roll my eyes. "I'm not brave—"

"You are, kiddo." He smiles, a tear falling down his cheek. "Thanks for giving me another chance."

My lip quivers. "You're welcome, Dad."

Meera

It's barely nine a.m., and I've been pacing in front of Lucy's front yard for the past half hour, wondering if I still have the right to knock on her door and apologize. I spent all of yesterday shut in my room, blasting the "MRG" playlist through my earphones and pretending I didn't screw up the lives of my ex-crush and, well, my now crush. Or has Lucy been my forever crush?

"All right, Meera. You've got this." I shake out my body, roll my head, and walk up to the doorstep. My hand is an inch away from the door when it swings open. Lucy's mom blinks at me in confusion. She's dressed in a floral dress, a purse hanging from one wrist. She puts her hand on the edge of the door as though she doesn't want me to come in, then smiles tightly. "Meera. What a pleasant surprise."

Her tone makes it clear it's absolutely *not* a pleasant surprise. She's never liked me; my being Brown and the daughter of two gay men probably doesn't sit well with her so-called moral values. When Lucy and I were friends, we never hung out at her place. Ms. Miller was always shut in her office, coaching clients who looked and acted and thought just like her. It wasn't a safe space for me to be around that energy, and Lucy knew it.

My stomach flutters at the thought. Her betrayal notwithstanding, Lucy was always a good friend. Sometimes I wonder if she ever hated me until now—after all, she looked after me when I got too drunk at Seth's party, and she accepted my help when her dad showed up.

"Meera?" Ms. Miller snaps her fingers to get my attention, still fake smiling. "I asked, to what do I owe the pleasure?"

I suppress the urge to roll my eyes at her pretend niceness. "Um, I wanted to see Lucy."

Ms. Miller frowns. "Lucy's not here." When she doesn't

elaborate, I raise my eyebrow, waiting, and she adds, sighing, "She's visiting her father in LA for spring break."

"Oh." I take a step back. A cool wind blows, goose bumps sprouting up my arms. I rub along my skin and sigh. "Well, thanks anyway, Ms. Miller."

I make room for Ms. Miller to lock the door behind her; then she nods at me and walks away, her high heels clip-clopping their way to her car. She looks back once, probably to check if I'm still loitering around, so I head home.

Dad and Appa are both sitting at the dining table, midway through a breakfast of poha and curd, when I step in and take off my sneakers. "Where did you run off to so early in the morning?" Appa asks. He's got a drop of curd hanging from his mustache. I'd laugh and point it out if I weren't so miserable.

I put my hands on my knees and take a few deep breaths, trying to calm my racing heart as their curious eyes regard me.

"Meera?" Dad sets his spoon down and turns his chair to face me. "Are you all right?"

I shake my head, surfacing again. "No. I—I need to tell you both something."

My parents stand up in unison, worry sprinkled across their faces. Dad opens his mouth, then closes it. He gulps.

"I'm not pregnant," I quickly say.

Dad lifts a hand to his chest. "Oh, thank God. But if you were, we'd still love you and help in any way we could with the—"

"I'm bi."

Dad pauses midsentence. "Oh."

"And . . . and I think I'm falling for a girl."

Appa tilts his head, a smile on his face. "It's Lucy, isn't it?" he asks.

"That obvious, huh?" I laugh, pressing a hand to the back of my head. "Yeah. It's Lucy. I guess I never loved Sushant after all. Just . . . the idea of what we could be."

Dad grumbles something under his breath, then pulls out his wallet and hands Appa twenty dollars. "Fine. You and your stupid psychic abilities win. Again."

Appa pockets the twenty-dollar bill and grins. "Told you."

"Wait, wait, wait." I gasp. "Did you make a bet on my identity?"

"No, of course not." Dad quirks a brow. "It was pretty obvious to us that you were bisexual. The bet was Team Sushant"—he jabs a thumb to his chest—"versus Team Lucy." He smacks Appa on the head playfully.

"Ouch!" Appa laughs, then pokes Dad in the ribs with a finger. They exchange a look that's full of familiar love and fondness. My heart clenches. I wish I had that too. I wish I could have found my forever person during senior year, just like they did.

But if it isn't what the Universe wants for me, then I'll have to come to terms with it.

Somehow.

"Wait, so you knew?" I ask Appa, wide-eyed. "This whole time, you knew I loved Lucy and not Sushant? You knew even before I did?"

He comes over and wraps me in a soft embrace. "I always

had a feeling. I just didn't know if it was intuition or"—he cracks a smile—"hope."

Dad joins us to bear-hug me from the other side. "Lucy's a wonderful girl. We're so happy for you—"

"Don't be." I gently push them away and blink back my tears. "I didn't tell you this earlier, but I went ahead with my Plan, and she found out about it. She hates me."

"Ah, well . . ." Dad quiets, biting his lip. I'm so sure he's holding himself back from saying *I told you so.*

Appa shrugs and musses up my hair, and I let him. "Then, putta, you need to remind her of what you once had. What you can have again someday, if she forgives you."

"That's not going to be easy, but"—I slump down at the dining table, my head in my hands—"I guess it wouldn't hurt to try."

"You hungry?" Appa asks. When I nod, he rubs his bald spot. "I'll make you a plate of poha. Sit tight."

Dad bends to kiss my forehead. "We believe in you, okay? You'll figure this out."

"Thanks, Dad," I mumble. But I'm not so sure he's right.

CHAPTER TWENTY-FIVE

"Nobody Compares To You"

by Gryffin feat. Katie Pearlman

Lucy

I'm in no mood to return to Madre Maria after spring break. Disneyland was wonderful. I hadn't been in years, afraid of revisiting old places and memories, but with Dad and Jade, it was like I was a little kid again. We took selfies and ate cotton candy and corn dogs; Jade and I waved and booed at Dad from roller coasters he refused to join us on, and I felt at home with him after so many years. I'm glad I decided to give him another chance.

Touring UCLA was even better. The library is huge, they have a thriving book club, and the campus is beautiful. I can't wait to experience college life.

As for going back to high school? The only thing I'm looking forward to is telling Natalie and Julien about spring break at my dad's.

What I dread is people knowing Sushant and I broke up—or, worse still, the reason we broke up. I trust Sushant not to say anything. He would never out me publicly; he loved me so much that any resentment he feels toward me will remain in his heart and not linger on his tongue.

But I don't trust Meera. After all, her plan did say she wanted to "dethrone" me. Wouldn't that include painting me as the villain for cheating on Sushant?

"You didn't cheat," Natalie's voice echoes in my AirPods as I drive to school. "Sushant asked for a break from you, remember?"

"Technicality," I mumble, stopping at a traffic light. "Julien, what do you think?"

Natalie's put the call on speaker so Julien can chime in while he drives them in his rental car. "I do not know," he says, coughing softly. "But we'll get through today together."

I exhale. He coughed, which means he's lying. He does think I cheated. I don't blame him—my anger toward Meera in no way compares to my guilt and disappointment in myself. I broke the heart of the best guy in the world. I don't deserve his forgiveness.

When I park my Honda in my usual spot and get out, Natalie and Julien are already waiting for me. They envelop me in a group hug, and we walk into school together. Heads turn and hushed whispers follow in my wake, but when we get to my locker, no insults are spray-painted on it, nor does anyone say anything to me.

I see the football team standing by Sushant's locker with him. With his head down, shoulders slumped, and dark circles around his eyes, he seems . . . miserable. Not to mention that it looks like he hasn't shaved in days. Some of his friends notice me and whisper to him. He turns to smile weakly at me, then walks away, a textbook tucked under his arm.

People around us notice the interaction, and the whispers start again. "See?" Natalie says. "Now everyone can see you're on good terms."

"I guess," I say. My eyes fall on the glittery huge blue-and-gold *Senior Prom!* banner hanging from the ceiling, and my stomach coils. "Sushant never got to ask me to prom. He said he'd planned a whole promposal and everything."

Julien clears his throat. "Everyone deserves a promposal."

Natalie squeezes my hand. "I'm sorry, Lucy."

I grab some books and shut my locker. "Shall we head to class?"

"Um . . ." Julien shuffles in place, tugging on his collar. "Natalie, don't you want to check your locker?"

She holds up her handbag that hangs from her left wrist. "I've got what I need here."

"Buuuuut," he says, stretching out the word, "I have a feeling we should check your locker anyway."

"Julien, it's getting late—"

My eyes fall on his bobbing throat and his crossed fingers. Has he planned something? "He's right, Natalie," I say. "We should stop by your locker."

The look on Julien's face is immediate relief and gratitude. "Oui! Let's go."

"What—"

We all but drag Natalie farther down the hallway. A small crowd has already gathered around her locker. When we push through and stop just short of it, she gasps, her hands flying to her face.

A heart-shaped red piece of paper with the letters **J + N** is taped to her locker. She turns to Julien, her eyes misty. "Did . . . Did you . . . ?"

"Open your locker, Natalie," he says, smiling, his hands in the pockets of his well-cut black trousers.

She does as he says with trembling fingers, and over a dozen multicolored Post-it notes fall down at her feet. We bend to gather them, and she reads some of the messages on them out loud. They range from **Natalie is so pretty** and **I could look at her forever** to **She is everything** and **I think I am falling for her**. Tears are streaming down Natalie's face as she scans note after note.

"I wrote one every week since we first met," Julien admits. "But I have one final note for you." He pulls a piece of pink paper from his pocket, unfolds it, and holds it up for everyone to see. **Prom?** "I love you, Natalie. Will you go to prom with me?"

Natalie howls with joy, "Yes! I love you too!" She drops the notes, wraps her arms around him, and kisses him. Students in the hallway cheer and clap, but I'm the loudest of them all, because nobody deserves true love more than Natalie and Julien. Not even me.

Just as I have that thought, Meera pokes her head out from the back of the crowd and waves at me. "Lucy! Can we talk?"

Natalie pulls away at the sound of Meera's voice, her lips in a snarl. "Let's get out of here." She takes Julien's hand and mine, and we walk to class. I look back once to see Meera still standing there, mouthing, "Please?" at me. I hold my head up and turn, eager to put distance between us.

Meera

This sucks. School is almost done for the day, and all Lucy has done is ignore me, with Natalie acting like a defensive, furious, scowling bodyguard. Julien was by their side the whole time, and although I was hoping he'd side with me after our conversation in his car, he's clearly Team Natalie after that promposal, which means he's Team Lucy by default.

So I need to plan ahead. Ten minutes before the dismissal bell rings, I tell my Calculus teacher, Mr. Saxe, that I have agonizing period cramps and need to grab my pain medicine before I collapse.

His face pales, and he swallows as his eyes dart to the wall clock. Old male teachers never know what to say when the topic of reproductive health comes up. "Grab your things and go," he says, waving me away with his hand, then mumbles, "Uh, take care."

I sling my backpack over my shoulder and race for the door, one hand still clamped around my stomach like the pain is unbearable. I pass by my locker and head through the front doors, toward the parking lot. Lucy won't have cheer practice now that the final game of the year has ended. If I just wait for her by her car, there's no way she can avoid me.

I stand under the shadows of the trees, tapping my shoe restlessly until the buzzing chatter of students fills the parking lot. Five minutes in, there's no sign of her. *Ugh.* Should I just leave? No—I can be patient. I'm patient. I'm as patient as anyone could ever be. Right?

Finally, when most cars have driven away, she walks into my line of sight, and I run ahead to intercept her.

She puts a hand to her chest in alarm when she spots me, but her expression quickly fades to anger. "Go away!" she exclaims, heading for her car.

"Lucy, please wait!" I tug on her arm, letting go within seconds when I feel that burst of electricity between our skin.

Lucy blinks and steps away, putting some distance between us, though she's at least facing me. She rubs the side of her elbow where my fingers were seconds ago, as if the ghost of my touch still remains, and raises her gaze to mine. "What more do you want from me, Meera?" Her voice is hardened, defeated. "Haven't you taken enough from me already?"

I look around us at the almost-empty parking lot and lower my voice. "I know you were in my room that night."

"What night?" She blinks in mock confusion. "The night you kissed me in front of my boyfriend so you could check off the fourth bullet point on your master Plan?"

Words fail me. I was right; she saw everything. She knows everything. "Lucy, I—I can explain."

"Explain what?" She grips the hem of her dress with a fist

and takes another step back. “How you waltzed right back into my life when I clearly did not want you in it in the first place, and then played me like a fool just to get your revenge?”

“It might have started out like that, but I promise you, I didn’t kiss you to—”

“I shouldn’t be talking to you.” Lucy shakes her head and wipes the side of her eye. “I have to go. Let me go.”

“Please let me explain,” I beg as she turns to leave for her car. “Just give me a minute of your time.”

Lucy stops in her tracks. Her chest heaves, and then she walks back up to me. “I hated how our friendship ended, and now that you’ve proven what kind of person you are, I shouldn’t have any regrets. But it breaks my heart that I still—”

“The kind of person *I* am?” My voice is shrill. “Did you forget that all this happened because being popular mattered to you more than our friendship? Because *you’re* the one who replaced me with Natalie and then started dating the boy I thought I had loved since forever!”

She pauses, her sleek fingers on her car’s door handle, her head bowing in defeat. “I did that so you’d never talk to me again. I didn’t have a choice.”

“What are you saying?” I run a hand through my long hair, frizzy from the humidity. “Why would you want that?”

“I’m . . . I’m pansexual, Meera.” Her voice cracks. “And I didn’t want to have feelings for you then any more than I want to now.”

She’s pansexual. I gasp, my heart somersaulting in my

chest as the second part of her sentence hits me. "You . . . you had feelings for me?"

She gives an offhanded shrug, but her gaze is narrowed. "I guess nothing's changed, has it? Because I know if I spend even a minute longer in your presence, I'll . . ." She exhales, her eyes closing. "I'll fall in love with you. Again."

I suck in a breath at her words. She—did she just say she loves me? In spite of all this? I smile and start toward her, to touch her, to hold her, to tell her I love her too, but then she speaks, and my world comes crashing down.

"And you'll break my heart. Again." Lucy chuckles sadly. "But this time, Meera, you'll do it on purpose. Because that's just the kind of person you are." With that, she unlocks her car, slides behind the wheel, and drives off, leaving me in the parking lot, my jaw slack and my heart thudding painfully in my chest.

There's nothing left for me to do but go home. I don't dare stop by the café, because I can't face my parents in this state. One look at me, and Appa will know everything. I'm not ready for Dad to tell me I should have seen this coming or for Appa to remind me that I was my own undoing—just as he'd predicted.

I walk home in the sharp sunlight that stings the back of my neck, drenching my black T-shirt in sweat. When I unlock the front door, Raj runs over to me, wagging his tail and jumping high enough to lick my face. I smile ruefully at him and head upstairs. I'd usually crumple into bed and sleep my pain away, but instead, I head to my desk.

Appa gifted me my own tarot and oracle decks during sophomore year of high school. I've only pulled cards for myself twice over the years—the first time was when I got the decks, to see what the future held for me and Sushant; the second time was when Lucy ended our friendship, to figure out why she could have done it. Both readings had the same message for me: Have trust in your Angels, because everything is unfolding in your favor.

In short, the readings were useless.

This will be the third time I read my own fortune.

I open Spotify and play the tarot reading music I found years ago that claims to strengthen your psychic abilities. Then I light a peppermint-and-rosemary-scented candle, arrange my favorite crystals like a frame around the decks, and, finally, start to pray like Appa taught me to.

"God, Angels, Universe," I breathe, tears pricking my eyes, "help me understand where you're leading me. Help me undo my mistakes. Help me change Lucy's mind. I am willing to do the work, and I am ready for your guidance. Please, and thank you."

My hands shuffle the tarot deck back and forth until three cards fall out on their own. I turn them around. Ten of Swords. Judgment. Ace of Cups.

A teardrop falls on the Judgment card. The messages staring back at me are clear as day: Something is ending, causing me suffering and pain, and yet something transformational and healing is on its way. The way through is weighing the situation at hand, repenting for what I've done, and choosing forgiveness.

But I'm not the one who has to choose forgiveness—Lucy is.

I shuffle the oracle cards next, whispering to myself while I do, "Spirit, what can I do to make Lucy forgive me faster?"

A card falls out of the pile within seconds. I flip it over and grit my teeth. It's the same oracle card that came up when I did the second reading, about my friendship ending. Archangel Michael smiles up at me, his wings unfurled, a sapphire-hilted sword in his hands. The message on the card reads *Trusting the Divine: You are loved. Your Angels will keep you safe. Surrender and allow a shift in divine timing.*

I throw down my hands and scatter all the cards on my desk as my cheeks burn with salt water. "Fuck you, Archangel Michael!" I yell, pushing my chair back and grabbing fistfuls of my hair. "Fuck you, Spirit! And fuck you, Universe!"

My door bursts open, and I jump. Dad stands before me, one hand on the knob, his eyes wide and mouth agape. "Meera? What happened?"

I shoot up from the chair and fall to his side, sobbing. Dad doesn't hesitate. He lifts me up in his arms and kisses the top of my head, murmuring that he loves me, that he's here for me, that we can figure it out.

Empty words. Because how can I figure this out when nothing is in my control? How can I undo the pain I caused Lucy? She said she loved me once—when? Was that all in the past?

Even the Universe has no clear answer for me except to

have trust. But where has trust gotten me? What have I gained from this Plan? Popularity? Confidence? How does that matter when I've lost not just Sushant and Lucy but also Ron and Valeria?

"I . . ." I pull away from Dad's grasp and wipe my snotty nose with the back of my hand. "I need to apologize to Valeria and Ron. For once, I need to do the right thing and be a good person, a good friend."

Dad bends down so he's eye level with me. Putting his hands on my shoulders, he says, "You *are* a good person. Go get 'em, kiddo."

I smile at him through my tears. "I will."

CHAPTER TWENTY-SIX

"How You Get the Girl (Taylor's Version)"
by Taylor Swift

Lucy

Mom's taking a lasagna out of the oven when I slam the front door behind me and storm into the kitchen. My stomach is growling, which makes Mom laugh. "Someone's hungry," she muses. She serves herself some lasagna, but when she goes to grab a plate for me, I stop her. Meera's pleading words ring in my ears over and over, making my head spin and my mouth dry.

"I don't feel so good," I tell Mom, avoiding her gaze. "Save some for me for later?"

Mom studies me, an eyebrow raised, and points to my stomach. "Honey, you're obviously starving. Is everything okay?"

I force myself to nod. "Yeah. I'm just not in the mood for lasagna."

"You're not skipping meals for prom, right?" She tsk-tsks, grabbing a fork. "Maybe your friend Natalie likes her outrageous diets, but there won't be any of that under my roof."

"I'll eat later. Promise."

"Speaking of prom, is Sushant coordinating his outfit with yours? My senior prom date matched his bow tie to my silver dress." Mom fluffs up her red hair. "I was prom queen. Should have married him instead of your father," she then adds, sighing.

"A silver dress sounds nice." I stand across from her and knead my knuckles with my thumb. "But, um, I'll be going to prom solo. Sushant and I broke up."

Her fork falls onto the plate with a clatter, her wide eyes trained on me, and then she races forward to hug me. "Lucy, I'm so sorry. How did this happen? When? Why?"

"Mom—"

She cups my face with her hands. "Did he break your heart? Should I reprimand him or call his mother?"

A laugh nearly escapes my lips. "Mom, we just weren't sure about the long-distance thing," I lie. "There are no hard feelings between us, I promise."

Mom shakes her head, stepping away to put her hands on her hips. The lasagna's getting cold, but she doesn't seem to care. "Do you want to skip prom and do a girls' night instead? I could try to finish my client calls early, or reschedule them, or—"

I hold up a finger to shush her. "I'm up for prom queen, so I can't skip it. It'll be fine. I'll just go with Julien and Natalie as friends."

"But it's your senior prom! You shouldn't have to go alone." She frowns. "What about that boy, Billy, from church? I've seen him look at you a few times during service."

"Mom. Hey." I sling an arm around her shoulder. "Focus on your meal and your clients. I'll . . . I'll be fine."

Mom returns the hug and air-kisses my forehead, probably to safeguard her red "girlboss" lipstick since she has another call in a few minutes. "You're a strong girl, Lucy, and you'll find a more suitable young man for yourself soon enough. Who knows, maybe he'll even be Christian."

"Yeah," I say. "I'll find someone else soon enough. I'll be prom queen after all."

"That's my girl." Mom smiles at me, then puts her plate in the sink and returns to her office, her hot-pink heels loud against the tiled floor.

I dump my purse on the kitchen counter and head upstairs to my room, shoulders hunched. My eyes fall on my bookcase. Jade bought me a new Austen-inspired fantasy novel from a romance-only bookstore near their house. Apparently, they found out about my obsession through my hundred #bookstagram posts.

But reading to distract myself isn't the right move. I need to process everything or I'll explode. I put on my headphones and open Spotify. Sushant hasn't removed me from our shared account yet or changed the password. He's so wonderful.

And I'm despicable.

I play the "MRG" playlist on loop, thinking back to my long-gone friendship with Meera and my everlasting, unrequited feelings. Tears drench my pillow as I let myself grieve the end of something I never quite got over.

I hope someday I will.

Meera

Mrs. Perez doesn't think twice about inviting me in, her eyes bright. "I haven't seen you in so long!" she gushes, pinching my cheek. "You look . . . pretty, mija."

She's obviously being nice—I cried the whole way here, and my nose is probably still red and snotty. But I smile weakly at her and walk inside, looking around for Ron and Valeria. Thank goodness for the Find My Friends feature, which told me they were both at Valeria's.

In the distance, the TV plays a song from a Bollywood movie I've watched with them at least five times. They're still watching my favorite movies without me. Maybe they do miss me. The thought almost makes me smile. I duck my head into the living room and clear my throat. "Hey."

Ron jumps, spilling popcorn all over the couch. Valeria lets out a choked gasp and turns to me. "Meera, what are you—"

"I'm so sorry for being a shitty friend," I say, holding back a sob. I don't have more tears left in me. "Can—can you both forgive me?"

Val's eyes widen while Ron frowns and hits pause on the remote. "You completely forgot about us, Meera," Valeria says, folding her arms as she stands. "Even though we were there for you this *entire* time."

"Do you really think 'sorry' will cut it?" Ron shakes his head as he also gets up from the couch.

"It won't, and I know it." I bite the inside of my cheek. "I was so focused on the Plan and my obsession with Lucy that I ended up doing exactly what Appa warned me about. I lost both of you. And now"—my voice breaks—"I've lost the love of my life too."

Ron shuffles in place, giving Valeria a look. She nods, and slowly, they come over to me and put their arms around me. I hug them back, resting my head on Valeria's shoulder. "I'm so sorry," I whisper. "I'll never do that again."

Ron pulls away first. "That was all we wanted to hear, Meera. That you accepted your mistakes and were genuinely sorry." He smiles. "Want to join us for movie night? Val insisted on watching that corny movie I hate. And, hey, it might help take your mind off whatever happened with Sushant."

"Yeah," Val chimes in. "I'm sorry that he doesn't feel the same way."

I hold back a grimace. Right. They don't know that *he's* not the love of my life anymore. So much has happened in my life since the Holi party that they missed out on, and I'm sure they've been up to a lot of things during this time too, all without me. I can't wait to catch up on their lives with them.

But first . . .

"You both need to know something," I say. "This may come as a shock to you."

Valeria squeezes my hand. "What is it?"

"Um." I swallow hard. "It's about Lucy." Ron is about to roll his eyes, so I quickly add, "I think I'm in love with her?"

They look at each other, then at me. "Oh," Ron says after a moment. He scratches his jaw. "That . . . actually makes complete sense."

Valeria gasps. "Wait, everyone at school is talking about Lucy and Sushant's breakup. Does that mean she left him for you?"

I sit down on the couch and draw my knees up to my chest. "Not exactly." When I'm done narrating the story to them, Ron lets out a groan and Valeria puts her head in her hands.

"Meera," Val says, voice muffled, "what the hell did you get yourself into?"

"I don't know what to do," I whisper, looking from Ron to her. "I love her, and I know she loves me too. I just . . . I think I've blown it."

"Of course you have," Ron scoffs, and joins me on the couch. "You need a new Plan."

"No." Valeria glares at Ron, then leans over the couch and puts her hands on my shoulders. "You need to apologize and tell her you love her. No more gimmicks. Please."

"Can you help me?" I ask in a trembling voice. "I have an idea in mind. It's sort of a big gesture, but . . . she won't even talk to me."

Ron leans his head back against his arms, thinking. "I'd suggest asking Sushant for help getting through to Lucy, but"—he laughs dryly—"he's the last person who'd want you and her together."

"Actually, that's not a bad idea." I stand up and dust cheese powder from the scattered popcorn off my clothes. "And I know exactly where he'll be."

Valeria raises an eyebrow at me; then she and Ron share another look.

"I promise I'm not bailing on you again. I just need to make this right," I say, biting my lip as they pause, considering it.

After a moment, Ron smiles and Valeria stands, putting her hand on my shoulder. "Go," she says. "We're here if you need us."

I borrow Valeria's bicycle and get to Gianni's Pizza. Sushant sits outdoors underneath a large red umbrella, stuffing a whole slice of deep-dish pizza into his mouth. His eyes are vacant, his gaze on the empty chair across from him, and there's tomato sauce on his scruffy beard. Has he shaved at all since I last saw him?

"Hey," I say, parking the bike and walking into his line of sight. "Is this seat taken?"

Sushant exhales, gesturing ahead of him. "Do you see anyone sitting there? Maybe the Ghost of Christmas Past?"

"No." I sit down, grateful for the creaky metal chair that distracts from the stifling air between us. "So, um, how's everything going?"

"How do you think, Meera?" He looks at me, one eyebrow quirked. "The woman I love broke my heart, I have no date to prom, and my parents are mad at me for throwing away my Berkeley scholarship and moving to the East Coast all for a girl who doesn't want a future with me anymore."

I duck my head. "I know everything is my fault, so—"

"And Lucy's." He snorts. "My friends all think I should be angrier at her than I am."

"Did you tell your friends that she and I . . . ?" My voice trails off. Nobody at school looked at me differently today, and though the thought of being out to the whole world isn't scary, I'm not sure I'm ready for everyone to know that *I'm* the reason the It Couple broke up.

"Nah." He sighs. "Just that Lucy and I ended things. It's funny. I feel like I should have seen this coming from a mile away, but how could I have?" He tries to chuckle; it comes out more like a sob. "I thought she was the One for me. Now I realize she always thought that about *you*."

I lift my eyes to his. "Not anymore. She made it clear she hates me."

"Why?" he asks, scratching his scraggly beard, smearing cheese and sauce on it. "She kissed you. And she told me she's never loved anyone like she loves you. How could that change so soon?"

I swallow. I don't have the energy to tell him the truth. Someday, I will. But not today. Instead, I say, "I can't get into that now, but . . . I need your help to win her back."

Sushant doesn't speak. He wipes his hands with a tissue and runs his tongue over his teeth. "I really should hate you both more than I do," he says. "But if you promise you'll make sure Lucy's happy, that you won't break her heart"—he lets out the smallest smile, finally—"then I'll help."

"I promise." I hold my hand out, and we shake on it.

He leans back and studies me. "So, do you have a plan in mind?"

I nod slowly. "What does Lucy love more than anything else in the world?"

"Besides you?" Sushant says, and I roll my eyes.

"Yes, other than me," I say.

He thinks to himself. "Books."

"And Taylor Swift." I ask a passing server for some extra tissues and a pen, then write, *The Plan 2.0: Get the Girl.*

"Two point oh?" He rubs his chin. "Was there a Plan before this?"

I cough. "Um, no. Anyway, here's what I'm thinking . . ." I continue scribbling on the tissues, laying out the Plan while Sushant sits there quietly. "And then I walk out from the tent and—" I look up and pause. "I know you're surprised, but, geez, close your mouth. I can see pizza."

He shuts his mouth, chuckling as he looks over the Plan. "You must really love her," he says. "I already thought of how I'd propose to her after we graduated college, but your Plan takes the cake."

"Propose? You mean asking her to *marry* you?" I exclaim, gripping the edges of the table. *Fuck.* Did I rob Lucy of not just love but also the perfect wedding?

Sushant shrugs. "Like I said, I thought she was it for me. But if I can't do a grand gesture for her anymore, it might as well be you, right?" He smirks. "So don't fuck this up."

I give him a small salute. "Roger that."

CHAPTER TWENTY-SEVEN

"Woke Up in Love"
by Kygo, Gryffin, and Calum Scott

Meera

A part of me has always dreamed of tonight. Not because I wanted to be prom queen or lose my virginity in a hotel room on a bed of roses, but, surprisingly, because I'd hoped it'd be exactly the way all the movies show it: I walk down the staircase in a sexy floor-length black dress and lock eyes with my date—the boy I love. He's waiting patiently for me beside my fathers. When he sees me, he puts a hand to his heart and mouths "Wow," too speechless to say anything else. And I blush, probably for the first and only time in my life.

But tonight, Sushant is neither my date nor the one I love. Nobody is waiting for me at the foot of the staircase besides Dad and Appa. My dress is formfitting and black, but I'm too restless and anxious to look or feel sexy.

I've spent the last two weeks hashing out the Plan with Sushant and my friends and looking out for any risks that might come up. But more challenging than that is finding the right words to tell Lucy how sorry I am, how much I love her, and how desperately I hope she'll let herself love me back. We had to cancel this month's book club after Lucy emailed Dad her resignation letter. It wouldn't be right to do the club without her . . . at least, not until I've shot my shot at forgiveness.

"You look beautiful, putta," Appa says as I walk down from my room, Valeria behind me in her ruffled seafoam-blue dress. A few people asked her to prom, but when she realized I was going solo, she turned them all down. "We'll go as friends with Ron and Brenda," she insisted. I can't believe I ever took a friend like her for granted.

I smile at Appa and Dad, who's wiping his tears from behind his glasses. "Thanks," I mumble. We let them take photographs on their phones until we're sick of posing, and then Dad drives us to the hotel ballroom where prom is happening.

The hotel is one of two fancy five-star places in Madre Maria. A crowd of excited, dressed-up teenagers swarms the entrance. Faint dance music drifts into my ears when we get out of the car and say bye to my dad. Ron and Brenda stand by the front doors, probably waiting for us. He's wearing a tux that looks uncomfortably large on him, his fingers playing with the yellow corsage on Brenda's wrist. He leans down to whisper something in her ear, and she smacks him on the arm, her face pink with laughter.

When they spot us, they wave us over. "It's nice to meet you, Meera." Brenda hugs me, and I return the gesture. We head inside, following the loud beat of remixed pop songs thrumming from one of the event rooms.

The place is packed, the ambiance vibrant and energized,

and a disco ball hanging from the ceiling changes colors every few seconds—neon green, red, orange, blue, silver. But despite the music, the cheers, the flashing lights, and the hundred people dancing around me, I sense Lucy standing with her friends across the room. She's dressed in a sparkly pink ball gown that outshines every single speck of glitter on the disco ball. She cups a hand to her perfect pink mouth, stifling her giggles at one of Julien's witty remarks, then nods at Natalie's comment. Her red hair hangs in a half-up, half-down style, swaying with the movement. *Wow.* She's so . . .

"Earth to Meera." Valeria jabs me in the side with her elbow, and I exhale, biting my lip. "Sorry," I say. "I—"

"So all those times you'd just stare at Lucy with that intense look in your eyes," she says, lowering her voice, "it wasn't because you hated her guts. It was because you couldn't stop admiring her. Damn."

I smile, my lips wide. "She . . . she didn't bring a date, either."

"Come on," Ron calls out to us, "let's grab some punch."

"In a bit," I mumble out of the corner of my mouth, letting them go. I stay there, still watching the girl I love, taking in the silver glint of her heels, the red roses in her corsage, and—

And the tall guy with the swimmer's body who hands her a glass of orange punch, tousling his perfect wavy hair and nudging her shoulder when she thanks him.

Fuck. Seth Simons is Lucy's date to prom?

A popular TikTok song starts playing, and everyone cheers in unison. My eyes zoom in on Seth's hand on Lucy's back as Julien ushers them all to the dance floor. I can't help but notice her perfect smile directed at Seth. His loud, boisterous laughter, audible even from this distance. And the small jerk of her head when she spots me looking, as though she's taken aback and didn't expect me to be here. After all, I've kept my distance since we last spoke. Sushant said it was best if I gave her time to cool off.

She takes me in now, her mouth twitching, her gaze going from my wavy dark hair falling loosely down my shoulders to the long black dress with a slit up to the thigh that Valeria and Ron promised made me look hot. Well, Valeria promised. Ron said it distracted from my resting bitch face, which is better than nothing.

Seth tugs on Lucy's hand, which breaks the staring contest. She turns to him, a polite smile on her face, and doesn't look back at me at all.

Shoulders hunched, I head to the refreshments table, lean against Valeria's shoulder, and groan exaggeratedly. "I hate this."

"Are you okay?" Brenda asks, concern knitting her forehead. "Do you want to sit down?"

"No," I say, massaging the back of my neck, "I want the girl I love to love me back."

When I'm met with silence, I look between the three of them. "What?" I ask, quirking a brow. "I can have two gay dads, but I can't be out and proud myself?"

"You can." Ron grins. "Shit, we've missed you, Meera."

I punch him on the shoulder. "Missed you too."

A romantic pop song plays, the lights dimming, and Brenda

drags Ron onto the dance floor with a giggle. Valeria watches them, a soft smile on her face. "They're good together."

"Are things still awkward between you and Ron?" I ask tentatively.

"Nah. He might have had a crush on me once, but I think he could really love her. Besides"—she laughs—"we've been friends for years at this point. Nothing can change that."

I nod. I wish that were still true in my case. Forget love—even friendship might be off the table for Lucy and me. She loathes me. The back of my neck prickles, and I rub my skin self-consciously. "Is Lucy looking at me?" I whisper. I don't want to check for myself and be proven wrong.

After a beat, Valeria checks for me. "Yep," she confirms. "She looks miserable."

"And whose fault is that?" Plucking a dog hair from my dress, I add, "I don't know if my Plan will work. Sushant thinks it will, but he obviously doesn't know about the original Plan and how much Lucy hates me for it." Even as I say it, I think back to what Appa once said: *Some emotion will always tie you to your twin flame. The only emotion you will never, ever feel for them is indifference.* Love and hate are often two passionate sides of the same coin, right?

Val makes a low growl in the base of her throat. "Meera, I told you to cut the Plan nonsense out and just . . . communicate. How hard is that?"

"It's hard to communicate when Lucy refuses to be in the same room as me," I point out. "And after what she saw on my whiteboard, can you blame her?"

"I really can't," Val agrees. "Come on, let's dance. It'll take your mind off things."

"All right," I mumble. I hold myself back from returning Lucy's gaze, which I suspect is still fixed on me. *I'll find my way to her*, I promise myself. I just have to wait a little longer.

Lucy

I've never been as fond of parties as you'd expect a head cheerleader to be. Maybe it's the introvert in me that prefers to find solace in books and music, not alcohol and dancing. But when you're popular and a pathological people-pleaser, you go with the flow. What other choice do you have?

So I put on a brave face on prom night and dance to five different songs with Seth, Natalie, and Julien. I smile through the pounding of my heart when I hear the loud laughter of Meera's friends from the dance floor. I avoid searching the crowd for Sushant, who has also found a backup date to appease everyone the way I did by bringing Seth. And I try and fail to keep my eyes off Meera in that stunning dress. It's unfair how she manages to look good in anything black—ripped jeans, leather boots, band T-shirts, and evening gowns that curve around her body like every stitch in the fabric was custom-made for her. More than that, it's unfair how many times I've listened to the "MRG" playlist since my talk with her. Why can't I just delete that playlist and be done with her? Why can't I stop loving her? She doesn't deserve my love or forgiveness . . . right?

But they're announcing prom king and queen now, which means all eyes will be on me. I just have to put on the It Girl façade for a little longer. After a few more songs, I'll leave and let go of Madre Maria, both emotionally and mentally. I promise myself I'll never look back.

Hannah, the president of the student committee, ushers everyone to face the stage, holding up an envelope in her hand. "Class of 2026, are y'all ready to find out who our prom king and queen are tonight?"

People cheer, some hooting and screaming names while they clap. Hannah waits for the noise to die down, then opens the envelope and screams into the microphone, "Please welcome to the stage this year's prom king and queen: Sushant Khera and Lucy Hughson!"

Hushed whispers accompany the thundering applause. Two exes winning the crown, mere weeks after their breakup? We'll be the talk of the town before the night is over. But I know everyone saw this coming. It could never have been anyone else walking up to the stage tonight but Sushant and me.

Natalie and Julien nudge me forward, and I lift both my chin and my dress just the slightest to ascend the stairs. Ahead of me, Sushant walks to the stage in his formfitting tux and pink tie that matches my dress perfectly. My heart leaps to my throat; a bead of sweat rolls down my back. His date's dress isn't pink. What does this mean? Does he still love me? Does he still hate me?

I study the wide smile on his face that's clearly meant for everyone else. His beard is mercifully clean-shaven again, which makes him look healthier and more put-together than he has since our breakup. I hope he's doing better.

Vice Principal Montgomery crowns us and places the prom court sashes across our bodies, after which we pose together. People cheer and click photographs. I sense Sushant's gaze on me from the corner of my eye, but I stare straight ahead, fake smiling.

"Well, let's see our king and queen's first dance!" Hannah says, but Sushant stops her and gestures for the microphone. "May I?" he asks.

What's this about? I swallow, my mouth dry.

He taps the mic twice, making sure it's still on, then speaks. "So, uh, this is nice and not at all awkward."

People laugh. Sushant grins and continues. "I didn't expect to be crowned prom king with my *ex*-girlfriend by my side, but, hey, a win is a win." He exhales, his eyes moving over the crowd until he nods at someone in particular. I can't tell who it is. "And for all of you gossip-hungry folks wondering, there's no-body else I'd rather share the stage with."

When he looks over at me, I press my hand to my chest and mouth, "Me too." And I mean it. How was I ever lucky enough to have this boy's love?

He smiles as he adds, "It's funny how sometimes you don't

realize you're a secondary character in someone else's story until you're too close to the ending."

The room is so silent, you could hear a pin drop, until murmured voices grow loud. My heart beats faster in my chest. Is Sushant about to tell people about Meera and me? *No,* I remind myself, *there is no "Meera and me." And he wouldn't do that . . . right?*

Slowly, Sushant takes my hand in his, a pained wince on his face, and people grow quiet again. "I'll find my own story someday. That's not the point. But, Lucy, as we stand together, quite possibly for the last time, promise me you'll let yourself love and be loved by the right person. Promise me you'll give them a chance, even when it seems like the odds are against you or when it feels scary. Because nobody deserves love like you do."

The audience bursts into applause. Sushant must have talked to Meera, probably that night when I saw them in his room. Nonetheless, his words are so pure and unconditionally loving that I choke on a sob. I distinctly hear Julien's and Natalie's cheers before Sushant steps away from the mic, a tear escaping his eye.

"Well, that was something," Vice Principal Montgomery says, laughing, and then we're shooed off onto the dance floor for our king and queen's dance.

"Thank you for that speech," I whisper, winding my arms around Sushant's neck as romantic music swells around us. "But you don't know what really happened."

"All I know is, you love someone who loves you back," he mumbles in my ear. "Doesn't take a genius to see it."

“I’m tired,” I admit. “Tired of loving her, of breaking your heart, of . . . this party. I wish I could go back in time and—”

“Hey, the past is in the past.” He shrugs. “And if you’re tired, go home early. Maybe . . . maybe think about what I said.”

“Maybe.” We sway to the beat in silence, letting the floor fill up with others who want to dance. I rest my face on Sushant’s chest, soaking in the scents of cinnamon and soap on his tux, knowing we’re dancing far too intimately for two exes. But he’ll never be just an ex to me. He’ll be a friend. A real one at that.

I spot Natalie and Julien slow dancing in my peripheral vision, their heads bent, foreheads touching. He’s leaving for Paris on Monday. I don’t know what’ll happen between them, if they’ve already talked about trying to make it work despite the distance, but I’m glad they found each other, even if it was only for this short while.

The song ends, and Seth taps me on the shoulder. “May I cut in?” he asks Sushant.

“Of course.” Sushant smiles, and I feel a rush of love for those dimples and all the times they were directed at me. “My date’s probably waiting too.”

Seth and I dance for a few songs that get progressively faster and louder, after which my social battery dies and I bow out. I look around for my friends, but they’re still slow dancing like nobody else exists. Smiling, I slink out of the ballroom. I’ve had enough of prom night, and all I want now is to be calmed by books and music in the comfort of my room.

CHAPTER TWENTY-EIGHT

"Fearless (Taylor's Version)"
by Taylor Swift

Lucy

There's something about the way the world looks after a rain shower. I step out of the hotel, my heels tapping against the damp ground. Petrichor-scented air wraps itself around me like a humid blanket. The streetlights shimmer with lingering water droplets, and familiar music plays in the distance. Taylor Swift?

I turn back. No, it's not coming from the hotel, but, rather, from somewhere outside. I shuffle, weighing my options. I'm exhausted, especially after that talk with Sushant, and I could do with an early night's sleep. But the music . . . it's calling to me. It's my favorite song.

Maybe I'll just see what's going on, then be on my way. I lift the hem of my sparkly pink dress to avoid puddles and walk forward to find the source of the music.

Just up ahead and to the right of the hotel is a fork in the road, leading to a secluded part of the beach. I've been there many times during the day, although not at night. Maybe there's a private party happening. I shouldn't disturb them. But curiosity gets the best of me, so I take my heels off and walk down the soft, sandy path toward the music.

I stop a few feet ahead of the waves at a table with a plastic covering, probably to shield the books on the table from the rain. To my right is a large Bluetooth speaker playing "Fearless (Taylor's Version)"; to my left is a cozy tent aglow with bright yellow fairy lights. There's . . . nobody here.

This is definitely a romantic surprise somebody planned, and I'm the third wheel about to ruin it. As I turn to leave, I notice the titles of the books on the table, and my jaw drops. There are at least twenty paperback copies of romance novels, all of which are inspired by Jane Austen's books: *Match Me If You Can, The Secret Diary of Lizzie Bennet, Austenland* . . . and *Prada, Purrs, and Prejudice* sits at the very top. A sticky note is taped to the front of its cover.

I gulp. Is all of this . . . for me? Slowly, I uncover the wet plastic, pick up the book, and read the sticky note.

> *You have bewitched me, body and soul, and I love, I love, I love you. I never wish to be parted from you from this day on.*

It's from *Pride & Prejudice*, the 2005 film adaptation of the book. I know that movie by heart, and this scene specifically is my favorite. Did . . . did *she* do all this? For me?

The music stops, and she calls out my name. "Lucy."

My vision blurs. I set the book down, take a deep breath,

and exhale as I turn. Meera stands in front of the tent, her chest heaving. That beautiful black dress is plastered to her body. Droplets cling to her hair, frizzy and wild in the salty ocean air. She's shivering; it's so windy here. "Hi," she says.

"I—you—" I sigh, wishing I could form words. Any sensible words. "What is all this?"

"Exactly what it looks like," Meera says. She takes a hesitant step forward. "It's a confession of love . . . and an apology."

I'm so stunned by what's going on that I let her take my hands in hers. They're cold and clammy, but her touch sparks something buried deep in my heart.

"I'm sorry I tried to sabotage your relationship. I'm sorry I tried to bring you down. I'm sorry I broke your heart. But"—her gaze falls to my mouth—"you know what I'm not sorry for?"

"What?" I ask.

"I'm not sorry I kissed you," she says. "I'm not sorry that you were my first kiss. I'm not sorry for wanting to kiss you again. And I'm never going to be sorry that I love you."

I blink back my tears. "I thought you loved Sushant. Not me."

"I liked him," Meera agrees. "Sushant was the cute Indian boy next door I had a crush on because I thought he'd be perfect for me. But you were *actually* perfect for me. You were my best friend, my . . . my soulmate, my favorite person. All the shit I pulled—it was because I couldn't let *you* go. Not because I hated you. In fact, it's the opposite. Even after we stopped talking, I never got over you. I never got over us."

A tear trickles down my cheek, and I let it. "I never got

over us, either," I admit. "But after what I saw that night, how could I possibly trust you again?"

"Honestly? I don't know." She bows her head, her grip on my hands loosening. "But if you give me a chance, I promise I'll earn back your trust. No matter how long it takes. Even if it's just as friends."

"Meera . . ." I look around the beach. "This is all wonderful, but love isn't about the sweeping grand gestures you see in the movies. It's about the little things—"

"—like talking about books with you and the club you're leading. Being by your side when your estranged father wants to get Froyo. And"—she smiles—"giving you the space to vent when you're sad and crying, even though we're technically supposed to hate each other. Right?"

I pull my shaking hands away and wipe them on my dress. She's right. Meera has been a friend to me even when I've tried to shut her out. She stuck around on the worst days. It couldn't have all been for her Plan. Not if she really does . . . love me.

"I want to do the little things," she says, "and the big things, and everything in between. I'll go to Taylor Swift concerts with you and memorize the lyrics to her songs so we can scream them together. I'll watch movies with you until two a.m., then hold you while we sleep. And . . . and I'll stand in the closet with you until you're ready to come out." She walks closer, until there's nothing between us but mere inches, electric with anticipation. Her voice lowers. "Will you let me, Lucy?"

No matter how much I love books and music, I don't answer

her with words. Instead, I step forward, cup her face with my hands, and kiss her.

Meera

I used to think, years ago, that Appa's beliefs about soulmates and twin flames were bullshit. He always says you're tied to the One by an invisible string pulling you to each other again and again despite the odds, that being with them will feel like you've finally found home.

Turns out, he's been right all along.

Lucy's mouth is soft and warm against mine, her hands tenderly raking along my skin and over my wet dress, and I shiver for a whole other reason. My fingers find their way into her glossy hair, the base of her neck, her lower back. This is home. She is home.

When she pulls away, her eyes are heady; her lips are red and swollen. I don't need a mirror to know I look the same. "I love you too," she whispers, swallowing. "And I'm scared."

I nod. "Me too."

We head to the table so Lucy can pick a book of her choice. "How long have you been planning this?" she asks as we duck inside the tent and snuggle into the pillows and blankets.

"Couple of weeks." I smile. "Sushant helped."

She laughs. "So that's what his speech was about."

I rest my head against her shoulder. "I'm also sorry he ended up being a casualty in all this. If it weren't for me, you two would have ended up together."

"I'm not so sure," Lucy admits, wrapping a blanket around us. "The guilt would have always hung over my head, eating me up on the inside. Part of me thinks this—us—was inevitable."

"I think so too," I agree. "I was scared you'd see the table and walk away."

Lucy blushes, her lips grazing the top of my head. "It didn't even cross my mind. Maybe I'm nosy, or maybe I just love you that much."

I lift my face, and we kiss. I have nothing else to compare our kissing to, but I can't imagine it being better with anyone else. Smiling, I pull away and leaf through the book she picked. "Do you want to read something to me?"

Her eyes light up. "Yes!"

Lucy reads out her favorite lines from the *Emma*-inspired rom-com novel for the next hour, and we steal kisses in between. Sometimes, as she's reading, her eyes flick toward me, as though she's making sure I'm listening and I like the book. She's adorable.

And she's mine.

By the time she closes the book, it's just before midnight—almost our curfews. We pack up, still talking about the book, before heading back. People mill about the streets, so we maintain some distance. Our hands graze as we walk and chat about her going to UCLA, my staying here for the café. Every touch makes me want more of her.

"I'm gonna try to visit when I can," Lucy says, avoiding my gaze. "But long-distance is hard, no matter how big or small the distance is."

"I'll visit too," I promise, squeezing her hand, then letting go as someone cycles past us. "We can make it work."

She shoots me a small smile. "I really hope so, Meera. I don't want to lose you again."

"You won't," I assure her. "Now, can we get to my place already so I can kiss you good night?"

Giggling, Lucy leads the way, a skip in her step.

CHAPTER TWENTY-NINE

"All You Need To Know"

by Gryffin and SLANDER feat. Calle Lehmann

Lucy

Mom doesn't miss the wide grin on my face over breakfast the next morning as I serve myself some bacon and pancakes. "I'm guessing winning prom queen felt great, huh?" she teases. "Sorry I didn't stay up for you, but I saw all the photos on social media."

I swallow a mouthful of food and nod. "It was a night to remember." And that's all the information she gets about last night. Mom doesn't need to know about Meera's beach surprise or the good-night kiss we shared at her doorstep. The mere thought sends a flutter down to the tips of my toes.

"Come on," Mom says, slapping the air with a hand, "tell me more! I want to know everything."

I fiddle with a bottle of maple syrup, shrugging. "You probably saw that Sushant won prom king. Seth was a nice date; he dances really well. That's about it."

Mom daintily sips her tea. "Winning prom queen in senior year is a big deal. I'm proud of you, Lucy. I'm sure you'll be the talk of the town at UCLA too. You should join a sorority like I did."

"I'd rather focus on my classes," I reply. My phone buzzes on the counter, lighting up with a good-morning text from Meera and a kiss emoji. She must have just woken up. "Besides," I add nervously, "I might visit every other weekend. To see Natalie, you, and . . . Meera."

Her eyes snap up to mine, narrowing. "Meera?" she repeats, a forkful of whipped cream and pancake nearly at her mouth. "I thought you weren't friends with her anymore. You haven't mentioned her in months."

"About that." I push my half-empty plate away. My stomach lurches at the thought of coming out for real. But I don't want to hide who I am anymore, not even from Mom. Not just because nothing stays hidden in Madre Maria, but because . . . she's my mother, and I want her to know. Even though I'm terrified she won't understand. So, with a deep breath, I let out the words, "Meera's my girlfriend now."

My mother's fork clatters onto her plate. Her mouth falls open. Her lips move, but she doesn't speak.

"Mom," I say, sighing. "Please don't—"

"You mean 'girlfriend' like a girl who's a friend, right?" she asks, dropping her voice low like she's afraid someone will hear us through the bushes outside our house.

I grip the sides of my chair and hold my head up high. "I mean 'girlfriend' like a girl I'm in a relationship with. A girl I'm in *love* with."

"Well, I never!" Mom stands up to pace around the room. "This makes no sense! You were so happy with Sushant, and you gave up a future with him for—for—" Chest heaving, she clutches her head with her hands. "Honey, is this because of your father? Has he . . . influenced you? Lord, I shouldn't have let him into your life again—"

Red flashes before my watery eyes. "Dad has nothing to do with who I love."

"Lucy, maybe you're confused," she reasons. "As a life coach, I know how normal it is for people to have rebound relationships that aren't genuine or healthy—"

"Stop." I grit my teeth, tasting salt water as the first tear slides down my cheek. "This is who I am, Mom, and if you can't accept that, then I guess it's good I'm moving out in the fall."

She forces herself to smile, but her eyes are still wide like she hasn't processed what I've said yet, and her lip is quivering. "We'll discuss this later. I have another conference to prepare for." She hurries back to her office, and a loud sob echoes through the room as her door slams shut.

I rest my head on the table. That went about as well as I thought it would. I'm not sure if Mom will ever come around, no matter how much she loves me, but it's not my job to hide who I am to keep the peace with her. I know that now.

Sighing, I get up, blow my nose on a tissue, and put our dishes in the sink, running water over them. Meera's text still needs responding to. I reply, asking if she'd like to meet up at the café later today.

Meera:

I'd love that 😊

Lucy:

Soooo I came out to my mom just now

Meera is typing . . .

Meera is typing . . .

Meera:

WHAT!!!!

Meera:

Are you ok???

I smile through the tears clouding my vision. Yes, I text back. Or at least I will be. See you around noon?

Meera:

See you ❤

I stretch my arms. As I start for my room, wondering how to tell Natalie and Julien everything when I see them next, the doorbell rings. Mom calls out from her office, "Can you get that, Lucy?"

"Sure!" I yell back.

Natalie is waiting for me on the doorstep. "Hey," she says, her face pink. "I need some girl talk. Can we go to your room?"

I grin. "You have perfect timing."

By the time I'm done narrating the beach surprise and my kiss with Meera to Natalie, her eyes have gone from narrowed, to widened, to lit up. "Oh my God!" she shrieks. "I can't believe Meera did that for you. But are you sure she meant everything she said?"

"Yes." I turn on my bed, lying on my side so we're facing each other. "I really think her feelings for me are real, the way mine are for her."

She rests her head on her hand. "If you trust her, then I trust her."

"Thank you," I say. Then I sit up, fluffing my pillow. "Now, what are the updates with you and the gorgeous Julien Perrin?"

Natalie burrows deeper into my bed, pulling my comforter over herself. "He rented a hotel room for us after prom," she admits, her voice muffled from underneath the covers. "And we, um, had sex."

"Whoa," I say, my voice hushed. "Wasn't it your first time?"

Her face peeks out at me. "Yes."

"And?"

"Oh, Lucy, it was perfect." She finally sits up, giggling. "Julien is so . . . experienced. I've fooled around with my exes before, but it's never been like this."

I intertwine her fingers with mine, hesitating. "He's leaving tomorrow, right?"

Natalie wipes a tear with the back of her hand. "We're going to try long-distance. I know we're just two teenagers living on different sides of the world and we have our whole lives ahead of us." Her voice quavers. "But I've never been loved like this before."

My arms wind around her body in a tight embrace before she can finish that sentence. Long-distance is a terrifying concept, one I've been ruminating on as well. There are so many what-ifs and variables you can't control. Feelings fade. Fights happen. People grow distant. And yet, sometimes, love can be stronger than inevitable change. Meera will be only a three-hour drive away from me. Our love will survive it.

It's not that simple for Natalie and Julien. Flights aren't cheap, and time zones make relationships harder than they should be. But if anyone can do it, it's them.

Natalie pulls away, her cheeks wet. "Maybe I could visit him in Paris over the summer. It would be so romantic. And I'm already looking up photography courses in France. Julien really thinks I have what it takes to do it for a living."

"I think so too. Also, you'd better send me a photo of your Eiffel Tower kiss," I say, poking her in the shoulder. "I'll live vicariously through you."

"Or we could do a double-date vacation," she muses. "Meera, you, Julien, and me."

I smile. "I'd love that. I don't know how I'll say goodbye to all of you in the fall."

"It's not 'goodbye,'" she reminds me. "It's 'see you soon.'"

She's right. No matter the distance between us, these people will always be my home, and I'll be theirs. That's love.

Meera

I'm distracted throughout my morning shift at Café Kismat, so much so that I mess up three drink orders. I can't stop replaying last night in my head. The beach surprise. The walk home. The good-night kiss. God, Lucy's lips are soft.

"You know what?" Danny snaps when I pour oat milk into someone's Earl Grey tea order. "You're off duty. Just take a break, enjoy your date, whatever."

I take off my apron and toss it aside. "Why, thank you, Danny. I never pegged you for a romantic."

He makes a face as I slip out from behind the counter. There are only a few minutes until noon. I frown when a thought hits me. Is this my first official date with Lucy? Should I have brought her flowers? Offered to pick her up? When I text them to ask for help, Ron and Valeria don't think it's a big deal, but to be on the safe side, I pluck a daisy from the café's back garden and roll the stem around between my thumbs, waiting in anticipation for my girlfriend.

I'm sitting at a table right across from the door, daisy in hand, when Lucy walks in. She spots me and grins so wide, I want to squeal and kick my feet with joy. "Hi," she says, a little breathless. "You look so pretty."

"Really?" I tug at my black T-shirt, giving my jeans and worn-out sneakers a once-over. "I look like this every day."

She smiles. "Exactly."

I tuck the daisy behind her ear, and when she blushes, I hesitantly wrap my arms around her, inhaling the scent of flowers that always follows where she goes. "Did it go okay with your mom?" I whisper in her ear.

Lucy pulls away, shuffling her feet. "As well as it could have gone," she mumbles.

"How come you decided to tell her?"

Her eyes drop to our feet—my sneakers, her pink kitten heels—and she blushes. "I didn't want my feelings for you to be a secret any longer. From anyone."

Those words warm me from head to toe. "I don't want us to be a secret, either," I admit. "But are you sure you're ready?"

"I'm ready," she agrees.

I look around. The café is moderately busy with our fellow classmates and a few other residents of Madre Maria scattered across the establishment. People are deep in conversation, some laughing as they sip their coffees; others are typing away on laptops. We would have never been able to turn the café's fortunes around without Lucy. My Lucy. I lean forward and brush my lips against hers, and she reciprocates, her thumb tracing a line along my cheek. If people notice, they don't make a big deal about it.

We pull apart seconds later, both red in the face, and head to the register hand in hand.

"Two iced ginger turmeric chai lattes, please," Lucy says, smiling.

"On it," Danny mumbles, ringing up the order. Then he peers at our linked fingers and adds, "Are you two, like, a thing now?"

"Yes," Lucy says confidently, raising her chin. "In some ways, we always have been."

Midway through our chai lattes, Appa calls us over for a tarot reading. "Putta," he says to Lucy, his eyes crinkling, "I haven't drawn a single card for you in months!"

She sits down cross-legged beside me and cringes. "That Tower card really scared me."

He raises his brows, a chuckle in his next words. "Does it still scare you, though?"

Lucy's eyes meet mine, her gaze softening. "Not anymore. You were right, Mr. Rao. Everything worked out the way it was meant to."

I squeeze her hand. "I love you," I say.

"I love you too." She beams, then turns to face my dad, peering at the tarot and oracle decks. "All right, I'm ready for my first-ever couple's reading. Mr. Rao, if you please?"

EPILOGUE

"Rule the World"
by BANNERS

Lucy

"There it is!" Meera exclaims, pointing at the large tower lit up by twinkling yellow lights in the distance. She grabs my hand, and we race forward, Natalie and Julien following in our wake.

We stop a few feet away from it, panting. Natalie whips out her camera and tripod for a selfie, then pauses. Julien's already told us photographing the Eiffel Tower at night is illegal. Sounds silly, but, hey, who are we to argue with the French?

Instead, we stand and admire the beautiful tower, the French architecture, and the crowd swarming it. Then Julien leads us to the grassy lawn near the tower, and we lounge on blankets, chatting idly about the hawkers and the (quite possibly) scammers who are shoving Eiffel Tower trinkets in the faces of passersby.

This night is flawless, one I'll remember for the rest of my life. I'm in the most romantic city in the world with not just my two best friends, but also the girl I've loved for longer than I can remember. Meera and I have been together for nearly four blissful months now, and every day, I find I love her more and more. Mom's still not happy about this. Our conversations are getting shorter by the day, and I'm making no effort to accommodate her bigoted feelings. Maybe she'll accept Meera someday, or maybe she won't. It isn't my problem to fix; it's hers.

Julien hooks his arm around Natalie, pulling her closer and whispering sweet nothings in her ear. They're adorable, and now that Natalie's gotten into a six-month photography course here in Paris, I know they'll make it. I reach into my bag for the queer young adult rom-com Meera and I have been reading together. Café Kismat's book club is still going strong, especially now that Meera has a bigger role in the business and has nearly doubled their revenue in the months after graduation. Although I won't be in Madre Maria for the next one, since college starts the week before it, I want to be part of the experience just the same. I'll tune in over Zoom.

"Where were we?" Meera asks absentmindedly, flipping through the book until she gets to the dog-eared page. She's not one for bookmarks; she's more likely to misplace them than actually make use of them.

I rest my head on her shoulder and listen to her read the next chapter aloud. She looks so beautiful in the moonlight, with her dark hair in a messy braid and her curious eyes scanning every word on the page.

Two weeks until I leave for UCLA. I gulp. Meera's voice fades as my worries set in about what's next for us. Mr. Rao's tarot prediction months ago said navigating a long-distance relationship would be a roller coaster, like they often are, but as long as we're strapped in and ready for the ride, it'll be worth it.

But what if I lose her? What if we can't make this work? What if we go from friends, to enemies, to lovers, to exes?

"Hey." Meera's lips brush my temple. "You know I can sense when you're anxious."

I stifle a weak laugh. "Yeah, you aren't Mr. Rao's daughter for nothing."

A wrinkle appears between her brows. "What is it?"

"Same as always," I whisper, nestling my face into the crook of her shoulder. "The future scares me."

"Me too," she says, tilting my chin up for a quick kiss. "But I'm very hard to get rid of, Lucy Hughson."

"And thank God for that." I refocus my attention on the book and let her voice bring back my hope. Despite the tumultuous year we've had, this love came back to us. This love is ours to keep. And I will never, ever let go.

Lucy's MRG Playlist

"After You"

by Gryffin and Jason Ross feat. Calle Lehmann

"Need Your Love"

by Gryffin and Seven Lions feat. Noah Kahan

"You Were Loved"

by Gryffin and OneRepublic

"Nobody Compares To You"

by Gryffin feat. Katie Pearlman

"Woke Up in Love"

by Kygo, Gryffin, and Calum Scott

"All You Need To Know"

by Gryffin and SLANDER feat. Calle Lehmann

"Forever"

by Gryffin and Elley Duhé

"Safe With Me"

by Gryffin and Audrey Mika

"Just For A Moment"

by Gryffin feat. Iselin

"Feel Good"

by Gryffin and Illenium feat. Daya

Acknowledgments

Okay, this is my third time writing the acknowledgments for a book with my name on it, and I don't think it'll ever stop feeling surreal. And incredible. And mind-blowing. Thank God for that!

It's funny: I wrote a coming-out story about these messy, chaotic queer girls who make mistakes and learn from them—sometimes the hard way—but if you'd asked me seven years ago if I would ever write something like this, I'd have said, "No way! After all, I'm . . . straight."

Oh, how clueless you were, twenty-three-year-old Swati.

Before I thank my wonderful publishing team, my friends, and my family, I need to thank the bestselling author whose queer young adult romance helped me come to terms with my bisexual identity. In a moment of impulsiveness, I DMed her on Twitter, telling her about this life-changing revelation, and to my surprise, she actually responded. Sophie Gonzales, you're the first person I came out to, and I thank you for your constant support and kindness over the years. This book wouldn't exist without *Only Mostly Devastated*.

Now I need to thank the greatest literary agent in the world, Rachel Beck. In the time it takes me to write the acknowledgments for whichever book is coming out next, you somehow manage to get me another book deal. Five contracted novels with Penguin Random House so far—how do you do it? We're the perfect team!

Thank you to my incomparable editor, Alison Romig, whose enthusiasm and passion told me she was Meera and Lucy's champion as early as our first email interaction. Also, you are SO cool, Ali! I hope we get to meet in person someday.

It takes a village to publish a book. Thank you to the entire team at Delacorte Romance: Kaitlyn San Miguel, Colleen Fellingham, Trisha Previte, Michelle Canoni, Tamar Schwartz, Natalia Dextre, Marla Garfield, Sophie Bennet, Andrea Baird, Jasmine Ferrufino, Sarah Lawrenson, and Shameiza Ally.

The very first person who read *As Long As You Loathe Me*, in all its flawed first-draft glory, was and still is one of my biggest supporters. Anahita Karthik, I know I dedicated this book to you, but I still can't thank you enough for the many hours you've spent commiserating with me when I was at my lowest, and for celebrating me whenever I had a publishing win. I'm glad we have each other as author besties, and I hope we always will.

Thank you to my dearest friends in real life and around the world: Amrutha Raja, Darshita Agarwal, Sambhram Puranik, Anshuman D Gopi, Ananya Devarajan, Kalie Holford, Noreen Nanja, Aishwarya Tandon, Melly Sutjitro, Kathryn

Harris, Stephanie Downey, Shannon O'Brien, Krishna Betai, Anirudh GP, Deeraj Ramchandani, Siddharth Jeevagan, Aastha Sharma, Vasanth Kini, my therapist Veena Nobbay, and many other people I'm definitely forgetting.

Most Indian authors unfortunately don't have family who support their dream of getting published. I feel lucky every day that this isn't the case for me. Appa and Amma, I will be indebted to you forever not just for encouraging me to try my hand at writing when I was a little girl, but also for your unbridled and unwavering enthusiasm two decades later. To my sister Kavya, thank you for pushing me to do better and be better every step of the way. I wouldn't be the writer I am today without you.

Thank you to Taylor Swift, whose music video for "You Belong With Me" served as inspiration for this book. I hope that, just like you, I can have a successful long-term career doing what I love most.

And lastly, dear reader, thank you for making it to the end of this book. *As Long As You Loathe Me* is the most personal and raw book I've written yet, a love letter to the queer teenager in me who never got to admit her feelings to that popular girl in high school. I hope that just like me, no matter who you are and who you love, you find your people—the ones who make you feel like you belong, even when the whole world is against you. You've got this. We've got this.

Don't you ever forget that.

About the Author

Swati Hegde is the author of *As Long As You Loathe Me*, *Match Me If You Can*, and *Can't Help Faking in Love.* She is also a freelance editor, mindset coach, and self-proclaimed coffee shop enthusiast who lives in Bangalore, India, and can often be found at the nearest café with a mug of hot tea or singing her favorite songs off-key at karaoke night. She looks forward to a long career bringing Indian stories and voices to light.

swatihegde.com

: @swatihegdeauthor

: @SwatiHWrites